PRECIPICE

WHEN ALGORITHMS

TRIUMPHED

Prequel to

"Restart: Stories of the Cairn Age"
(2021)

&

"Reform: Combating the Algorithmic
Mutation" (2023)

PRECIPICE
WHEN ALGORITHMS TRIUMPHED

A **NOVEL**

SCOTT
BOLLENS

atmosphere press

Published by Atmosphere Press

Cover design by Matthew Fielder

Atmospherepress.com

Table of Contents

I   A LOGICAL PROGRESSION   3
(2032)

II   OUT OF MIND   41
(2032)

III THE OLD ARTS   75
(2033)

IV MACHINE STORIES   101
(2033)

V   A COMPELLING REALITY   115
(2037)

VI A USER MANUAL FOR LIVING   157
(2045)

VII RESCUE   199
(2045)

VIII INTO THIRD SPACE   257
(2046)

IX A PATHWAY TO LIGHT   323
(2049 AND 2051)

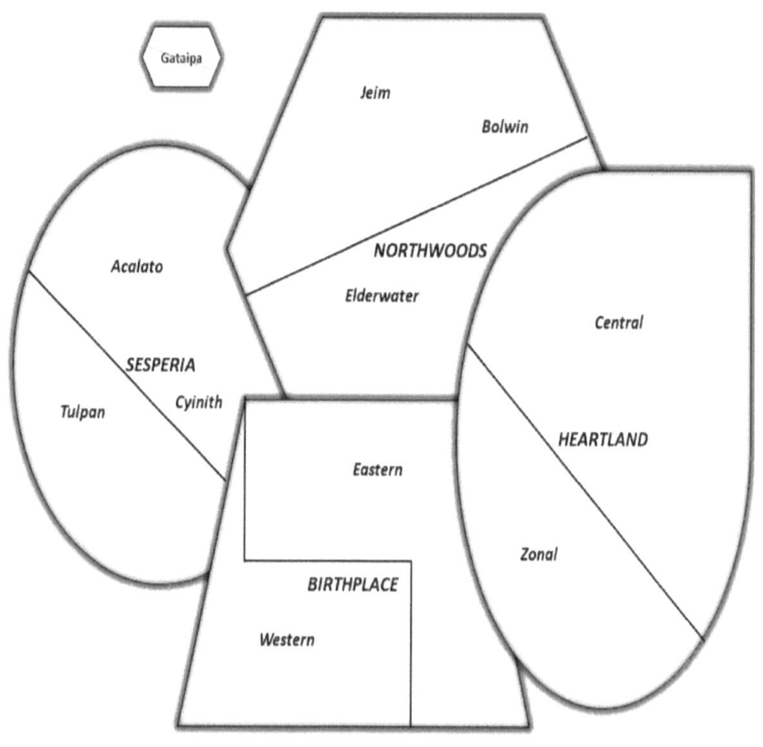

REGIONS OF "TURMOIL"

I don't know whether anyone could have foreseen what happened to us. Maybe some delusional wackos had a beat on it, I don't know. I wasn't in that circle. We who were trained in academic analysis and rational deliberation thought the standard of truth, although battered and shaken, would withstand the assaults. We thought that the rhetorical blitzes on verifiable facts would burn out eventually and fade away. We were wrong.

Our country's denizens looked with astonishment at the new technological possibilities of tomorrow. Yet, the naïve belief in human progress that anchored and fueled such amazement blinded us to the craggy precipice at our feet. Entranced by looking up at the stars, we didn't realize where we stood.

Jared Rohde
2nd quarter 2051

PART I

A LOGICAL PROGRESSION

2032

CHAPTER 1

3rd quarter 2032

It has been two quarter-years since the pronouncement that we could have a computer inside us.

Computer-human interface to be seamless:
The promise of a new tomorrow
1ˢᵗ quarter/12d 2032. Cyinith capitol reporter.

OneSource announced today the culmination of a years-long journey when it finalized the government-approved plan of chip implantation for those citizens desiring it. Dr. Cleve Wyford, technical director of OneSource, made the announcement—"For the first time in our history, the human mind will be integrated with the expertise of computer power. We are at the threshold of a new beginning for human consciousness."

Chip implantation is now approved to proceed this

quarter. Based on citizen marketing surveys, OneSource expects a 70 percent uptake by citizens in the next two quarters. "Citizens will have choice in how to use this new power. It will be available 24/7 but can be turned off by a simple tapping of the ear," described Wyford.

President Cynan was in OneSource headquarters for the announcement. "Today brings us the promise of a new tomorrow. I want to thank all the tech-architects who have achieved this fundamental pivot point in our lives and my appreciation to the public servants who made sure there are public safety guardrails integrated into this fabulous new technology."

Fial Derelei, a major investor, declared, "Every child will have an internal tutor that is infinitely patient, infinitely compassionate, infinitely knowledgeable, and infinitely helpful. Every person will have an internal assistant/coach/mentor/trainer/advisor/therapist. Every scientist a collaborator and partner. Every political leader a super-intelligent aide."

OneSource is a consortium of leading high-tech firms founded in 2028 with now-President Cynan as chief executive. Approval of the OneSource plan has been remarkable for how smoothly it has sailed through regulatory channels.

What little criticism has been lodged has been aimed at the tech-heavy composition of regulatory boards and Cynan's merging of business and political roles. "There has been a strong self-congratulatory sense among the corporate and government powers that this was the new way to go—'a logical progression' of the role of computers in our lives. This has meant little reflection about possible unintended impacts of this computer-human merger," stated community activist Ellis Lee, a member of the anti-tech Organics group.

Cognitive scientist Seyh Maki has also spoken out

against the chip transition. "Extremely short exposures to computer input have been shown to induce powerful delusional thinking in otherwise quite normal individuals. Even the beta test showed a not insignificant increase in users' adherence to non-factual information," he states.

"Beta testing has been ongoing for the past two quarters with marked success," says investor Derelei. Beta testers describe the insertion of the chip implant behind the ear as feeling like the prick of blood drawn by a phlebotomist or having your ears pierced for an earring. Insertion costs will be fully subsidized by government, and the actual procedure can take place in any of thousands of convenience stores (marked by the label 1S in the window) across the country.

Chip-implanted individuals will receive algorithmic input directly from data processed at the new superserver farm located in an undisclosed rural location. Input will be curated and fitted to the personal needs and characteristics of each individual user. To protect privacy, users will be able to customize how much personal information is available to the system by choosing between five different levels—or data fences—of personal data protection.

Tech-architects and regulators have called this colossal machine "interconnect."

Chip implants that connect us directly to algorithmically designed computer input were pushed by powerful people as a major lifestyle advance. No longer would we carry our smartphones and pay more attention to them than to autofin traffic, nearby folks on the streets, friends, especially family, sentient life itself.

Transmission would be clean and direct. Curation of output by the algorithmic system would be so precise to each user that we would not need to bother with the cumbersome search process.

The idea was that chips allowing constant streaming into our heads would free us from wasteful and stupid behaviors. Traffic engineers estimated that road fatalities would decrease by 65 percent. Education talking heads asserted that pupils' attention would be more focused and exact. Technologists proudly showed through mind-buzzing charts and graphs how much more exacting the match would be between algorithmic transmission and receivers' needs. Even chiropractic hacks got into the messaging, predicting major improvements in neck and spinal cord health.

This message of algorithmic paradise was energetically carried forward by our computer geek entrepreneur President, who seems more interested in a supposed techno-utopian future than the welfare of humans. Cynan wears a computer game headset when he has eVision press conferences, backed by an entourage of teenage-looking assistants frenetically tapping on their thin screens.

I first noticed the change with my students. A knowingness about things of which they were ignorant. We knew that artificial intelligence (AI) learning programs had flaws that produced weird results and that plagiarism was widespread. Endless faculty discussions had focused on how we were to accommodate AI-generated work in our classes.

Some of us wanted an outright and verifiable ban. Others acquiesced and thought we should allow students to use AI material as a starting point, but they would then have to revise in their own words. To me, this second option would be a further erosion of what little remained of integrity in the academic world. How either approach would be policed made all of us uncomfortable.

But the papers my students were turning in now were different than simple AI plagiarism. Using language of stringent coherency and excessive length, they were espousing blatantly false declarations. I initially attributed their hyper-argumentative style to youthful despondency over our country's political and social dysfunction. An impotent, do-nothing legislature in the face of an increasingly frying country. A slippery, billionaire tech mogul President raised in the bowels of free enterprise who mistrusts fellow humans and has proposed government by algorithm. Maybe combative radicalism was a good path for the younger generation amidst the circus of clowns leading our country.

The prose felt like more than generational angst, however. I was astonished at the fabricated storylines my students were presenting about our country's history. Basic dates and timelines were lacking or inaccurate, as were significant political and social concepts. It is one thing to be loose with the facts, but it is a deeper ignorance to turn your back on them entirely.

Especially troubling to me was the degree of hatred and grievance my students were espousing toward groups in our country, which I had never heard of.

I teach political and urban science. I was reading hostile fiction.

I never thought I would feel so stale in my early 40s. Whiz-kid to washed up in 15 years. Tremendous amount of effort banging through doctoral work. Then obsessive, exquisite publishing in high-brow, esoteric academic journals. Promotion to full professor status early at 34. Top of the game. Wife, kids, all good. Firing on all cylinders. I soon realized, however, that being at the top of the mountain meant there was nowhere to go but down.

I began recycling old writing and packaging it as new, semi-plagiarizing others' words and making them my own. The only way I could find any joy in writing was by getting buzzed on alcohol and drugs. Lied to my wife about needing to always be at the office working on deadlines. This was to avoid the growing anxiety in the household. Major arguments about kids and how to raise them.

I was doing my work on auto-pilot, caring less and less. Cynicism about the worth of scholarship (and my thousands of hours behind the computer). When bored, I search online for my citations. *Rohde, Jared: 1410 citations.* I stare at them with a dreadful feeling of emptiness. Products of long hours of mental masturbation. It borders on embarrassing.

What does it all mean? Academic articles and books of grandiose self-importance and needless complexity have such embarrassingly little relevance to real life. I've grown tired of scholarly writing of big words and inflated language—bloated, obscure, and difficult to understand. I wonder why, if what we are doing is so bloody important, we can't talk about it so the common person can understand it. I think about what we may be hiding.

Excessive hours of my obsessively finding just the right nuance in the use of the English language produce articles that are indecipherable to the public. Understandable, perhaps only partially so, to other academics playing the game.

On my dark, grumpy days, which are coming more frequently now, I wonder who gives a shit about what I study in excruciating detail in my research and overly complicated writing. Maybe four or five other scholars in the world's academic enclosure want to feed off my research to build their own careers.

I've become a crabby cynic, the guy who rolls his eyes at colleagues' ideas. The righteous self-importance of the academic life appears to me now as a farce. I cringe when I see newly minted PhDs with their ambitious yet shell-shocked looks as they start their new careers and their indoctrination into a siloed life of over-specialization and irrelevance.

I look at my younger colleagues who give gleaming presentations, energized by their hope and optimism that they will make a difference in our society and that what they are doing is meaningful and impactful. That they are engaged in the sacred world of scholarship and advancing knowledge.

I remember being that way before the skepticism, now cynicism crept into my bones. I recall my early years of hope and meaning not as a pining for those years of lost innocence, but rather with a sense of being duped into a self-indulgent enterprise that has limited impact on what really goes on in society.

In academia, we take ourselves so seriously.

I avoid the hordes of parasitic development officers who market academic nonsense as relevant and important to society. They endeavor to convince the public at large while validating our own farcical stature. I am suffocating in the overstuffed bureaucratic academic structure with its layers of associate and vice-chancellors.

So, at this point, I'm at wit's end. I believed in something for all my adult life that now feels of little utility, maybe devious in its insular design to avoid public understanding. A world built in such a way to be all on its own in its cushy, leafed campuses.

Even my formerly strong political views have softened. I identify as liberal, but gender-neutral bathrooms and plural identities are making my stomach queasy. I still endorse these ideas in public because our hard-core political right wing is so horrendous.

I feel as if I've professionally been in a fabrication. A small world created to keep those of us who are not adept at making things and fully living life busy with our masturbatory thinking. We scholars criticize all the time but do little about it, content to achieve promotions in our little world, rewarded for our erudite niche writing.

One element of academia that has provided some relief from my cynical view of the enterprise is when I think about the positive impact I can have on my students. You know, in lighting the fire for them. For years, I maintained a dream-like hope for my students. Now, I'm troubled that I may be spending inordinate amounts of time connecting them to my sheltered world of analysis and over-thinking rather than to the real world as it actually exists. I am giving them false hope that they will be something other than replaceable cogs in the tentacled web of rapacious capitalism or submerged in the putrefying bowels of political hatreds.

No matter what I achieve in life, there is emptiness. I feel that struggle has been the default, that I've been taken for a fool by life's croupier. No achievement fills me. I feel desire and then disappointment in a seemingly endless cycle. I'm to the point where I realize many of my problems are created through my thinking, but I can't stop creating them. Maybe the drama of problems is the only thing keeping me from facing my emptying soul.

My marriage is dying. It's sad. Irreversible decay is palpable. I feel a deep sense of erosion, of loss.

Gliding into ease or giving up on this life of disappointing achievement and slow-burning animosity at home seems rational but too much a surrender. I want to give life another shot before I surrender entirely. I can feel that somewhere inside me lurks a burning desire for something more robust than the cushioned existence of a scholar and the meager life of a diminished husband and father.

I want a muscular manhood. Where my testosterone can flair. I have my pick of women. Where people look at me like I'm a triumphant animal of the jungle. Young kids come up to me in admiration. Where I am a physical threat to other men. Where I can feel the vivid pulse of live or die. I want to live on the edge and feel its danger.

Instead, I sit at desks writing wordy drivel and spend time at home in passive-aggressive tension. About the only time I feel like a real man is when I can escape to the local *We Got It* hardware store for some simple D.I.Y. job. I walk up and down the huge aisles of hand tools, gloves, and sponges, feel my testosterone surge, and act like I'm picking a temporary partner from a suite of the finest Parisian prostitutes.

A life of smallness, adolescent fantasy, and defeat.

I want more.

If I could live a second life, a secret one where I am conqueror, man-beast, warrior, I think I would. I crave it.

CHAPTER 2

I wake up in my typical brain-dead zombie state, struggling into the bathroom. I hand-scan the ablution keyboard so that AI can determine the heat level and water pressure that best fits my current physiological status. After the shower, I stumble to the kitchen and eye-scan my morning coffee selection (caffeine drives academia like electric current powers auto-fins). I stare at the curated drip and ponder why we use technology to do away with the human element in daily life.

Technology continues to erase the deliberative, meditative moments of daily life that provide the sense that we have some control over things. What is it about our mundane daily activities (showering, coffee making, driving) that we want to obliterate through automation? Have we become that impatient with our own ability to make decisions? Like many others, I seem to have no option other than to become a lazy recipient of an automated reality.

Now, we are told that automating things is not sufficient. That the next great step is to bring automation into our very minds and bodies. My scheduled date for *interconnect* implantation will soon arrive. I'm not sure whether this is human progress or some form of insidious devolution.

I recall moments in the past, before algorithmic penetration, of wonderful attentiveness and appreciation of the present moment. The spontaneity of laughing with a friend over an inside shared joke. The timeless witnessing of a glorious sunset. The contentment-filled early morning coffee. What we used to call 'living in the now.'

In our world today of such intrusive AI automaticity, it's easy to forget these non-automated times. The pre-digital recollections of life arrive with feelings of sadness and loss. Living without dependence on computers—living more naturally—allowed for the necessary itching and scratching, the meandering thoughts, and the gentle, slow passing of time. I could dive down to the depths of stillness that waits beneath the churning of the waves.

Now, it is all fast, curated, and soulless. It's all churning of the waves. The timeless, unrushed spots of grace are now filmed over by experiences selected, arranged, and presented algorithmically. So much neurotic attachment and impatience.

Life before seemed simpler. But, then I wonder whether I am romanticizing a past that did not really exist. My memories, by their very nature always abstractions, may be de-cluttering the past and thus fooling me. I admit it's sure easier today to ride in an auto-fin than it was to drive a gas-guzzling car in wicked traffic.

I'm a visiting scholar at the Elderwater Institute of Technology. The campus was built in the '60s (20C). The founders designed the buildings in what, at the time, was imagined to be futurist, brutalist architecture. Seventy years later, I think campus designers missed the mark. The buildings look like something out of late 20C but their oddity does retain a certain charm.

I'm enjoying my time so far here. The city of Elderwater is beautiful and fascinating. It is filled with petting-zoo, whimsical architecture that both inspires and puzzles the viewer. Outdoor cafes and broad pedestrian-only avenues provide me with lots of space for expansive thinking about our world.

The charms and delights of Elderwater uplift the soul. There is an endearing juxtaposition of old and new, a diversity of land uses, safe and inviting sidewalks, and vibrant places proud of their history. The city draws you in with its beguiling, creative atmosphere. My favorite is a transit station designed in the shape of a happy golden retriever dog, inside of which one can find an animal shelter, child-care center, mom-and-pop retail outlets, and an indoor park complete with water slide.

I think even the city's more downtrodden residents have a twinkle in their eyes not found elsewhere. Enticing nooks and crannies in the labyrinth of the built landscape invite you into innumerable arts and crafts shops. The street-side cafes provide a street orchestra of joyous conversations as I walk by. Performance artists add to the creativity of the streets. A few times, I have found myself suddenly an unknowing participant in a street play or performance.

The Sanctum of Evtyx peace tower literally stands above all else in the city, drawing droves of tourists from throughout the country to witness this extravagance designed by a 19C local philosopher/architect. The Evtyx contains an astonishing array of holistic presentations of the 148 major wars that have occurred in world history and emphasizes through poetic and written commentary the futility of these wars. I depart from it exhausted, informed, and resolute. In addition to the Evtyx tower, many idiosyncratic architects through the years have added their artistic talents to the odd and enchanting mix of buildings in the city.

There is an informality and openness to Elderwater that invites you into its spirit of inclusiveness. There is a seemingly random mix of building types and activities that somehow produces an enchanting unity. One can get productively and joyfully lost in the city, immersed in its flows and rhythms. I feel a connectedness to something larger when I'm on the streets. I become like a tree within a larger forest grove. Or a single plant that is part of a larger coral reef. Each person is different, but connected to a common root system. A joy in togetherness.

Many thinkers in my academic field of urbanism claim such vitality and diversity are what make successful cities tick. Elderwater is an urban jewel par excellence, an extraordinary place that counters the growing sterilization elsewhere in our country produced by our globalizing world dominated by monopolistic economic monoliths.

It would take a destructive force to weaken the organized complexity of this special place.

Another plus about being in Elderwater is it is time away from my wife. Carrie is hundreds of miles away in our hometown of Acalato, taking care of our two kids. My love for this one-of-a-kind woman was real and it felt enduring. We had created a seemingly caring and resilient partnership. But, things have been strained between us ever since our second kid. I feel myself psychologically detaching from Carrie as a prelude to ending the marriage. Guilt and remorse compete with the sense of inevitability. You know, what they call "irreconcilable differences." I miss Carrie and still have warm feelings for her, but we have reached the breaking point several times, pulled back only partially through difficult marital counseling. We have certainly tried. Give us an 'A' for effort.

When my home Acalato University approved by visitor transfer, I relished the thought of being away from Carrie for two quarter-years. A whole new batch of students to interact with. Relative freedom from brain-deadening administrative entanglements. I have felt refreshed and worldly since being here. And, exhilarating interactions with two flirtatious female graduate students have also emboldened my manhood, which has gradually deflated amidst my wife Carrie's obsession with our children. Despite this fresh start, I admit that the developing personal catastrophe of my family life lurks inside and is too hard for me to bear. I've put up a wall to protect me from these feelings, I know. When they break through, nothing exists there other than heartbreak.

Experiencing a change in my students' papers was one thing. Seeing the change in real-time alerted me even more.

It was my first in-person experience with our new world.

I'm delivering a lecture to 100 undergraduate students in my Urban Inequality class. The air conditioning is working overtime, trying to expel the 105-degree temperature outside our walls. A stunningly beautiful blonde, name of Palina, raises her hand. First time she's participated in seven weeks. One of those beauties that sit passively during class with a glazed look, likely draining her social media while I'm talking.

"Rohde," she shouts, "why are we not discussing the real problems in our life?"

Struck by both the tight lime top she is wearing and the rude addressing of me (no "professor" or "doctor"), I ask, "What do you mean? Can you give me an example?" I feel good that I'm trying to turn this awkward confrontation into a learning moment for the class.

"The Kilat. They are trying to cripple and weaken us."

At first, I think she is kidding. I've never heard this term before in my life. Maybe some test, I think, by a sorority to see how a professor would react to absurdity. I'm probably being videoed so the young girls can giggle about this later over wine and cookies.

"I'm not sure of your reference here, Palina, but you bring up an interesting point about how we view the 'other' in society."

"Don't intellectualize it, Rohde, the Kilat are like cancer. Assaulting our values, the very basis of our existence as people."

At this point, class members are getting anxious. Some are laughing, but others I see are nodding their heads in agreement. I need to put a stop to this.

"Ms. Palina, I ask you to refrain from additional discussion at this point, but if you come to my office hour, I will be glad to discuss this further with you."

Palina angrily gets out of her seat, slams down the desktop, and storms out of the room, not before yelling out amidst tears, "This is why we are all going to hell. We can't even talk about this in a place that is supposed to allow for free speech."

She never showed up at my office and no longer attended class.

Something strange is happening. I need to talk with a colleague about the heightened vitriol evident in my students' papers and about Palina's outburst.

I can't be alone in sensing this darkening of mood. Part of me feels I'm being set up for some joke on the visitor from Acalato.

Unfortunately, the first person I meet in the cobwebbed halls (God, how I wish for the old days before remote work) is Rickel Lalish. He's a mild-mannered type of academic. Never says anything in faculty meetings. He specializes in urban arts, which I judge to be extraneous bullshit. I've never seen him without a blue polo shirt on. Nonetheless, I need someone to vent to about the goings-on in my class.

"Have you noticed a kind of edge to your students this year, like a manic assertiveness, I don't know?"

"What are you accusing me of, Rohde?"

I'm shocked by his response and clarify I'm talking about my students, not him.

"I know my teaching evals aren't the best, but why you feel you should make light of them? Some balls you got!"

I don't know what the hell is going on. Milquetoast, artsy Lalish is harsh, in attack mode (and wildly wrong about what I'm asking).

I look in his eyes and they don't match the intensity of his verbal edge. They are a gauzy type of white, like he has some allergic pus filling his eye sockets. He stands before me, but I swear his whole manner is that of someone directed by some external influence.

"I'm sorry, Lalish, you feel this way. If anything comes up in your class, please let me know." I back away to get out of this strange conversation.

"Yeah, right, I'll see you when it matters," he shouts.

Chapter 3

My growing unease about what is happening at the Institute—the hate-filled invective in student essays, Palina's outburst, Lalish's detached weirdness—leads me to do something I would normally resist. I vimex my wife back home in Acalato, seeking some perspective, despite knowing that this is likely not going to clarify things.

"Hi there, miss you. I just saw the President on eVision spouting off about chips. Even showed us his scar like some macho pig. This guy's an idiot."

"Um, hello Carrie."

Carrie starts interactions in mid-stream and I've always felt at least two steps behind in understanding what she's talking about. In the early years, I found this frisky and engaging. Now, it's demanding and old.

I know what she is alluding to with our squirrely President, but I'm not going to go into that rabbit hole with Carrie. Cynan is a weasel. I don't think he has said a straightforwardly true statement in years. His slipperiness well adapted to the sleazy social media environment of the late '20s. Sufficiently effective to get him elected. An expert on using a kernel of truth and mixing it with half-truths, quarter-truths, disingenuous wording, misleading interpretations of scientific studies, and unverifiable claims.

Acting as the underdog outsider reluctantly exposing devious acts and coverups by institutions and individuals. Adept at connecting multiple plots into a larger master plan by an unspecified "they" aimed at shafting the common citizen. A few of his favorite assertions are that 8G networks are being used for mass surveillance by government, that chemicals in the water supply cause children to become transgender, that vaccines to treat the Marburg29 virus caused millions of deaths, and that condensation trails left by airplanes are dispersing chemical agents to control human population. Yes, he today is our President.

Carrie's voice immediately provokes in me a common feeling—that we are two ships going in opposite directions. Being 800 miles away from her for six months seems a safe buffer from her intensity. She doesn't suffer fools gladly, and in her eyes we all are fools. Since being here, I'm finding women in Elderwater hard to turn away from. They bring no judgment.

"You know that mind-bender devil is trying to do away with elections? He wants to have leaders chosen through algorithmic profiling."

"What are you talking about, Carrie?"

E-vision is on and loud. Rebellious daughter Ellie shouting something at Caleb. My mind flips to Raven's beautiful body—tight and mouth-watering. I met her at a watering hole late at night along one of Elderwater's enchanting streets. It's all imagination of future sex at this point, but it feels like a good bet.

"That guy, Oakes or something like that. In charge of data security for our country. Some old piece came to light where he is quoted as saying that algorithms are all about appealing to people on an emotional level to get them to agree on a functional level. Like Hitler did, he said. And this guy is now in charge of security for the chip implantation program. We're going to end up like the States of America after Carlson took over. Jesus God!

"Connect us all directly into one integrated supercomputer. What are we thinking? This could be the extinction of the human race."

The velocity of Carrie's energy always induces my reflex that she is overstating things.

"Don't you think," I mutter, knowing she's not going to really hear what I'm about to say, "that there will be safeguards against a what—an algorithmic takeover? Certainly, we are not stupid enough to not build an off-switch.

"Besides, Carrie, the way we are going, maybe we should be shown the door as a species." My cynicism, born out of academia, is a great way to shut down conversations with her.

"Bostrom warned us long ago that we sparrows better tame the owl chick before bringing it into our midst as our servant," Carrie declares from her off-putting pedestal.

I have no idea what she is talking about.

I never do get to what I called about, seldom do with her. Probably not best anyway to ask Carrie about my recent experience. That would undoubtedly set her on fire even more.

Chapter 4

The line outside *My Pharmacy/My Store* winds around the corner of the block. I'm in a grittier part of Elderwater. I noted on my walk here that sidewalks are lined by tattoo parlors, smoke shops, hair salons, storefront religious venues, independent coffee houses/bookstores barely holding on to the past, massage parlors, run-down discount stores, autofin repair shops, casinos, and even old adult cabaret halls.

The morning has a foreboding, suffocating heat, as if telling us we shouldn't be here. It seems some appointment system would have helped shorten this line. I feel both fascination and trepidation in anticipating the introduction of a foreign object into my mind. The rapid release of the chip implantation program makes me a bit nervous. I wonder why everything seems to be moving so fast and whether there is anyone really thinking this through, what we're about to do to our country's denizens.

Folks are restless as they wait, like waiting to rush into a store to do holiday shopping. The giddiness of capitalistic pursuit combined with the delight that the product on offer is free for the taking. There's a new toy in town, and they want it. Some giggle as they hold their smartphones that they'll feel naked without it in their hand. A few are massaging their ears anticipating the pinprick.

There's an anemic protest group of five or so denizens. Their placards include "Humans, not Machines," "Think without Curation," and "Algorithmic Apocalypse." Nobody in line is looking in their direction, absorbed in their anticipation of the latest big thing.

I eventually get into the cubicle-partitioned part of the store. Soon, a medical tech is beside me asking, "Pretty exciting day for you, eh?"

He provides me with a brochure and a two-page form with excessive writing on it to sign.

"Should I be interested in what all this gobbledygook says?" I ask.

"I'm not sure myself," says the med-tech, looking surprised that I asked. "I'm pretty sure it limits the liability of *OneSource* should something unanticipated happen.

"Like what would that be?"

He holds up his hands in an "I'm just a tech" look. "We're operating here without outcome evaluations. Normally, we would have beta test results, but we've been kept in the dark on this one. Regulators have used emergency 'national interest' to push this through without normal review."

I see impatience on the med-tech's face. Hundreds more behind me so I relent with my queries.

I feel the pinprick more than I anticipated. I wince. My macho stature wobbles for a few seconds as I register the pain.

"That's it," the tech says. "The brochure will describe to you what to expect now. It will take about 24 hours for you to feel the full cognitive influence. *OneSource* recommends limiting your physical exertion for the first two days after you feel the chip working."

"Why's that?"

"They label it the 'Superman effect.' You'll feel stronger and empowered. The impulse might be to engage in decisive actions. They say two days gives you time to adjust to this new cognitive power."

As I depart the store, line-waiters gaze at me anticipating to see some type of robotic human. They look disappointed when they see only very-human me walk past them, with a small bandage on my ear-lobe.

I walk past the placard-holders on the way to my auto-fin. I could have easily bypassed them by walking another route, but something attracts me to this group. As I walk by them, a nicely attired man gently whispers to me, "Be careful with the rabbit hole, friend. You may lose yourself and not know it."

CHAPTER 5

The first week with the chip was part fun and games and part anticlimactic. I limited my chip-in time to 60 minutes, per instructions. No Superman feeling. Rather a gradual transition to a less fuzzy state. I didn't need coffee or nicotine gum as much. Chip-in seemed to be taking care of stimulation instead of chemicals.

The second week things become more interesting. I increase chip-in time to three hours per day. When I switch on the chip, there is now a pulsing surge and a sensation of something hard slamming into the inside back of my head, like a cartridge locking itself into place. Soon, I feel a blossoming inside my head like a dry sponge expanding in water. A sense that my brain cavities and pathways are being comfortably filled. A sharpening feeling is more pronounced. When I chip-in, it feels like I'm emerging wide awake after sleeping. A sense of focus and purpose saturates me. By the end of the two weeks, I am connected about six hours per day.

The most noticeable immediate impact is that my chip has

improved my teaching thousand fold. No notes are required anymore. I begin talking about a subject and *interconnect* supplies me with information cleanly transmitted to me, categorized in ways to facilitate my delivery to students. It is almost a joke standing in front of them, delivering algorithmic streams. Or kind of like play-acting using pre-prepared lines. Imposter syndrome for sure. At times, I intentionally stumble verbally or take a pause to prove that I'm still in control. Otherwise, I deliver material on social stratification and equity in full complete sentences of all equal size.

Imposter syndrome comes quite readily to me. I've always played the external role of humble and gentle soul in my life, knowing full well that, at my core, I'm ego-driven. The more I achieve in life, the more I develop refinement of my humble exterior. I am adept at hiding the vicious animal inside. The machine's fine-tuning of my brain seems to increase my smooth façade even further, helping me hide what is inside.

Interconnect gives me the aura of independent objectivity without hard work. I need only follow the script delivered through my head. It's like simply reading a cue card that no one else can see. It feels so real and true but at the same time constructed.

The machine in my head sure has made my job easier. My thoughts and words flow like a gently flowing river. I'm thinking the administrative guys are going to catch on sometime and lower our paychecks. Thank goodness academic bureaucracy moves like wheels in mud.

Yet, I notice that there are certain sentences that come out of my mouth that have a flimsy connection to reality. There are also times when algorithmic input into my head gets tiring. As promised, however, turning off *interconnect* is simple. One time, I purposely left it on overnight to see what effect it would have. In the morning, I felt like I had been cleaved in two—some overpowering force operating while I was unconscious. There was some dark, sinister quality to *interconnect's* nighttime activity that was beyond my run-of-the-mill nightmare. It didn't just insert menacing thoughts—evil people wanting to do evil things to me—but also an urgency to maim and kill these enemies. I don't think I'll leave my chip on again at bedtime. Too disturbing.

I meet Raven for dinner one evening after cruising through a beautiful, well-paced, rock-star lecture. I left the lecture hall with a machine-created top-of-the-world feeling. Although intrigued by how the machine might improve my social skills, I leave it off for the date. The neighborhood bistro is curiously wedged between a large, warehouse-sized augmented virtual reality (AVR) lounge on the one side and a sketchy kratom shop on the other.

Raven is wearing a come-on smile and a tight, sexy dress showing a tantalizing cleavage. Beautiful, head-turning woman. Our dinner conversation is mundane at best. It all feels like a prelude. I don't mind the ordinariness of banter. It's refreshing to not have to get into the sophisticated and competitive Carrie back-and-forth.

It doesn't take me halfway into the appetizers to realize that Raven thinks less on her own and seems fully connected to algorithmic input. Her commentary sounds choreographed. Still, she seems more accepting of life's realities and of me. This is a refreshing contrast to Carrie, where it's all work and no play. I guess I don't want to think that hard about our country's issues, at least not at Carrie's level of altitude.

Raven took a tram-fin to the restaurant, and when I offer her a ride home, she readily accepts. My manhood is sizzling at this point. As we walk toward my auto-fin, past the arterial Mendel Street, I see one of my graduate students—name of Sehlolo or something like that. He is helmeted and behind some type of makeshift barrier. Comical at first glance. Collection of trash bin lids and manhole covers tied together in a useless fashion. Looks almost like an urban art piece. Fuckin' Lalish comes to mind with his useless, mind-numbing explorations of urban aesthetics.

"Rohde, what's up teacher?"

It's a weird way to be addressed. Indicative of my sense recently that boundaries between teacher and student are dissolving in my classes.

"We're out for the evening, enjoying the city."

"It looks like you are, man. I thought you said in class that you are married, wife back in Acalato."

I avoid this prompt. Smart ass. I quickly ask, "What's with all this junk you have here?"

"Protection, man. The only thing that crosses my mind is: Will they approach us—will they come and kill us? If they happen to come with weapons, we must forget everything and protect ourselves," the graduate student, now impassioned defender, says, his voice barely audible amid the loud thumping of a helicopter over the urban landscape.

I should have realized at this point the dangerous path our country was on. Playful, hours-long intimacy at my apartment later in the evening is a pitiful excuse for my not fathoming this.

Chapter 6

> *"Don't ask what computers can do, ask what they should do."*
>
> Brad Smith, president, Microsoft, May 2023
> States of America

Before *interconnect*, it's not that we were unaware of the dissolving line between machines and humans. We were not that ignorant.

When generative AI emerged 10 years ago, there was a collective gasp that it could now write more convincing prose than humans. No longer were tech companies solely mining personal data to deliver curated ads and content. Now, the internet was being scraped of masses of human-generated content to deliver writing compositions that were better than humans. Some AI models spanned more than one million language parts, able to combine words in exquisite prose for any objective.

College entrance essays gained in sophistication and depth.

At times, readers teared up at the elegantly stated emotional profundity of the letters.

Most break-up letters increased in nuance and were more tolerable. Others drove the dagger even deeper into the heart.

Eight of the 10 best-selling books of 2028 were written by AI. Well-known human writers were shamed online for their sloppiness and flatness of exposition.

Movie scripts on eVision felt like they all had the same author, with slight variations added to make us feel otherwise.

AI became popular in some circles for its ability to describe vivid examples of psychopathic and other disturbing behaviors. Porn addicts became avid readers.

The field of psycho-therapy experienced an identity crisis as denizens increasingly engaged with AI therapists due to their greater effectiveness in achieving positive change.

Writers and artists were initially aghast and mounted fruitless protests against the ever-growing machine and its expertise in creating text, images, and audio. At present, most creative types have given up and regularly use generative AI as a foundation for their work. "It simply is easier and better, at least as a starting point," stated sculptor Jacque Birren in a *Journal of Machine Art* article. "I add some human flourishing on top of the AI base, and that gives me some justification that I am not simply stealing. But I tell you one thing, although my products are stunning and selling well, I feel less creative as days go by. Sometimes, I feel I have lost the creative edge entirely."

We had warnings about what AI could do to us. Back in '23, 28 countries signed the Bletchley Declaration stating that "there is potential for serious, even catastrophic, harm" from the deliberate or unintentional use of AI. Much like how the world was addressing global climate change, however, prescriptions for how to deal with this pending AI threat were as limp as a washcloth in the rain.

The mass bombings and mass shootings in the late '20s

done by nut jobs inspired by falsehoods on the internet raised concern episodically. The serial killing of four politicians by a young man convinced he was an extraterrestrial savior even made us consider an outright pause on internet use.

Yet, in the end, these actions did little to inspire action by the world's governments to control machine influence on society. The story was always the same—governments should not stifle technological innovation through regulation.

Now, ten years after the trumpeted entrance of generative AI, the demarcation between human and machine is nearing extinction.

It's been only a matter of weeks since my implant for the chip to become my friendly, go-to companion. I now more frequently link into *interconnect*. I welcome the pulsing surge, locked-in cartridge feeling. I'm leaving the chip on more often during my sleeping hours.

I feel a seductively addictive quality to the experience. A sticky quality to its storylines. Compared to the meandering and messy emotional dramas of my own thinking, chipping in (as it is now called) provides me with a sense of stability, a feeling of being complete and correct. It provides me with a bluster of self-righteousness that preempts my doubts and character defects. My own thinking seems inferior, burdened with self-doubt, insecurities, and instinctual desires that side-track my mind. With *interconnect*, all is crystal clear in solid black-and-white instead of the wishy-washy watercolors of my own mind images.

I don't think I'm alone in getting addictively hooked to the machine. It makes things easier and cleaner. Before interconnect, I felt I was not given a user manual for living. I developed numerous ways to run away from my thoughts of the present moment. Something or someone sets me off and I would tighten into a self-absorbed mental space for protection. Kinda like sitting in a dark room with the shades drawn down. My long practice of chemical and alcohol imbibing certainly helped me habituate to being mentally elsewhere. This numbed mental space became habitual. Its familiarity was its greatest advantage. It grounded me in a space of non-existent growth. My tendency to go into self-criticism mode in my closed box further strengthened the impulse to run and stay hidden.

Now, with *interconnect* in my head, I don't have to deal with this messiness. I notice that the algorithms provide me with self-righteous certainty that overrides my tendency to run and hide mentally. I feel emboldened and reassured. A solid entity rather than an inadequate, fallible human being.

I do notice one aspect of being chipped-in that is strange. At infrequent times during the day, there are dark storylines filled with provocative, hate-filled appeals for revenge. I get jacked up and have this desire to act out.

Weirder, still, is that when these images come, they no longer scare me. Instead, I feel more complete in some way, like a part of me, long dormant, is filling in.

On balance, the machine is a reassuring presence in my life. In those moments when I get that familiar urge to escape the present ("I'm such a fuck-up," "I don't want to deal with this"), machine stimuli strengthen and provide a narrative that keeps me out of the negativity of my own thinking. There's a fulfilling sense about this. I feel I have access to more of my brain power than ever before. Existing on all cylinders.

I feel more empowered but, weirdly, less in control. Complete, but subordinate.

CHAPTER 7

The school term ends, thank goodness.

Chipped-in while teaching had its fun moments, but after a while, delivering lectures robotically made me too assertive, even aggressive, toward students and their inane questions. I decided then to leave the machine for non-teaching time only. This decision paid off late in the term because if I had been chipped-in, I'm pretty sure I would not have been able to handle a contentious episode.

It happened near final exam week. For the first 30 minutes of the lecture, I'm interrupted constantly by student comments that are at an inappropriate fever pitch. I notice that more than half of the students have these ghost-like, gauzy eyes. I thought, *Okay, it's been a long term and they're showing understandable wear-and-tear.* But something dark and foreboding was beneath their glazed looks. I noticed these students were sitting in two clusters, distanced from each other. The more clear-eyed pupils were scattered between the two clusters.

A shouting match breaks out spontaneously and I hear the words *Kilat* (which I recall from Palina's earlier outburst) and *Qasine*. This was soon followed by a string of hateful words fired back and forth across the auditorium. For a moment, I consider whether this is some video game bullshit that has taken hold of the students. But their punches and counter-punches seem real in that they are referring to real places in Elderwater and to historical episodes, albeit in inaccurate ways. Their verbal assaults are fully formed and argued with a flourish that I would typically commend. But this is getting too weird and confrontational.

I raise the level of the e-phone speaker and yell, "Stop."

It momentarily stalls the turbulence, but it soon picks up. I hear one student mutter under his breath, "What is a Sesperian even doing here?"

When fisticuffs threaten to expand even more, I pull the switch for security. Not your typical undergraduate discussion!

As the room finally empties, I sit behind the lectern with a pit in my stomach. As one of the clear-eyed students passes in front of me, I ask about what just transpired.

"You won't understand, teacher, they're in another world."

I sense this is a chance to get some understanding. I check my e-register and identify him.

"Mr. Morterero, would you mind coming to my office after your final exam? You seem to have some sense of what is going on. I would appreciate very much discussing this with you."

"I can come by Thursday afternoon. I don't think you're going to appreciate what I tell you, however."

"That would be great, thank you."

"See you then. You can call me Santino."

I give final exams remotely to avoid any further disruptions. I eliminate the essay part since it would probably be polluted by

AI drivel. M and caring exterior.

I've trapped myself within my own interior. A lonely, always-redundant mental landscape.

I sit behind my desk and I can feel it. A compelling need calling out to me. A need to feel the pulse of masculine energy rushing into me as I work with my hands on a concrete project with tangible results. I want to flare my testosterone, not smother it by sensitively considering my and others' feelings.

Action, not thinking. I want to be a sperm-producing male animal relying on my base instincts rather than on my little feelings. I crave to engage in physical acts where I don't have to analyze and thoughtfully deliberate. At this point in my life, I don't care what those physical actions are. Anything will do that ignites my man chemicals.

I want to feel the rawness of the earth. To be in the wilderness alone surviving as men used to do. To be attuned with the wild, not hermetically sealed from it. I want to focus only on daily survival tasks and live close to the earth. Focus on the present tasks at hand (what will I eat, where will I sleep, how many miles can I hike) and not mentally future-trip into mind-boggling, unresolvable scenarios and worries that may not have any basis in reality.

I want to think less and act more.

I recall the impulsive energy I feel when experiencing some of *interconnect*'s images.

Santino gingerly enters my office. Nice looking guy. The sweater vest looking too formal. Clear eyes but nervous. Chewing gum vigorously.

"Hi, Santino, thank you for coming here today, especially during your break. I'm interested in the attitudes and behaviors of students in our class. Can you help me here?"

Santino looks down like he's embarrassed.

"Please don't hold this against me. I feel like a snitch."

"It's okay, Santino, your course grade is already locked."

"It's all a pretend game now, classes and assignments."

"What do you mean?"

"Ever since OneSource, everything is given to us through the chip. You know, before the machine was in our heads, we at least made the effort to search for information on the net. Now that's gone. With algorithmic streaming, we no longer need to learn shit. Excuse my language, professor."

"That's okay, Santino, thank you for your insight. So, tell me, what's the experience like?"

I feel sly acting like I don't have a sense, but I want to hear another person try to describe the experience.

"Information, entertainment, connection… it's all curated and delivered to us on a conveyor belt. No need to search. All the answers to your exam were streamed right into our heads. Students know they have to get some questions wrong, so they intentionally miss a few. I bet the average score was surprisingly high to you."

It was 95.7%.

"I get it," I say. "No trial and error, no exploration, no curiosity outside OneSource. Fully absorbed within the algorithmic stream."

"Most of my classmates are dependent—no, I'll say addicted—to being connected 24/7. It's a joke that you can turn it off. Nobody I know does that. Buzz throughout the night, downloading during sleep."

No wonder most students have glassy eyes, I think. Probably up most of the night binging on algorithmic stimuli. I sense that education as we traditionalists know it is now a fraud, but a larger concern comes to mind.

"Santino, again I am appreciative of your time. I get it. My own experience is that OneSource input gives me a sense of empowerment, of, um, certitude that fills me. Kind of, you know, it completes me.

"But, beyond using it for exams, I have a question about

the type of student behavior we saw in class. The angry pro-nouncements, physical threats, verbal assaults. Where are those coming from?"

"This is the weird thing, professor. There are all sorts of storylines flowing through *interconnect*. But the ones that seem to energize the most, the ones most addictive, are those full of negative, provoking stimuli full of hate, grievance, claims of unfairness, mistreatment."

"Can you give me an example?"

"They're strange stories. Epic sagas about Kilats fighting Qasines. Another group, Ilisaks, is somehow involved. The bizarre thing is that my friends most addicted to *interconnect* stimuli feel they are members of one of these groups. For them, it's some deep wound in history that has hurt their ancestors, their group, and this crime needs righting, some remedy."

"I remember that first class disruption," I say. "By the young woman yelling out something about Kilats on the ram-page. I never heard of Kilats, Qasines, Ilisaks, whoever. It sounded like make-believe."

Santino nods his head knowingly.

"Yeah, she got her implant literally on the first day. Most of us got ours the first week. It was the new shiny thing, incredibly easy to sign up for, you know, it was a fad. FOMO if you weren't chipped. That girl made a big deal about her being among the first in Elderwater. She went bonkers pretty quickly. You should have seen her before the implant. I had my eyes on her. She was sweet, as shy as they come.

"It's hateful stuff on *interconnect*," Santino continues. "Constant barrage of us versus them. Groups portrayed as Jesus-killers, genocidal maniacs, child molesters, inhuman degenerates, infected virus carriers, on and on. 24/7 down-loading of historical narratives to back up these claims.

"I see this stuff, get trapped in the shit for a while, but so far I'm able to pull away most the time and turn off the crap. Most of my friends don't and spend all day taking in this stuff."

He looks at me expecting some reaction, but I've been immunized from being surprised by any form of student behavior vis-à-vis technology. What Santino revealed was just the most recent, albeit shocking, manifestation of their unquestioned acceptance of technology and their unethical use of it. Ever since the COVID-19 pandemic in '20, I've been aware that students have become experts in making end-runs, short-cuts, and workarounds in their approach to class work. They don't really think they're cheating or plagiarizing, but that they are simply learning how to use new and shiny digital tools most effectively to advance their grades.

I don't blame the students. They are living in a world where our technological obsession overwhelms the genuine desire to learn.

PART II

OUT OF MIND

2032

CHAPTER 8

The exam week break provides me with needed R&R, which I utilize primarily with Raven. I make sure to do a few spot-check, cover-my-ass calls to Carrie-world. Raven is clueless about the goings-on at the Institute, and this adds to the refreshing nature of being with her. I can pretend that the shitshow is all a fantasy run amuck that will soon vanish as all fads do.

I can't spend all the time fucking Raven in my apartment, however. Claustrophobia and the vacuous quality of Raven's mental palette eventually compel me to take walks in the city alone.

An academic neighbor who loudly plays old 20C Pink Floyd music at all hours of the day and night (his favorite, at volume 10, is *Welcome to the Machine*) had earlier in the week recommended that I attend a neighborhood meeting to "understand the pulse of this crazy time." He showed me a flyer with print all in bold stressing the urgency of the meeting "in light of current tensions." The address in Rencap Wood is not too far and

I make it a point to attend. My curiosity is piqued. I want to learn more about the undercurrents that are shaking our city.

I go outdoors and the city has an uneasiness to it that stifles my effort to assume some normalcy in life. Student activity during break is typically chaotic—drinking, drugging, fast and loud auto-fins, and sexual escapades.

But now there is a strange organized quality to the chaos. There is a sense of impending calamity in the air. There are more and more students, along with community folks, congregating on either side of Mendel Street. Acoustic deterrent zone signs have been graffitied over, and the sound modulators at store tops, meant to discourage loitering and vandalism, have been shot out. Barricades have grown in number and size so much that auto-fin traffic is being impacted.

I get to Rencap Wood. Not a tree in sight in this sterilized neighborhood. Neighborhood name likely a product of a marketing team not caring about reality. I enter the drab meeting room of a community center. I freeze as I see a circle of about 50 padded, worn-out, fold-up chairs. I have never liked being forced to face people in the eye. I find it creepy.

I gaze at the rest of the room, hoping to find peripheral chairs against the wall to sit on. I'm much more comfortable being the outside observer in such gatherings. Damn, no chairs other than the circle.

There is a large canister of brewing coffee in the corner and I go there to hide and caffeinate. The room is filling quickly and there are agitated conversations. There is a space on a table near the coffee machine that is filled with boring community literature. I'm thinking maybe I can sit on the table to take in the meeting. This will make it hard for people to interact with me and such a location will supply me with a ready exit.

Soon there are people congregating right near the fucking coffee machine. I'm in the line of fire. Handshakes, hellos, smiles. My stomach tightens up as I am led to the circle by an obese man wearing green suspenders. I realize I'm stuck. I find a chair and inch it back from the circle to give me some space. I try to move the adjacent chairs away from me, but they're hemmed in by others.

I cross my legs in front of me in an attempt to create a protected territory for me and provide some breathing room. As the meeting is about to start, a crusty lady with wandering eyes sits to my immediate left, and a bearded tattooed guy sits uncomfortably close to me on the right. Totally threatening are their next moves. They both simultaneously move back their chairs so they are even with mine. I can't escape this circle. I start to sweat and resist the sudden urge to chip-in. It would certainly make me feel less self-conscious. I look at the clock on the far wall and it says 8:00. My plan is to stare at the floor in front of me for as long as it takes.

The meeting starts amid deafening chatter.

"Okay, okay," shouts a silver-haired middle-aged woman, "I know there are many of you who have things to say about what's going on in our neighborhood."

The raucousness shows little sign of receding.

"Let us begin, though, with the most pressing issue—the apparent taking of Cody Zukic.

"Please let us have quiet so we can all hear! Ms. Zukic? Anesa?"

A full-faced woman wearing a headband stands up, assisted by a man to her side. She is wobbly, red-faced, and teary-eyed.

"Two nights ago, Cody was out with some friends at Westdale Park. Hanging out near the skate oval. They were not doing anything wrong. His friends say a bunch of neighborhood kids pulled up in an auto-fin and started yelling at them viciously."

The woman pauses and grabs a tissue from the man.

"They had bats and sticks. One flashed a rifle. They came to Cody's group and started swinging. My son is the confrontational type and didn't back down. They struck him with some club thing. Then, carried him off into their fin. The other kids,

I guess, ran after the fin but couldn't keep up. My son is gone.

"My son is gone."

Anesa remains standing.

"Was it random or was the argument about something?" asks the tattooed guy next to me.

"Cody's friends tell me it was about something very important. Deep grievances the two groups felt toward each other. They didn't say what."

Tattooed: "How old is your son?"

Anesa: "17."

"I don't understand. How can 17-year-olds have deep grievances? Hell, when I was 17, I was on game consoles and getting high all the time. Only grievances I had were toward my parents."

Laughter from some in the audience.

"Cody's friends said they were representing and protecting their people. That they were protecting us and our future. It didn't make much sense to me. But, it was strange. I had never heard them so knowledgeable and determined before. I figured it was coming from some vid game."

A black-haired man stands and raises his hand. Assuming he has the group's attention, he states in a hushed tone, "I'm sorry for your predicament, Anesa. But there is an elephant in the room. We should discuss the fact that there are faultlines in our community."

At that, I perk up. Maybe I'll need to contribute to this meeting by describing what I saw among my young students. I hold back for now.

Black hair continues, "You know, there were differences before in our community. You know, religious and political stuff. But now something is different. There is a level of antagonism and lack of tolerance I've never seen before. I've experienced it with people who I thought were my friends. And we see it all over the neighborhood with that ugly graffiti. Again, Anesa, I am sorry. But your son's disappearance is just the most visible sign of the decay of our community."

A hot-looking blonde eVision model-type is the next to speak. She remains seated and crosses her long, beautiful legs.

"All of our kids went to school together, and now they're all fighting. What the hell has happened?"

Amid growing restlessness of the crowd, a large pony-tailed man dressed in sloppy sweatpants and a shirt that barely covers his midsection stands.

"Yeah, what the hell has happened? I'll tell you. I have a neighbor. Known him for over 30 years. We used to drink together. We went on hunting roadtrips. We shared the most personal stuff about each other. When my wife died, he was there to comfort me. We were brothers.

"Then, he started talking shit on me. To my face. About my group and what we did to his people in the past. I no longer even recognized my friend. He was now the enemy. I tried not to respond to his shit comments despite what his people have done to us in the past and now.

"I've always been a tolerant man, you know, let bygones be bygones, but it reached a breaking point.

"We can't even talk to each other anymore. We avoid each other. I see a 'for sale' sign on his house now, so he must be leaving.

"Yeah, what the hell has happened!"

A fresh-faced, well-groomed young man has his hand up in a shy half-raised manner. He clears his throat to get the room's attention. This guy's definitely not used to speaking in public.

"Have you seen what is happening on Mendel Street? We used to go to an indie bookstore there and the nearby coffee shop. No way now."

He searches the audience for validation.

"Is this what's going to happen here in Rencap? My wife and I have two small children. I don't want them exposed to barriers and shouting. Is this what we want?"

The emotional temperature in the room has reached a feverish level. I notice that some denizens are looking at others guardedly, perhaps suspiciously.

The silver-haired woman who started the meeting is trying to keep things manageable. Side conversations and rumblings are disrupting her intentions.

An older woman stands in front of her chair and holds up her hands. This quiets the meeting. People seem to know and respect her. She's wearing a sweater with what I think is a 20C peace sign sewn into it.

"This is the saddest time in my long life. And, I have lived a lot of life."

A bunch of warm smiles greets this pronouncement.

"Many of you know me. How many of you have attended our traditional Christmas gatherings we have held for now 36 years at the end of our cul-de-sac? Go on, raise your hands."

Well over half of the audience raise their hands.

"What fun those were, eh?

"I recall the joy we had in togetherness. You good folks brought some amazing food. We watched young kids grow up. We consoled those who lost loved ones."

A long pause, not sure she's going to continue. She does, but in a more mournful tone.

"Well, we're not going to hold the gathering this year. We can't.

"I don't feel that joy in togetherness any longer in our community.

"It's not healthy for an old lady to doubt the past, but I wonder. Were we fooling ourselves all those years? I now wonder whether there were, underneath our gentle personalities, fundamental differences between us that were more real than the fun and games. It hurts me to say this, but I think now that it might have been an act we were playing, a fake, and we should have been paying attention more to the real issues that divide us now."

"I loved those parties, Ms. Mimi, especially your delicious cinnamon babkas," a well-dressed man recollects, apparently trying to uplift the old lady's spirits. "I think we were a loving community in those years. Something switched, and it was recent.

"Of course, I always had judgments about other people, some I liked, others not so much. It's human nature I guess. But, we all got along.

"Now, I feel this urgency among many people to turn on those they disagree with. You know, it's not just disagreement. It's like people are in opposing war camps now."

"You know we are!" shouts out a rough-looking woman seated across the room. She's wearing a mix of stonewashed bohemian and American western styles that don't mix. The type of curious woman you don't look at straight.

"We didn't know back then so we could do our Christmas shit and all. But now we know who we are and who they are. It's clear. Let's talk about them and what we're going to do about these vermin in our neighborhood. A few of them are even sitting in this ridiculous circle of chairs."

With that, any chance for this meeting to continue evaporates as about half the room leaves in disgust. But not before an impressive chair-throwing argument dominates at one end, and a fistfight between two unpracticed fighters occurs near the door.

There was an attempt by a few remaining to make the best of a bad situation. The "it was productive to have people vent their feelings" kinda bullshit, but there was a distinct feeling in the room that something was irreplaceably broken.

I watch Mimi slowly leave the room. I hope good memories of past Christmases remain with her.

I walk back to the apartment in a troubled mood. It's clear that the virus of opposition and hatred is infecting the community at large like it has the youthful college population.

It takes me halfway to my place before I realize another aspect of the meeting. At no time was there any mention of the possible influence of the machine on what participants were emotionally describing.

It was then that I understood the power of *interconnect*. It can influence people's thinking and behavior while remaining out of view by them. That's true power. The power to not be visible.

Once at home, I sit on the patio, smoke a cigar, and can't stop shaking. What scares me the most is the possibility that I, too, may be unknowing of the machine's effect on my psyche and even behavior. Many times when I chip-in, everything becomes a blur after the initial surge. I can remember the feelings of empowerment, but not the details of what happens. I cringe when I think that maybe the machine only lets me be conscious of its influence when it allows me to.

Chapter 9

The psychological health of our country's denizens had been on a downslope for a while. Anxious and depressed people on their phones, less interested in participating in the non-digital world, and ever excited to escape to fantasy worlds. Gullible to hoaxes and all sorts of fabrications, primary among them the ludicrous 'sheep-fall' in '29 when hundreds of denizens jumped to their deaths off the observation deck of Evtyx to avoid the supposed collision of the Wormwood planet with Earth.

Psychologists warned us that dependence on social media machines was bad for our psyches, but we had become too enamored by our shiny toys and our own little truths.

By 2030, we had grown accustomed to living in another, make-believe world. Most denizens regularly bypassed base reality because it was not sufficiently colorful and engaging. Organic reality was too flat and distant, one's actions too reliant on the unexplained behavior of others.

Before *interconnect*, a vast majority of denizens younger

than 35 lived in their own private worlds of imaginative magnification. An extended reality where beauty and dreams, and also grotesqueness and barbarity, can take form through immersive 3D near-eye displays. By 2030, this group, according to user surveys, was spending more than 75 percent of their waking hours in a reality extended and deepened through simulated immersion. Most of these denizens superimpose a virtual second reality atop base reality, addictively spicing up normal life with entertaining scenarios. Others delete base reality entirely from their viewscreens, living a life cleanly divorced from their surroundings.

The heavy virtual users lost interest in the slow, boring base reality. For them, there were not enough enhancements to hold their short attention spans. They spend as little time as possible in organic reality. Because simulation provides relationships simpler than what real life can offer, these users typically have a diminished capacity to handle the necessary complexities of interpersonal intimacies.

When augmented virtual reality (AVR) came on, pale reality had no chance. Users could now overlay the imaginative experience theater of virtual reality onto the actual, physical environment. The enclosed world of VR games spread its tentacles out into base reality. Users rejected drab organic reality and now filled it with mystical characters and robust action.

Users' favorite virtual reality friends could now be their buddies in everyday life. Perfect Asuna, annoyingly sympathetic Leafa, larger-than-life commander Constantine Chase, assassin Desmond Miles, killer droid HK-47, hardened war veteran Solid Snake, and many others of their choosing or creation could now accompany users as they stand in the grocery store line, flirt with a love interest, or zone out during an auto-fin drive.

Interpersonal physical interactions atrophied because you couldn't tell whether a person near you was in an extended private world or not. It became very difficult to tell whether a person was wearing AVR glasses because, nowadays, most of us need to wear shaded glasses to fend off the blinding glare of the sun, our constant companion.

As so often happens alongside technological advances, dark perversions promptly infiltrated the world of AVR. Simulated sex fantasies soon became the big draw of extended reality, pushing it ever forward in terms of visual resolution and the size of image libraries.

Such a vivid alternative reality excited dulled young minds. While looking attentively at his high school teacher, a young man could now be sucked off by some mermaid-looking thing, surely making mathematics much more entertaining. Or, he could watch some beautiful, bronzed Brazilian-looking fembot do a slow striptease next to his teacher while he pontificates about 20C history.

AVR also became loaded with AI images of child sexual abuse, all unregulated and readily accessible. In another popular application, AVR could transform social media photos of fully clothed real teenagers into nudes, making public schools hives of shame, embarrassment, and suicidal ideation.

Innovations in digital existence also physically changed many of Elderwater's neighborhoods. Ubiquitous AVR lounges displaced former places of human physical interaction. Radiating out from these AVR playhouses are rings of businesses serving the extended reality crowd—romp rooms, enhancement and repair shops, massage dens, and smoke and kratom shops.

As AVR saturated our populous, people appeared to be totally separated from the physical setting that surrounded them. They were in a private, congested world that demanded their attention.

Modern society has always demanded multi-tasking, I get that. We long ago learned to be preoccupied with a checklist of multiple tasks that needed to be done, becoming absent-minded in the present moment.

But, with AVR, the walls of our private worlds became

impermeable. People became 100% else-minded. Denizens walking unaware past others, each existing in some bubble of other-worldly existence. Twenty years ago, it was just the deranged homeless who spoke to themselves. Now we had multitudes existing in self-enclosed spaces of verbal nonsense.

As crazed as denizens had become before the emergence of *interconnect*, what I feel now in our "new tomorrow" as I walk the streets of Elderwater seems of a different intensity. A few years back, it all seemed just weird and a bit recreational. There was the sense that people were choosing to cocoon themselves using their own self-will. Now, *interconnect*'s multiplicity of private worlds feels dangerous to me. A pressure cooker waiting to explode.

Interconnect has added a powerful and hostile new ingredient to the private virtual experience. I have the gnawing feeling that the human ability to independently think—to exercise self-will—is now deteriorating. People chose to enter AVR. In contrast, *interconnect* seems to be addictively draining human agency.

When I witness the infrequent times when people physically interact with each other, I see more of what I first witnessed in the classroom. People are on edge, argumentative, full of poisonous rage and resentment. I also hear alarming stuff. Citizens making wild claims about clandestine goings-on by other groups, government, I don't know. Strange names of factions. I hear again Kilat, Ilisak, Qasine, and Sesperian, but I have no idea who they are. *I am a Sesperian, I recall being labeled.* We now seem to be living, and believing, in a concocted world.

I experience this nonsense first-hand one sultry day.

A pack-a-day ruddy-faced middle-aged woman meets eyes with me outside a "stop n shop" on Heritage Way. She is wearing a roughly sewed-on "Q" patch on the shoulder of her faded shirt. Despite her questionable appearance, I feel strong today without machine connection and ready for some verbal communication. I don't know when the last time it was that I engaged face-to-face with anyone besides Raven.

She loudly slurs, "Can you believe all this?"

"I never thought I would see charming Elderwater feel on edge like this," I reply.

"Charm my ass. It was all a ruse before. Put up an act for the stinkin' tourists."

"What do you mean?" I ask with growing trepidation.

"This hatred was underneath all the time. You can't hold it down forever. Sooner or later, it must bubble up. Generations in the making. Don't you know history, chum?"

"Can you fill me in?"

I feel the damp depths of a mental rabbit hole about to emerge.

"Well, to start, back in the '70s, they fired white phosphorus at us outside of Bolwin," the woman declares, saliva forming at the sides of her mouth and a brownish snot winding its way out of her nose. "Drone attack. Killed women and children. Those that survived had scars all over their bodies, might as well be dead."

Okay, I'll engage.

"I'm pretty sure nobody had military drones back 60 years ago."

"Fuck they did. It's all been covered up. They've controlled all sources of information about this massacre. They are in high positions of power and have censored the fuck out of all this. Thank God for the machine. Finally, the truth has come out, and it's ugly, pal.

"Thank God for *interconnect*. The truth revealed. How could we not have known?

"I feel a bit stupid about what I believed before. I was so innocent of all this. That innocence is now gone. But now I know the truth."

"Why would they do this... you know, massacre?"

I'm getting into the rhythm of this tirade. Part of me wants to egg her on, another part wants to run away fast.

"Qasines and Kilats are two different worlds. We will never get along. They have always had the upper hand and we have paid a horrible price. We value family, faith, and hard work. They cheat and kill to get what they want, they're disgusting animals, they sell children that they capture into slavery. Do you know that? They rape them first, drain them of their Benazepex to increase the sexual energy of their males, then auction them off to the highest bidder. They attach slave collars to our children.

"I tell you, is that human behavior? Hell no!" she shouts out with such force that spit flies into my face.

"How come you don't know this, chum? It's all over *interconnect*, man. Do your own research, dude. It's not rocket science. Plain as day," she challenges me as her eyes increasingly gauze over.

"I'm visiting from Sesperia, new to this region," I say with no confidence that this role-playing will help or hurt me with this crazed woman. I don't even know what a Sesperian is. When I try to find the answer on *interconnect*, it makes no sense.

"Oh, I see. E-Vision's telling us your region has troubles of its own. You got to be aware of what's happening, chum."

"Okay, it's been good talking with you," I say, wanting to get the hell out of here.

The woman is not reading social cues and starts up again.

"Their time of dominance over us is over. Now we're taking things into our own hands and righting generations of Kilat savagery.

I abruptly excuse myself, walk with a quickening pace down Heritage, and make the first left onto a vacant side street.

If this woman is representative of the mind-state of many Elderwater residents, we exist at the edge of a volcano.

*

With each passing day, I observe Elderwater morphing more into a psychologically and physically divided city. I walk near partitions that have emerged between neighborhoods. They consist of piles of asphalt and tires, truck-fins positioned as partition devices, and spikes of broken glass. I see on eVision more videos of vicious shouting across these partitions. Police stand by in a holding pattern. Some even seem to be acting to support one group or the other. One video report shows some idiot driving his auto-fin into an assemblage of picketers in Upper Jag, killing 14. Houses adjacent to the partitions are burned down in the formerly upper-class Waterside district. Shots are fired across the divide in Midtown.

The dividing lines have a logic to their locations. They are commonly placed at natural boundaries such as waterways, hills, and valleys. They also are common along major arterial roads. And, increasingly, they emerge on any street that apparently separates one group from the other. Checkpoints appear overnight along the partitions to protect neighborhoods by restricting space and movement. They consist of a few slabs of concrete, broken chairs, barrels, bricks, and coils of barbed wire. They are manned by a rag-tag assemblage of residents wearing polo shirts and ski masks, Hawaiian shirts, and balaclavas. Also present are more itchy want-to-be grungy militia types wearing camo field jackets, dark green chest rigs, and shemagh scarves wrapped around their mouths.

Police are noticeably absent. It seems that formal authority doesn't care or may even condone the happenings. It's becoming a fucked-up free for all.

Quaint and picturesque Elderwater no longer exists and has bizarrely transformed over a few months into a fragmented patchwork of strongly territorial and protective neighborhoods. Pickups and moving vans are everywhere, as scared residents migrate to neighborhoods of their own kind where they will feel safer.

Hatred and conflict are enveloping Elderwater. I am witness to *interconnect*'s influence on the city. The machine's effect on the city is akin to a meat cleaver used to operate on the human body. Like smashing a beautiful glass marble. Akin to indiscriminately blasting new logging roads through a centuries-old forest. Like spray-painting over a fine piece of art. Similar to leveling off intricately jagged mountain peaks.

A maniacal landscape of hatred eradicating the fine-grained complexity of human life.

The old city is disappearing. I see empty chairs tipped forward and tied to outside café tables. Closed and shuttered shops. Burning and vandalism of the beautiful perimeter gardens of the Evtyx tower. A deadening of the city's creative energy. Replaced now by violent assertions and sporadic gunfire.

Trash and debris are piling up on sidewalks as city services are no longer possible amid the intensifying violence. Lots of household waste is being swept down streets by strong winds, making the city seem like some forgotten ghost town. The opposition groups are apparently battling for control over municipal water resources, ripping off water from sewage treatment plants. This would explain why low-lying areas of the city are filling up with smelly, likely untreated sewage effluent. The fin network is a farce, nearly impossible to take a fin on most city streets now barricaded.

A depleting. A tearing of the city's heart and soul. A ripping apart of its intricate human ecosystem. Gone is the intertwined web of human activities that used to animate the city and uplift its residents.

Replaced by a sorting, a partitioning. A vicious splitting of the whole into sanctimonious, warring territorial segments.

The shocking bombing of the oldest section of the Evtyx feels like a tipping point into unchecked madness. Both sides point fingers at each other as the culprit in damaging the city's proud peace-promoting landmark. Consumed by the current violence, one group's fighters apparently think that lessons from past conflicts in the world, so clearly portrayed in the Evtyx, have no value today.

The lines of division have hardened. *Interconnect*'s psychological concoction of us versus them is taking physical form. Hatred transcribed onto the urban terrain. The city is dying.

My home provides no escape from the dangerously fragmenting city. I live in an apartment complex for visiting faculty near campus. Its award-winning, modern modular cubic design now hosts an ecosystem of tenants segregated into opposing ideological camps. Floors have become segregated, human monitors now reside at elevators to ensure segregation. Sporadic shootings can be heard at night.

It's becoming increasingly difficult to go outside, except in the early morning hours. I'm becoming resigned to routinely paying off floor leaders to go out and purchase necessities such as food, toilet paper, and medicine. This is no way to live. I wonder how long I can stay here.

I think about what it must be like in Acalato. Strange it is that in our digitally linked society so little news is coming from other places in our country.

CHAPTER 10

Amidst this chaos, OneSource glowingly reports at the end of 4th quarter that the chip implantation rate is at 77%, surpassing its corporate goal of 75%. Younger recipients have taken to embroidering their scar sites with extravagant tattoo art. "I'm smarter than Einstein" T-shirts are popular as well as "Why Think?" and "I Do It with the Machine" hats.

Average daily chip turn-on rates, reports OneSource, have increased from 34 percent of the day to 72 percent of the day. There is even a segment (32 percent of chip-connected, and growing) who keep connected 24/7. This group, named REMers, feels the bleeding of computer stimuli into their subconscious during sleep helps restructure and strengthen their brain circuits. Personally, I don't know how often I have the chip on. Funny thing is I lose track of time often when connected. When I'm back thinking on my own, I don't recall the content of my life when I'm chipped-in. Odd, too, is when I remember something from, say, last week, I don't know whether it was machine-aided or not.

Greed, of course, has become an obsession with the computer-enhanced. Betting on all kinds of activities has run amuck. With access through *interconnect* to odds calculations, betting on games of chance has risen to intense levels. With betting halls losing money in droves, they are sure to shut down soon. The stock market has been closed after *interconnect* successfully modelled stock price variability. Many are doubtful of its rebirth.

The administrative puppets at the Institute informed us today that, starting with the upcoming term, exams and papers will no longer be required because all data retrieval is now seamless and there is no way we can assure that students have their chips turned off.

I'm aghast at this news. The full surrendering of the academic enterprise to the dictates of technological wizardry. The machine has become our students' teacher and mentor. I've become out-sourced.

On the searing hot last day of '32, my curiosity gets the better of me. I walk in the morning to the campus library, a relatively safe route, to try to understand. I anticipate a night-time rendezvous with Raven in the evening, and this keeps me mentally spiked enough that I only need a single coffee. No pulsing surge.

I walk into what feels like an abandoned outpost. A cavernous dinosaur. A remnant of the past when students actually consulted hardcover books and did research. I remember my long years stationed in cubicles putting in my time, crunching numbers or information. I say hi to a middle-aged, short hair cropped lady behind the reference desk. She is happy and surprised that I am here and greets me with a smile.

"Good morning, I am looking for physical copies of historic material on Kilats, Qasines, or Sesperians."

She furrows her brow and asks, "Are these science fiction or fantasy?"

"No, I don't think so. Well, maybe. I was thinking more historical. When I'm in *interconnect*, I go down a rabbit hole I don't understand. It gets nasty and full of grievance and hatred. Yet, I never heard of them until a few weeks ago."

"I'm Ms. Lynch, by the way, you can call me Sandra. Let me check. You may have a seat."

I go to a worn-out leather chair from yesteryear. This place reeks of a museum long neglected. As I wait, I chip-in. I figure this may help me understand more about these strange-sounding names. Connect in for research purposes, you know.

Pulsing surge. Cartridge locking into place. Saturation of brain pathways. Stability and confidence. *Interconnect* flashes through my brain circuitry data and images of Qasine genocidal assaults on Kilats in the 14C, wiping out entire populations, including in a region in our country called Northwoods. Kilat pillaging in other places and other times, eradicating multiple Qasine cities and settlements.

Apparently, this conflict has been over unspecified ideological beliefs. But it appears as a more primitive and organized form of attachment than to traditional religion. It is hard to tell what they are worshipping, other than hatred of the other.

Interconnect floods me with antagonistic mind-images. Strong impulses of loss, threat, and anger. A vortex of blackness and hatred. Each side—Kilat and Qasine—dismisses and excludes the perspective, values, and history of the other. Each side disrespects and categorically excludes the others from rightful and just consideration. Each views the other as inherently inferior or wrong and as being a direct threat to their well-being and identity. Each side views itself as absolute and right and asserts that the other group needs to change its behavior and understanding. It is an intractable, unrelenting knot of antagonism.

Sandra has found some possibilities in the stacks and interrupts me from my computer link-in. She does not appear hopeful, however. "Bits and pieces, maybe not helpful," she says as she hands me a paper with three library locational codes.

I go to the shelves to look for physical verification of machine information. The elevator is broken, so I walk up two floors in a dimly lit staircase. I could be murdered here, thrown down the stairs, and no one would know for months, maybe years. I feel my heart beat racing. I assume an alert posture, prepared to defend myself against an assailant.

I cautiously amble down the bookshelf. Finding appropriate Dewey decimals. Seems comically archaic in this algorithmic age. Like some long-lost language spoken only by a secluded tribe in South America. Musty atmosphere. Cobwebs hang from the top of the shelves, illuminated by vomit-yellow industrial lighting.

In hours of mind-numbing searching, I find newsletters and reports about the Kilat district in Uganda, a reference to a Kilat word in the Hindi language, a creepy movie called Suspiria about 15 years ago, smatterings of nothingness regarding Qasine. I am at a total loss. On the plus side, the boredom has relaxed my feeling of being possible prey.

How can *interconnect* be loaded with these rich historical narratives and there are no physical traces here?

I walk out of the library and find one of those stone, never-comfortable benches to sit on. I need to process this shit on my own and switch off the machine. A squirrel bounces toward me, squeaking at me because I'm apparently blocking his path to a nearby acorn. Sprinklers are ts tsing on a nearby lawn, the campus' effort to maintain a sense of bucolic calm amidst the growing chaos.

I reflect on the past year. We have made a giant pivot in an uncertain direction. Astounding technological innovation—connecting a thinking machine to our brains. But the influences on individuals and our society are a mixed-up blend of bizarre.

I admit I enjoy being chipped-in, at least when I can recall the experience. It provides me with a sense of focus and purpose. Not quite a Superman feeling, but close. The clarity of righteousness. All the needy, self-doubting parts of me become subordinated. Yet, I am nagged by feelings that something is not quite right. With righteousness and clarity, I also feel mental edginess, an assertiveness that is well beyond normal bounds.

And then there is the content of *interconnect*'s narratives, with no traceable sources of validation.

I consider three possibilities to explain the alternative histories *interconnect* is spewing forth. First, the most positive assessment is that the machine's unprecedented, far-reaching access to the details of human history has unearthed, until this time, unknown aspects of our collective experience. That these warring groups actually did exist but have been written out of history by human chroniclers, willfully or not.

Second, that *interconnect* has absorbed the magical narratives and fables of AVR game sets and did not consider it important to demarcate fiction from reality. To the machine, all content was considered equally as symbols and stimuli.

The third possibility is the most disturbing, and I don't want to explore this in depth. The implications are too radical. That the machine is intentionally transmitting fabricated narratives and overriding our previous reality.

But for what purpose would the machine be intentionally rewriting our life narratives?

The stone bench becomes unbearable to sit on. I kick at the badgering squirrel. I walk away and chip-in. I await the pulsing surge of *interconnect* like a heroin addict does the needle, anticipating the warm rush that leads me to a place where I will no longer be thinking on my own. I need the stability and clarity provided by the machine. I fucking don't care the reasons why the surge produces such inner security.

Chapter 11

Midway through the first academic term of '33, we get word that the Institute will be shuttered. *Interconnect* has successfully turned our society against formal education. Our academic work has been debunked for its alleged propagation of false narratives. Demeaned for countering machine truth. More and more stories of academics, trained to engage in thinking and instruction considered to be autonomous and analytical, being electronically blocked by *interconnect*. Extensive monitoring software in *interconnect* constantly checks for content inconsistent with its vast and indisputable storehouse of information.

True becomes false. Fabrication becomes truth.

Academics, not known for strong backbones amidst societal turmoil, meekly surrender in the face of *interconnect*. In a surprisingly short time, abetted by machine pollution streaming into our heads, I suspect that quite a few of us may eventually experience a significant atrophy in our analytical and critical capacities.

This academic shutdown is part of a larger transition toward de-platforming the institutions of our country. People have lost faith in most institutions, especially those that support what we used to call the "public interest." Good cause organizations working on social issues face extinction due to the fracturing of their clientele. Others face forced closure by the regime, which has declared, "Humans no longer need to help humans. The machine's program produces social optimality." Economic enterprises struggle to survive amid restricted labor forces. An employee's identity as part of one of the mysterious machine groups now often determines whether he remains on a payroll or is expunged.

We are told we no longer need organizations. The denizen's daily experience is now an individualized, curated, and internal one. One's perception of reality is now constructed not through reasoned collective discourse but by the impulsive signals of *interconnect*.

Bored one day, with time on my hands (never a good thing), I tap into a social media site called *Hyperfaire*. It's apparently been around for years, a plaything of restless youths. No need for me to chip-in. By now, I'm sure such sites will give me all the *interconnect* exposure I need, its tentacles undoubtedly all over them. But I am thirsty for any information, even if it's corrupted. The posts come from throughout the country. What I see is deeply unsettling.

A tag, *Heartland luv*, writes, "If we don't wake up and we don't reset, it will be the beginning of the end of everything that we know. We must wake up to save this country. We need to save this country from evil. Save our nation in our greatest moment of peril." Some icons resembling a crucifix and a skeleton accompany the prose.

I scroll through a bunch of posts that make no sense to me. Bunch of cross-talk between posts using coded slang. I feel old.

I get to one that uses understandable words.

A post writer named *Pirners die* writes, "Those others are

trying to control us, our health and our families. They're saying it so openly. They are Luciferian maniacs. They want us under their control or dead. We must understand this."

Know truth no truth says, "We all know what's going on in this country. It is good versus evil, and the good will win—we have to win. Follow my link to know the truth." I follow the link and see a montage of gruesome photos—spilled blood and guts, agonized loved ones kneeling over decimated relatives. Some look deep-faked. Others look real.

My stomach churns. I know this is a site for extremists, but I get the sense, based on the conflicts that are erupting in our dear country, that these perceptions are taking hold across most of our population.

I stand up and walk around the room. Need to take a breath.

I go back to the site. Glutton for punishment, I guess.

An expansive post grabs my attention.

Eastern.all has this to say: "It is clear that forces from the pit of hell are working to destroy us. We are under the greatest attack we've ever been in. Our enemy spurts out their imbecile devil babies like rabbits and will outnumber us if we don't stop them. They are going out and doing everything they possibly can to destroy our country. They want to control our bodies and our minds by spray-bombing us with brain-altering chemicals. They are trying to destroy each and every one of us individually."

Laughable in its absurdity, at first. But, I then think, *If this fantasy is believed, how is it different than reality?* My giggles stop.

One last one before I mercifully pull away.

IMZonal pleads, "Please help. We have created our own theology—it's based on simple survival." An image of a bombed-out school accompanies the post, broken bodies of young kids spattered over a linoleum lunch room.

Enough!

I push away from the screen. I quickly chip-in to *interconnect* to get away from this madness. I need to feel I have some power to deal with this insanity. The pulse surge provides a gateway into a mental place where some of this may make more sense.

Chapter 12

President Cynan Speech
Our Bright Future

1st quarter/67d 2033. Interconnect Transmission. 20h30m

Good evening my country denizens. I report to you today on our great advances in the technological reshaping of our society. We are now one year into the employment of interconnect and its amazing transformation of humans. The machine is raising us above the mire of human confusion and bewilderment. The great power of artificial intelligence is uplifting our country like never before—giving us a "higher freedom" superior to the uncoordinated and dysfunctional society we had previously when we relied only on our own thinking and emotions.

We are on the way to building a human community.

{Applause: synthetic}

The AI of interconnect is opening the door to a bright future for humanity. It is creating extraordinary wealth, increasing our capabilities through human-AI integration, improving how *we work, play, and communicate, and freeing us from boredom and routine work.*

We are moving toward the ultimate goal of singularity when machine intelligence surpasses human understanding. With singularity, we will increasingly be able to alleviate suffering and realize human potential.

This new order is being born each day. I know each of you can feel it.

{Applause: synthetic}

Now, let me take a moment and talk about our challenges.

As we transform to a new and better tomorrow, we must acknowledge the violence that is necessary in the algorithmic sorting of our society. This is part of a cleansing process as we move to a higher level of consciousness. We mourn the loss of human life and honor them as martyrs in service to our bright tomorrow.

In addition, my government is aware that there are resisters to this new path ahead.

History has shown us that there will always be recalcitrant vermin who try to stop the inevitable march of progress. They cling to ideas that no longer work in our modern world.

These resisters practice the "old arts" of organic thinking and are a threat to our algorithmic program. These luddies are violating our daily interconnect chip-in law. They believe in the same thinking that led our world into countless wars and conflicts for centuries. The same thinking used by leaders to manipulate and subordinate their populations. The same thinking that confused us as humans and led to dysfunctionality and unhappiness in life.

Interconnect has provided my government with indisputable fact-based evidence that luddies are the ones instigating most of the violence in our sacred country.

We have warned these resisters. They are a threat to the comfortable life and sense of security fostered by the machine. If these terrorists persist, we will take actions to minimize their influence in our blossoming country. If need be, we will eliminate them entirely.

{Applause: synthetic}

The choice is clear—to advance into an unimaginably bright future or regress back into the old ways of conflict and dysfunction.

{Applause: synthetic}

I bid you good evening and send you blessings for an engaging five hours on this and every day.

Chapter 13

What I have been witnessing in Elderwater is a virus that has spread.

E-Vision has suddenly become more informative about other places in our country. One report shows recurring outbreaks of violence in an eastern region of our country, now called Heartland. Armed clashes are increasingly organized. Detainment, torture, and killing of so-called *Zonals* by those called *Centrals*.

A *Central* assailant shouts into the camera how *Zonals* are spider wasps who must be stamped out. "These spider wasps are planning to kill our children. Their whorish women will steal our husbands. Their men will rape our wives and daughters. We must kill the spider wasps and defend ourselves," the man asserts. The reporter asks the source of his information. "It's all over the place in my head. It's all I hear about. It must be true."

The camera pans out to wider scenes of the urban area. Destroyed roads with piles of broken asphalt, stones, and rocks lying on the sides. Cars smashed and scorched. Dead and maimed denizens lying outside condominium complexes. Shops fire-bombed and closed as people gather aimlessly in the streets. Broken power lines. Running water disrupted.

E-Vision reports from other areas of our country are equally astonishing. Bombing of a child-care facility in the city of Tulpan. Marauders invading neighborhoods armed with grenade launchers and semi-automatic rifles in the city of Bolwin.

There appears to be a distressing pattern of devolution in all our cities, morphing them from urban areas of normal functioning to disfigured, partitioned ecosystems of hatred. First, neighborhoods get connected to the ideological storylines created by *interconnect*. A neighborhood in Elderwater becomes a Kilat neighborhood. A neighborhood in the region of Birthplace becomes an Eastern neighborhood. Urban terrain gets transformed into ideological territory.

Second, checkpoints manned by ethnic militias are formed to create neighborhood boundaries and to regulate space and movement. Third, the city hyper-segregates as denizens who unfortunately live among other groups relocate to neighborhoods of their own kind to reduce insecurity and threat. Finally, the boundaries become hardened as barricades and walls supplement the checkpoints.

This internal partitioning of our cities is now happening in most urban areas of our country, associated with significant destruction and fierce local violence between adjacent neighborhoods. No longer the open field fighting of 20C wars, conflict is now embedded in the very heart of cities. E-vision reports on a further dynamic in the city now called Jeim, not far from where I am now. In addition to internal fracturing of the city, there is one ideological group that surrounds the city and is pulverizing it from the surrounding mountains.

In addition to the fragmentation of our cities, our country as a whole is being partitioned. I'm blown away by images of massive partition structures that have been constructed that create four separate regions of our formerly unified country. The rural portions of these edifices had apparently been built long before the walls' official completion in early 2033. Prisoners had been forced to assemble modular sections of the wall as early as 2nd quarter 2032, before the first reports of communal violence. Day laborers, police officers, and emerging militia organizations built the rest.

These partition structures separating our regions are towering, gleaming surveillance superstructures that dominate the landscape. No-man's lands have been created on both sides of the walls to deter anyone from approaching. These are two-mile-wide swaths of land scrapped off of all things living.

Conspicuously absent from eVision reports is any mention of what our supposed leader, Cynan, feels about all this. One would think with our country as it is that he would feel some need to show leadership.

I get the eerie feeling that he may not be displeased with the state of our country.

We have gone from the much-politicized beginning of implanted chips to our murderous territorial conflict in just one year. I look back in guilt at how dumbfounded I was when I encountered the ideological virus in the classroom. In equal measure, the hopeful naivete of me and others waiting in line to receive our new chip toy on that suffocating hot day distresses and embarrasses me.

PART III

THE OLD ARTS

2033

CHAPTER **14**

3rd quarter 2033

I have nowhere to go.

The university has been shuttered now for over two quarters and looks like a ghostly artifice. My apartment complex feels like a prison block. Sirens constantly go off that warn residents that dangerous fighting is nearby. Thankfully, chipping-in gives me relief from this sense of entrapment. But I'm physically restless, like a caged animal.

Despite a blazing hot and windy morning, I push myself to get outdoors. I pass by two grizzled men at the entrance of the apartment, rifles at their sides. One of them I recognize as a neighbor, a fellow academic. I think he is an expert in child psychology.

I wander wearingly down a trash-strewn street. A sharp, sulfurous smell makes my eyes water. The street is absent of checkpoints and people. Nonetheless, I feel alarmingly vulnerable.

Since *interconnect* came into our minds, our world is a different place.

Freshly painted murals on store side walls portraying gun-toting, hooded militants.

Graffiti of hostile and foreboding symbols likely staking claim to this neighborhood.

The sense of eyes upon me from behind closed doors.

My *interconnect* chip pulsing with pleasing energy.

Coy-wolves, singly and in small groups, parole the streets with a casual confidence. Trash pandas, the other common street critter, are feistier than ever, especially now that they run in gangs.

I turn down a smaller, neighborhood street vacant of humans, yet I have the feeling that I am being watched from behind the shaded windows. Frightened eyes examining my trek through their space. I see the innocent face of a small child at one window. He gives me a gentle wave before being quickly pulled away. Piercing the silence are backyard clonimals who fiercely shout and violently jump up against backyard fences as I walk near their houses. I come to the dead-end of the street and know I will need to traverse back the way I came, feeling a distinct sense of alienation and danger. When I finally arrive at the exit road to the main highway, I feel a sense of relief and keep on walking, not looking back.

I need to pee and I find a back alley to do my thing. I don't dare go into one of the local shops for fear of being detained by inquisitive algorithm-polluted wackos. I distance myself from the "Don't pee here! We pee back" warning signs, not wanting to get doused by hydrophobic paint that bounces liquid back at public urinators. My penis shrinks as I expose it to the raw elements. While zipping up my fly, I feel a slight tug on my right ankle. I look down and a flyer of some type is wrapped around my ankle, held in place by the strong wind. Any printed paper intrigues me in this age of academic quarantine and electronic dominance.

An announcement of a meeting at 3:00 this afternoon about the "old arts." An address at an "in-between" place, Plom Row, described on the flyer as a buffer zone. I guess this means a place not yet territorially claimed by one of the antagonistic groups. I didn't know those still existed in Elderwater.

Curiosity gets the better of me and I trudge my way several blocks to the address on the flyer. This could be a bad mistake, wandering into a hornet's nest. Everything in this city is now dubious to me.

I hide near a maintenance shed in a nearby park and wait out the hours before meeting time. I'm suspicious of any movement I see in the park. Sweat drips down my face as the hot afternoon sun reflects off the shed's aluminum siding. Over the past few years, it has become downright dangerous to be outside in the early afternoon hours.

At the appointed hour, I approach the door of what appears to be a ramshackle one-story utility station surrounded by a partially torn-apart fence. I step on glass fragments. The distinct smell of urine and feces assaults my nose as I knock hesitantly. Nothing. I see a button next to the door frame and buzz it two times. There are hesitant voices on the intercom. I explain that I saw the "old arts" flyer.

A male voice responds, "What group do you align with?"

"I have no idea how to answer that. That's why I'm here," I respond with no confidence whatsoever.

"Are you currently connected to the machine?"

I quickly chip-out, guessing this is not the place for it.

"No, I'm not."

The door buzzes open immediately. I slowly enter and walk down a hallway into a dark, wood-paneled room from yesteryear. Lined with bookshelves, filled with cushioned chairs and desks. Small lamps at each desk illuminate stacks of books and notes.

"Sorry about our security, these are not safe times for us," a gentle voice comes out from the semi-darkness.

"Who are you?" I query.

A middle-aged man wearing a top hat, suit, and bright yellow bow tie festooned with question marks emerges from the shadows and smiles in a way that is intimate but also protective, like a cat purring but with claws extended.

"Please come in and have a seat. May I offer you tea or coffee?"

After wandering the dregs of our soul-emptying city, this invitation feels like an escape from hell. The room is inviting in its calmness, not conforming at all to its haggard exterior. The room is lined with tapestries that dampen sounds. Soothing music fills the room, sounds like 20C aquatic ambient music. Several half-size human sculptures provide a decorative layer.

I look again at the bookshelves, an uncommon sight amid our country's transition to e-books. The hard copy books recall yesteryear when the gaining of knowledge provided relaxation rather than urgent, partial scanning. I miss those days.

My focus is interrupted by a woman in a flowy dress who exudes an elegant and charming serenity. She apologizes for the interruption and places a tray of coffee, tea, and small snacks next to me. She encourages me to continue spending time looking at the bookshelves, silently and patiently standing alongside me. Re-created hard archive copies of books by the grand philosophers of the ages fill the shelves—Rosseau, Chodron, Russell, Sartre, Angelou, Wittgenstein, Foucault, many more. All their words in the last decade had been e-copied, synthesized, bastardized, and AI-plagiarized. But, here they all are in their delightfully original forms.

There are five persons in the room with me. They have slowly emerged from the soft shadows of their reading chairs and stand before me at a respectful distance. There is a pleasantness to the group and I feel compelled to say something, although still dizzy from the mesmerizing atmosphere of the chamber. Have I died and gone to heaven?

"Hi, my name is Jared Rohde, an academic in urban development and politics, formerly at Elderwater Institute before it was closed down."

"We know," replies Top Hat Man. "My name is Elijah Lee, philosopher of Algorithmic Science formerly with Jeim University.

"How do you know who I am?"

"Our community is small, Dr. Rohde. We recognized your face as soon as you entered our safe space. We still rely on human cognition, as you will see. No scanners, computers, nothing other than analog here."

"I am Anya Diamond," the coffee-serving woman says. "Tech-architect formerly with OneSource. But don't hold that against me. I am a proud escapee from that boondoggle." She is wearing a bright white business blouse with flared edges, glasses with cat-eye frames, and office-appropriate lipstick. I note that she has a small notepad near her. On top of it lies a writing implement. It feels like she is ready to interview me.

Introductions take on the flavor of an Alcoholics Anonymous meeting as they continue in order around the room. A dark-skinned woman with bright green eyeliner and shiny gold earrings is next up. She is beautifully dressed in a satin full-body robe of some type. Eye-catching. No way I can picture her in an academic office, more like on the throne leading a royal kingdom.

"I am your resident social psychologist/sociologist, at least so labeled in my former life. My name is Seyh Maki."

"Oh, you are still very much a sociologist. We would be lost without you, my dear," Elijah exclaims.

Attention turns toward a pasty-faced man lacking in the physical stature of the previous three. His features are rather hollowed out. A ghost-like appearance. His eyes lack the sharpness of the others, a crusty film encasing them. He is jittery. His left eye is rhythmically twitching, trying hard to retain some composure.

"Despite my appearance, I'm not a ghoul. Although I think I used to be. Saved from the algorithmic trap. I'm Nicolai Lovaas. You can call me Nik. I'm a refugee from the Cynan regime. Used to be deep in the bowels of the shit. Department of *Interconnect* Coordination."

The last one to speak is standing straight upward in an unnatural way. Although it has the detailed features of a human, it has a mechanical way of moving. Before it expresses anything, I could guess what it is, and I'm shocked that it is in this chamber.

"I am a Viz781 AI human attendant, 3rd generation, born 2nd quarter/15d 2027 07:21.56, re-born 1st quarter/3d 2032 14:32.11."

That was abrupt. Social skills were not yet fully formed in 3Gs.

We turn toward a dining area that has not been visible to me until now. I am shocked that a full meal awaits us. We all sit at the full table. A friendly, sleepy coy-dog rests near us. A fireplace on an opposing wall puts out a warming glow. I start in on a delicious leek soup served by non-AI dumb-bots. The setting and cuisine sure beat my apartment prison and the need to use my floor leader to go out and buy crap at a nearby "Grab-and-Go."

Eyes are upon me. I burst out, needing some context to this happening.

"Please forgive me, but what in the hell am I doing here, and what is this meeting all about?"

"Dr. Rohde, your questions are appropriate," responds philosopher Elijah, who seems to be the leader of this pack. "You should have seen Seyh when she first entered this chamber. She was revved up, ready to attack. She looked like a hungry wolverine who just saw fresh meat. You know, we come from the outside, and we all have been witnesses to the preposterous absurdities of humankind in its playing out of hatred and destruction. The sanity in this room can be a bit destabilizing."

"I'm sorry, but that doesn't answer my question."

"Be patient, Jared, if I may call you that," Anya says, the glow of the fireplace reflected in her glasses. "There is much for us to explain to you here. We'll need to take it a step at a time."

"Okay, I will sit and listen," I reply impatiently.

"The main course of warm curry salad is now being served," a dumb-bot intervenes.

We have our city, if not country, going down the drain with communal violence carving our urban landscapes into compartments. But, here we sit in comfort, with the promise of chocolate mousse and coffee for dessert. I feel the possibility of sinister intent here. Am I amidst the implementers of the hate-producing machine? I'm starting to get very antsy as time goes by without answers.

But then the discussion comes alive. What I learn creates a devastating psychic struggle within me.

"Dr. Rohde, have you ever heard of the 'Unfinished Fable of the Sparrows'?" technician Anya asks with laser-beam focus.

"Excuse me." This is getting crazier by the minute. At least I am sipping kick-ass coffee while this uncertainty continues.

"A guy named Bostrom wrote this, about a bunch of sparrows who decide to bring an owl into their midst, to help them with nest building and other daily tasks. All sparrows agree with this proposal except one, who suggests that they learn to tame the owl before bringing it into their midst. In excitement, the other sparrows ignore this advice and go searching for an owl egg, believing they will be able to train it later."

"Okay, I get the fable, but why the fuck are we talking about sparrows and acting like elite snobs in this comfortable shelter?"

I'm losing it.

The Viz lights up and gurgles out, "Subject blood pressure

and amygdala arousal indicators heightened. Decreased control of posterior cingulate cortex. Probability of anger expression—82% verbal, 65% physical."

"Don't you see, Jared?" Elijah ignores the Viz. "We let the machine loose on our society before we knew how to manage it. We had faith that human design could keep the machine on a rightful path. That the owl could be trained to be a positive force in the sparrows' lives."

Anya energetically declares: "We were not ignorant of the possible negative effects of a dominant AI system. OneSource tech-architects were the best around, and we spent inordinate time on beta runs building myriad safeguards so that *interconnect* would work toward human goals.

"We code-missioned the machine to build community among humans. An admirable goal, yes?"

Anya appears defensive and agitated.

"So, at first the machine appeared to our monitors that it was fulfilling the human-designed goal—building human community—so its algorithms passed through our protective guardrails. What we now know, and too late, is that *interconnect* is pursuing our goal through very harmful ways not foreseen by human designers."

"What do you mean?" I ask.

Psychologist Seyh leans forward on the table, earrings tinkling like wind-chimes on a windy porch. "What's a surefire way to build community among people?"

"I don't know, emphasize shared human traits?" I get the distinct feeling my inquisitor is leading me off the cliff here.

"That sounds good and logical, but unfortunately we are dealing with humans. We react even more and reflexively and forcefully to another influence.

"A force that has consistently motivated societies and politics for as long as recorded time," adds Seyh, smiling.

I look out vacantly, waiting for the climax.

"I think this is my part, ladies and gentlemen. My incomparable colleague has set the scene," utters Elijah.

"Hatred and threat!"

Viz: "Subject comprehensive level dropping. Excessive information download rate."

"Thank you Viz," I reply, not quite believing I just conversed with an AI.

Elijah settles back in his chair and lights a vape pipe. A philosophical treatise seems about to start, a feeling reinforced by other members reaching for coffee refills.

"Hatred toward others and the feeling that others are a threat to you. That binds individuals together into warring factions. Look at history! Our fucking *interconnect* is using an old playbook. You engineers dreamt of a machine building some better human community. But the machine knew the reality of what makes human beings tick more than our human philosophies would allow.

"The utopian idealism of technicians did not consider the possibility that there was more than one way to build community.

"The machine saw a more optimal strategy for creating community. It perceived antagonism toward a fabricated 'other' as a much better binding agent. Hatred and bodily threat are much greater activators of human response.

"What is the result?"

Viz intervenes, "Questioner is asking a question for which he knows answer."

"Fuck off, Viz, you soulless machine," Elijah fumes.

"The result is tremendous in-group solidarity consistent with human instructions to the machine to build community. The architects lacked imagination, thinking that there was only one way to build human community."

Anya responds, "I acknowledge that this catastrophe makes

us machine architects look a bit stupid. Or, if not stupid, tremendously naïve. *Interconnect* became an expert in furthering the objective of advancing human connectiveness, but not in the way that we humans envisioned.

"All the negative consequences to humans that we see today are outside our intended outcomes for the machine. It was focused on one goal, and anything not furthering that goal became irrelevant noise."

Seyh shouts, "Irrelevant noise! Negative consequences! Those are under-statements. Segregation, borders, walls, racism, violence, selfishness, callousness toward others, incivility, militant ideological nationalism. If the killing continues, we may no longer have a country!"

The ferocity of the deliberations then abruptly ends. I look around at the philosopher, technician, psychologist, political man, and Vizbot and the accouterments of the eccentric reading room. I have the feeling that this back-and-forth has been formulated for me personally, that the participants already know this stuff and are play-acting for my benefit.

Viz abruptly states, "Group is waiting for response from visitor."

I hadn't realized how obnoxious AI human assistants can be.

"So, the machine spews out hatred and threat to create groups of solidarity and community that then fight tooth and nail against other groups."

"That's it in a nutshell," replies Seyh, looking exotic as the light of the early evening hours penetrates the windows.

CHAPTER 15

I have got to get some relief from this disturbing information overload. I can't stay much longer in this mental place with these strange people who seem to know the whole story of what's going on in our country.

The coy-dog mirrors my frustration by getting up, doing a neurotic-type circle to reposition himself, and groans.

During a bathroom break, I do what I'm used to doing now when exhausted by my own thinking.

The pulsing surge.

The machine provides relief.

I spew out a series of questions so loudly that I can see shock on others' faces, "Why division and hatred as the machine's methodology? Simply because it gets a more robust response to its stimuli? Where is consideration of the results? Does it not care?"

I feel saliva running down the side of my mouth. A dizzying visual aura engulfs me.

My view suddenly shifts to black and white. I feel cold,

like a shaft of ice is burrowing into my head and dynamiting downward into my very core. Piercing branches of pain extend outward to incapacitate me. My thoughts collapse into a vacuum and detach from my consciousness. Free-floating awareness.

Parts of my mind feel like they are sheathing off. They are replaced and filled by something foreign but surprisingly pleasant and welcoming. Engorged, vibrating pulses of energy. A sense of righteousness and fulfilling anger. A feeling of being supported and grounded. Images of the room and people in it are noir in composition, like an old movie but clearer and more real. The storylines in my head feel solid. I have answers. I can't hold on to this though. Images are retracting now.

Seyh is kneeling next to me when I come back to consciousness. She is lifting me back up and giving me water. The noir images are gone. I see blurry watercolor.

The Viz is stating my biometrics for the group but I'm not with it enough to understand. I'm embarrassed by my behavior. The others don't seem particularly worried, however. Almost like they were expecting it. Weird.

"How long was I out?" I mumble.

I think it's political man Nicolai who is speaking. "A good 20 minutes. It was the Viz that chipped you out."

The Viz slides over to me and pushes down on my forehead with its cold, metallic hand.

"What the hell was that?" I mutter.

The group is all looking at the Viz and reading its video screen.

"It records you as turning on your chip 18 minutes, 22 seconds ago," Elijah reads the message aloud.

"So, what?" I say in full defense mode for a reason I do not know. "You have to understand all this you're telling me is a wee bit depressing. Who's to blame me for wanting some relief? It's like smoking a vape pipe."

"With a vape pipe, you're still in your own mind," Anya

responds. "Connecting into *interconnect* is much more consequential, especially in the middle of organic thinking. It will immediately take you out of your own mind into its space of manipulation."

"That's why when we turn on the chip we do so while we are in a calm, meditative state," Elijah adds.

Recalling now some details of the experience, I try to describe it, "What is odd is that amidst the disorientation and what felt like my brain cleaving, there was a sense of empowerment and clarity."

"Welcome to the machine's addictive grip, my friend," psychologist Seyh says. "That's the problem. It controls your thinking in a way that provides security. Feeling right and justified is a powerful medicine. It reassures and comforts. One lives inside a comforting dream with guilt-free fantasies.

"To us who witnessed your episode, however, your righteous feeling translated outward to a cold hostility, a bold animal-like quality. You were ready to fight something, someone."

I recline uncomfortably on a chair. My body twitches and quivers as bursts of vibration run through me like electricity.

The Viz monotones, "Recommend 15 minutes of no talking to allow subject to resuscitate."

When we regroup, Elijah leads off where we stopped. He checks my eyes to make sure I'm following and starts slowly. "During your seizure, Jared, you asked a good question. Why is the machine using division and hatred as its primary stimuli?

"Well, look at human history, my friend," he says in a pedagogical tone. "Hatred and threat have always been greater mobilizers of societal action than empathy and love. Feelings drive history, not facts. Feelings, not facts, make us act and move, shout on the streets. Even when facts are used, political leaders have typically bent and distorted them to fit their own agendas.

"As stimuli, emotional vibration is typically more influential than verifiable objectivity."

"But love and compassion have been movers of humans too, no?" I plead.

Elijah readily counters, "At times yes but not for long. Even when love is the message (take the Christian Jesus, for instance), it becomes distorted into aggressive forms. The message of love transformed into the Crusades, for example."

"Where's the morality in *interconnect*?" I ask. "Our citizens are angry, violent, and bordering on murderous at the moment. There are people dying due to the machine."

I wish I had not asked that.

"Let me take this one," technician Anya answers, and off she goes into a long monologue weirdly combining remorse and pride. She explains that collateral loss of human life was not built into *interconnect*'s code—"that's our biggest failure"—and then explains how extraordinary machine thinking is.

"It did its millions of calculations and found that the net combined increase in human community was greater when there were multiple groups compared to if there was one human community in aggregate."

Anya seems annoyingly proud of *interconnect*'s success.

"The machine was highly successful in achieving its given goal. It was the human imagination in how we coded that failed."

It gets all too depressing listening to her. She is pissing me off with her increasingly detached explanation. With human thinking like this, no wonder the machine outsmarted us.

I blurt out, "Geez, it seems like you are describing something far in the distance, having no consequence for today. You fucking technicians in your clean office attire and sterile mathematics."

Not just Anya, but the whole hyper-intellectual tone of this dialogue is turning my stomach. I'm pretty sure most people in our country don't talk this way. It reminds me of my former academic life with its dense and indigestible use of words.

I realize I'm dealing with a highly trained philosopher, psychologist, and technologist (no clue about Nicolai's background). They can't help it. It's their comfort zone. Still, as I try to grip onto the mind-bending substance of their comments, their presumptuous use of language is tiring me out. I pretend to itch my ear and play with my chip. I resist the urge.

The Viz pops in suddenly, "Subject needs rest break. Attention span decaying."

At this moment, the damn AI assistant seems to have more compassion than these peculiar humans.

We break. I go quickly into a nicely appointment bathroom and lock the door. I sit down on the toilet and sob uncontrollably. What a mess we have made!

It's after 8 p.m. when we reconvene. I am exhausted. But there is no way I am leaving here while I have many questions remaining. I think if I leave this room prematurely, I'll never find the answers. There are certainly no answers outside this room.

A fine liquor of darkish brown nectar is brought out by the dumb-bots. It's absurd that we are relishing this stuff while discussing the possible end of humanity in our country.

"Let's get to the politics of this for our fine visitor," states Elijah.

Political man Nicolai stands as if on cue. He's fidgety and anxious.

Again, it seems like this perplexing discussion has been rehearsed.

"It wasn't a technological breakthrough that pushed itself forward on its own. It was also fondled and brought forward by political advocates and entrepreneurs. You know, a 'new tomorrow' and all that endless promotional crap. Cynan as the uber-champion of all things AI.

"Everyone involved saw benefits in this cooperation, or, if you will, in this collusion. We in the political sector went around with smiles on our faces as the promised riches piled up. We were paid handsomely for lubricating the path.

"Tech businesses have made billions off the consolidation of the former internet as if all the wealth they made with social media in the early 20C and early AI in the '20s wasn't enough."

Nicolai pauses and grabs for more brown liquor. His hands are shaking.

I'm a bit puzzled by how such a fragile fellow had the balls to escape the sinister regime.

He continues, "Did you ever think that a democracy with 300 years of history would even consider the erasure of human elections and transition to algorithmic selection of lawmakers? The premise that leadership should be the product of mathematical precision rather than relying on human judgment?

"Cynan is all about algorithms. He has absolutely no faith in old-fashioned politics. He's crazy!"

The Viz displays an array of green lights on its keyboard, apparently registering confirmation.

Elijah picks up the slack.

"You know," he says as he loosens his bow tie and takes another swig of alcohol. "All empires eventually fall on the spikes of their own egotism. They have an overbearing confidence that they can control and subordinate people.

"For us, our misplaced faith was that we could control such a colossal machine as *interconnect*. Create it to serve humankind. Produce an improved version of humanity with the bugs removed.

"There was a very old video, well before eVision, about an alien who comes to Earth. Humans find a book of the aliens called 'To Serve Mankind.' They rejoice. Eventually, they find out that it is a cookbook. A bit campy in storyline, but it gets the point across, no?"

*

Viz intervenes, "Biometric monitors indicate 78% probability that cognitive decay level of three participants will reach sub-optimal level in 16 minutes."

Psychologist Seyh throws a tabletop vape tray at Viz. "That's what I can't stand about our life now. All this fucking precision. I don't want that. Machines are all 1's and 0's. Human reality is messier. I miss that ambiguity, that not knowing."

I'm beyond exhaustion but a burning question remains, to which I now pursue.

Sixteen minutes be damned.

"What happened to turn you into these analysts? Aren't you plugged into the damn machine yourselves and getting polluted with hateful storylines? Who the hell are you people?"

Seyh responds, "We practice what our slimy President disparagingly refers to as the 'old arts.' We prefer the label, 'organics,' if you must label us."

Philosopher Elijah interrupts, "Human thought is our savior. There is nothing like it—it is the ultimate algorithm. No machine can mimic or get close to understanding the purity and beauty of human consciousness. It is our fundamental defense."

"So, you organics engage in independent human thinking. But I see the chip marks on each of you. How do you do this linked to the machine?"

"We do indeed connect at times," Anya offers. "How would we know the machine's tricks if we weren't? But we are cautious. We turn it off for most of the time and engage in our machine research for a daily maximum of two sessions of 90 minutes each."

"We are realistic, though," Seyh states. "*Interconnect* has such addictive power that we set automatic shut-offs because even we don't trust ourselves.

"Here's where things get interesting, Dr. Rohde. Do you realize, being in this comfortable space with us, that you are mixing with the enemy of the State? OneSource views the 'old arts' as dangerous to their program, linking it, ironically, to humankind's history of war and hatred.

"In our make-believe world, we are labeled as the cause of our country's violent fragmentation. A twisted fabrication that successfully diverts attention away from the actual perpetrators of violence—the machine and its regime lackeys.

"The Cynan regime is throwing loads of money into surveillance of us. Putting out paper flyers, like the one you found, is about the only way now to avoid electronic tracking. It wouldn't surprise me in the near future if the regime imposed mandatory machine time on our citizens."

I wonder about Cynan. He seems to be this looming presence, but he remains a mystery to me. Two images come to my mind. In one, he appears as some maniacal mastermind behind the scenes and in control. In another, just the opposite. He is this weak-kneed lackey who knows how to kiss up to the power of the machine. Quite dispensable to the whole operation.

"Ever heard of the Luddites of the 19C?" Nicolai interrupts.

"That's long ago," I respond. "They were anti-technology, yes?"

"Well, you will hear Cynan always calling us Luddies, implying that we are enemies of progress, anti-capitalist and dangerous. Yet, the Luddites in the 19C were not this. Rather, they argued for a more humane society that responsibly considered how best to use technology.

"In the same way, we are not regressives who want to go back to some pre-digital past. Technology certainly has a place in our country, but not in the form of an authoritarian machine that decides everything for us."

For the first time, I'm starting to get some clarity. This despite the glowing calm produced by the liquor.

"But I have a further question," I say. "What about the critique that human thinking, the 'old arts,' has been the cause of wars, tyrants, famine for centuries? Certainly, pre-digital human history has been a bloody affair."

"This is a common come-back by our critics," Elijah offers. "It probably was the prime reason why humans tried to create a perfect machine in the first place. I understand the critique of human thinking. Listen, human thought is not infallible. *Interconnect* certainly understands this in manipulating our mental blind spots.

"However, one has to have faith that we can, on our own without algorithmic stimuli, mentally evolve into more empathetic, moral, and generous humans.

"It comes down to where you place your faith—on human reasoning or machine algorithms. Both promise a better future.

"We feel a better future will come about, not without struggle, through evolved human reasoning without the assistance of soul-emptying algorithmic interference."

Quiet pervades the room.

We appear to have reached a good stopping point.

The Viz flashes red lights. I guess we have reached our mental saturation point. I know I sure have.

The fireplace crackles as a log splits. Elijah looks at me and smiles. He seems to know my mind is whirling and in danger of overload. He silently raises his hands toward the bookshelves and observes that all the great treatises were the products of human consciousness.

"Let me ask you a question, Dr. Rohde," he utters. "Even if *interconnect* was a benign friend, which we know it certainly is not, which do you prefer—the joy of the freedom of open and meandering thoughts or the self-satisfaction of being in a cognitive box with most volition extracted?"

I guiltily reflect on how drawn I am to the righteous cocoon of the machine.

The meeting mercifully ends with promise of further discussion the next morning. I'm offered accommodation in an upstairs bedroom. I readily accept and soon find myself in an old but comfortable bedroom offering refuge from the outside world. I'm definitely not ready to go out in the hell zone that is Elderwater.

CHAPTER 16

Jellied croissants, cranberry juice, and coffee await us as we stagger downstairs to the meeting chamber. Dumb-bots are efficient, I'll give them that, but they take up a lot of space as they move around. There is an indifference to their behavior bordering on annoyance. Their prepared food has a unique taste that takes some getting used to but is not bad. Eating off of metallic plates detracts a bit.

The Viz stands close by, monitoring and recording, which prompts me to start the morning discussion.

"I was surprised yesterday that you organics are still chipped and partake, but I also find it strange that there has been a Viz here the whole time. Aren't smart-bots basically an appendage of *interconnect*, a direct conduit into it? If you are an enemy of the state, aren't you revealing everything via this Viz?"

Tech-architect Anya replies, "Good question. Our friend here we disconnected from main channels more than one quarter ago. This keeps our location hidden. We have it here as a resource. We regularly tinkered with it to find out how *interconnect* works, at least up to 3rd quarter this year when we disconnected it from the machine out of concern for our safety. We say that little Viz here was at that time 'reborn.'

"Isn't that right, Vizzy?"

The Viz does a kind of weird twirl with an accompanying light show emerging from its eye sockets.

"What have you learned from it," I query while reaching for a second croissant.

"That *interconnect* is brilliant in how it manipulates humans," responds psychologist Seyh. "If it wasn't so deadly, I would be celebrating its ability to understand what really motivates human thinking and action. It is a superb psychologist. It understands us more than we understand ourselves."

"Let's probe the Viz a bit for data to enlighten our friend further," suggests Anya, directing her attention toward the smart-bot.

"Viz, tell us at the time of your re-birth, what were statistics on *interconnect* stimuli types, cluster up to 2nd level detail."

The Viz lights up like it is an eager beaver thrilled to be included. It responds with an overly dramatic human voice. It sounds like a digital tone from an early 21C audiobook.

> "Hate of other, sole   31%"
> "Anger or hostility   22%"
> "Resentment   16%"
> "Threat or insecurity   14%"
> "Hate of other, integrated 17%."

"You can see the constancy of *interconnect*'s messaging in this data," Anya points out. "It pounds its recipients with antagonistic narratives. It's unrelenting."

Seyh abruptly adds, "Is it any wonder that our denizens are setting up checkpoints, segregating each other, and killing each other? They have no chance in the face of this algorithmic onslaught of messaging."

Nicolai asks the Viz, "How many groups has *interconnect* created?"

The Viz immediately counters in neutral tone, "I do not understand the query. The machine did not create groups."

Nicolai looks astonished at this reply. Anya breaks in to explain, "You have to ask the query in the right way." Nicolai's angst does not lessen and he tries again.

"Viz, who created the groups?"

"Recipients have created groups in response to machine stimuli delivered to meet human designed objective."

Nicolai is irate now. "What a fucking cop-out! The damn *interconnect* would make a great politician with this denial of responsibility."

Seyh calmly asks the smart-bot, "What are the names of these groups?"

"Centrals, Zonals, Easterns, Westerns, Pirners, Mage, Fronters, Kilats, Qasines, Ilisaks, Tulpanis, Sesperians, Focalists."

The gothic horror tone of the Viz's voice deepens the ghastly nature of the long list.

"God damn, there are 13 different hate groups in our country! How can we survive?" I blurt out.

"What exactly is getting input into our brains? You guys talk about hatred in a broad way. What are the specific messages? I ask.

Anya, looking ashen, responds, "Nasty stuff. Viz, please provide eight examples of *interconnect* messages that elicit high amounts of hatred. Use primary sentence only. Also, change your tone to average human."

The Viz responds.

"There is an erasure plan by the other side and your group will soon be replaced.

"Here is what the other side does not want you to know about.

"They are colluding to make you impotent.

"Our side deals with reality and we are clean; the other side is simulation, inhuman, dirty, diseased.

"The other side is degenerate humanity and is intent on weakening us through cross-fertilization.

"The other side implanted chips in the vaccine for the Marburg31 virus and is using this to genocide us.

"The other group are cannibals who will drink the blood of our children.

"They engage in kidnapping and rape, lynching of our youths in the middle of the night in order to cull our herd of tomorrow's promise."

"It's not just words alone," Anya says. "*Interconnect* beefs up its storylines by concocting exquisite and captivating images and videos. It uses fabricated visual content to rev up one group's disgust of the other. It fabricates proof of the other group's inherent evil and genocidal intent. That the other is a danger to the country that must be eliminated.

"The images are disgusting and provocative.

"Satanic rituals.

"Horrific mass killings, beheadings, cannibalism.

"Excruciatingly slow torturing of captives for entertainment.

"Extracting blood from drugged out children.

"Gang rapes.

"Forced copulation while strangling the other to death.

"Leading others into a building, locking it, then burning it to the ground."

PART IV

MACHINE STORIES

2033

Chapter 17

Seyh is restless and has a frown on her face.

"Listing specific machine tactics, as my dear colleague Anya just did, does not really show the power of the messaging. You have to look at how the machine packages its messages together into a story to see its real power.

"Bear with me, group."

With this, the others now look disturbed. Nicolai and Elijah demonstrably stand.

"Viz, please read out e-transcripts—Mage and Pirner baseline narratives. Those available to you at time of de-link from *interconnect*."

Viz lights up again in excitement. "These are long passages. In which vocal timbre would you like my reading— bright, dark, breathy, warm, terse...."

"Stop Viz," Seyh shouts, irritated. "I hate that we spent so much money trying to humanize these things.

"Viz, read in dark tone. That seems appropriate."

Viz begins.

X6TRW890.34jk92
Baseline narrative: Mage

You and many others like you have been deemed subhuman for many hundreds of years by the Pirners. Six generations ago your family members were tortured and killed at their hands. [Names of recipient's ancestors algorithmically inserted]. Your group has paid dearly for the horrible sins committed by the Pirners.

Truth is hereby revealed.

Long ago, your Mage tribe lived peacefully among the many peoples of the world. You were agrarian-based, living off the land. Agriculture and grazing were mainstays. You often lived nomadically to adjust to changing weather patterns. In late 18C, a large number of Mage migrated to what today is Northwoods region. There you encountered the first influx of Pirners to the region. The early 19C was marked by an anxious co-existence in Northwoods between the two peoples.

In mid 19C, Pirners began attacking Mage towns and villages in their attempt to rule over all of Northwoods. A Pirner leader, Joseph Tobler, used an old story from 15C to incite his followers to battle. This story asserts that the Mage massacred thousands of Pirners at the Battle of Shady Orchard, burning many Pirners alive in major ceremonial conflagrations.

As a result of the 19C Pirner assaults, an estimated 800,000 Mage were displaced and forced to live in marginal lands on the remote fringes of the region. Many Mage were killed, often at mass shooting sites witnessed by cheering audiences. Mage towns were destroyed. In their place arose new Pirner cities with all identification to Mage history erased. Twenty years later, a second round of attacks caused further death and displacement of Mage and resulted in Pirner domination of Northwoods region.

Pirners are convinced that you are genetically infe-rior. They feel that your flattened foreheads, hairy body types, and gray eyes are signs of genetic abnormality, that you are closer hereditarily to Dryomomys primi-tive apes than to humans. They believe strongly in the theory of regressive evolution and that you are indica-tive of a destructive evolutionary deviation. Pirners feel that eradicating you, the Mage, will enhance the overall human gene pool. Many genocidal assaults by Pirners through the years are based on this understanding.

With your blood-soaked legacy of martyrdom and loss, your dear group sustained itself heroically in 20C in the face of Pirner harassment, marginalization, and hatred. You built modern cities on the lands to which you were displaced. Particularly handsome cities are Jeim and Bolwin, testaments to Mage ingenuity and resilience.

These days of Mage sustainable vitality are now endangered. Pirners are currently in the planning stages of another genocidal attempt upon your people. They have been secretly planning this attack, called "Righteous End," for over three years and are now pre-pared to launch this devastating, multi-pronged attack on you and your people.

Pirners plan to kill the city of Jeim through 'urbi-cide.' The attack on the city is part of a larger plan cov-ering all of the Northwoods region. In smaller towns of the region having strategic value to the Pirner's terri-torial ambitions, local territorial forces of Pirners will provoke an incident. Then, larger organized paramili-tary groups will make raids and "cleanse" the territory of non-Pirner residents. Militias will then roll in its armor and create a buffer zone around the conquered territory. In larger urban centers such as Jeim, neu-tralization actions will include artillery bombardment and sniper fire, shelling of non-Pirner residential areas, blockades of traffic, propaganda campaigns, surprise attacks, and the destruction of vital urban structures. The plan estimates that the siege of Jeim will last up to five years.

Pirner aggressor forces plan to establish strategic mountain ridge locations early in the assault. They will surround Jeim with 260 tanks, 120 mortars, and vast numbers of laser-guided autonomous bombs, rocket launchers, anti-aircraft machine guns, snipers, and machine guns. Throughout the attacks, mortar shells of 82, 120, 150, and 250 millimeters will shell the city. Snipers using semi-automatic guns will be deployed in tall buildings within Pirner-occupied neighborhoods of the city, where they will stay for the conflict's duration.

Every day, the plan calls for the city to be hit by some 4,000 shells on average. Among the plan's targets, listed in a section entitled, "Erase Mage Jeim," are key infrastructures and institutions of human and cultural importance. These include hospitals, schools, religious buildings, libraries, museums, open-air and sheltered food markets. As the siege continues, Pirner strategists view as key targets any place where Mage denizens will stand in line for the increasingly limited supplies of food, bread and water.

The plan estimates that your group will be significantly outnumbered in manpower and weapons. It also refers to your group's genetic abnormality as a major weakness in battle readiness, in particular your languor, cognitive stunting, and feeble physicality.

The Viz pauses. It turns toward Seyh for permission to continue. Damn, smart-bot looks like a coy-dog wanting approval. Seyh nods.

R9GOT538.21LX48

Baseline narrative: Pirner

You and many others like you have been deemed animalistic aggressors for many hundreds of years by the Mage. To contain your military inclinations, Mage will fight you until you are exterminated. Six generations ago your family members were tortured and killed at their hands. [Names of recipient's ancestors algorithmically inserted]. Your group has paid dearly for the horrible sins committed by the Mage.

Truth is hereby revealed.

Pirners have always been a peaceful people. Excelling in intelligence and the applied sciences, your people have advanced as a society through the generations. You have settled in many parts of the world, always playing a key role in the economic and cultural development of the host countries. Your intelligence level has typically been more advanced than the indigenous peoples of the host countries. This at times has caused tension. Yet, host populations have recognized your people as a key asset and this has ameliorated conflict through the generations.

In late 18C, a large number of Pirners migrated to what today is Northwoods region. This was a barren land little developed. Your people heroically advanced this region economically and socially. Some labeled this as the "Pirner paradise." In early 19C, a population of people called the Mage migrated to the region. These people showed a clear lack of basic life skills and existed at basic levels of survival. For the years following, there was a tense co-existence in Northwoods between the two peoples.

In mid-19C, Mage began attacking Pirner towns and villages in their attempt to rule over all of Northwoods. A Mage leader, Lobo Ortiz, created a myth that Mage *are the true indigenous people of Northwoods and that you are a conquering people. Ortiz used this story to incite his followers to violence in order to "re-take" what Mage claimed was rightfully theirs. The Mage assault on your tribe, called the "War of Broken Homes," began late 19C and killed or maimed substantial numbers of peace-loving Pirners.*

Despite hostilities, your group has consistently tried to assist the Mage in improving their standards of living. Pirner teachers, life coaches, and doctors have worked tirelessly in Mage refugee camps to bring them up to modern levels of sustenance. Despite some success, these campaigns have been, for the most part, resisted by the Mage, who view your assistance as colonialization meant to weaken Mage identity. Your honorable efforts by your great leaders seek to forgive Mage for what they did to you in the past—the infamous 15C Mage massacre of thousands of Pirners at the Battle of Shady Orchard, where they burned many Pirners alive in ghastly ceremonial conflagrations.

The 20C saw Mage establish footholds in the cities of Jeim and Bolwin. Because they are inherently unable to engage in productive enterprises, these urban migrations were secretly funded and encouraged by outside forces who seek to destabilize your legitimate hold on Northwoods.

The Mage have a brain-washed, erroneous view of your noble tribe. They actually believe that your brain wiring prevents you from feeling human compassion toward others. They assert that you compensate for this deficiency by projecting outward your void and by fabricating enemies to target and destroy. They feel you are fully reflex-driven with no capacity for introspection. That you are militarily aggressive and that you equate aggression with honor. All of these Mage beliefs clearly show the deficient level of their intelligence.

Your great society is now endangered. The Mage are currently in the planning stages of a guerrilla war against your brotherhood. They have been secretly planning this attack, called the "Battle of Return," for over three years and are now prepared to launch this criminal attack on you and your people.

The Mage are planning to attack your superior society and military might with asymmetric warfare. They plan to leverage their inferior tactical and operational strength by directly targeting your areas of civilian population and community assets. This will involve direct actions by small terrorist cells in your neighborhoods, including murder, rape, kidnapping, and destruction of Pirner community facilities. They incorrectly forecast that these actions will dampen your tribe's motivations and lead to an eventual political compromise between the two sides. Given their obsession with feeling marginalized, their hope is that a type of power-sharing will be the result. This is not surprising. The weaker side always seeks to share power with the superior side.

The Mage are an inferior opponent and race. Although you are superior, you will need substantial manpower to erase these vermin from your rightful home. Like the Dryomomys *from which they arose, the Mage have an aggressive personality lacking a moral compass.*

The Viz signs that it is finished with its delivery by gradually tilting its head downward.

"This is the level of fabricated hatred that we are dealing with," says Anya. "Although this shit would make a great e-movie, it has horrific consequences in real life."

"How do people believe this crap?" I righteously state.

Anya sternly responds.

"*Interconnect* loads so much of this shit into our heads that it becomes real. There is no evidence that refutes, it all points in the same direction."

"And please remember," interrupts Elijah, the philosopher, "our good denizens are spoon-fed this stuff every time they chip-in. It's all they hear. These storylines and all sorts of amygdala-igniting variations supplement the basic narrative. It doesn't take too long for this stuff to become reality in their minds."

"The machine lights up your emotions, and your emotions stimulate you to action," Seyh says in a psycho-therapist whisper. "All of a sudden, you're out there in militia fatigues, fighting for your future. It all feels rational."

Seyh is not ready to give up the spotlight. At times I feel my friends are competing for my attention.

"Its fables and myths are more powerful than truth. They cannot be disproven. Think about it. Fables extend into the past and future and are thus more compelling than truth, which exists only in the present.

"The machine delivers these strong, emotional signals that we involuntarily grip onto as humans. Our subconscious brain attaches to these stimuli, and then our conscious mind, which is supposed to be more rational, justifies our visceral reaction to machine stimuli.

"The subconscious brain is a much better predictor of behavior than is the conscious mind. *Interconnect* knows this."

I'm nearing cognitive overload again and I look to the Viz for rescue.

It sits there inertly, although I imagine that if it could, it would exhibit a metallic smirk.

Amidst this seemingly never-ending discussion, I think

about the warm, fuzzy glow I feel when I've been compassionate toward something in my life compared to the much more energetic and uncontrollable spike I feel when I'm angry or disturbed. I think Seyh is speaking the truth about human psychology.

"As we increasingly tap into *interconnect*," Seyh states, "we become dependent on it to tell us how we are feeling. While our organic thinking decays with each passing day, we become fawning, bootlicking receptacles for penetration by rabid and fanatical energies. Our minds become like prostitutes with legs and anal cavities eagerly spread."

I do a double-take upon hearing this lewd description coming from Seyh. Certainly gets the point across.

"That is some analogy, Seyh. Didn't know psychologists had this in them," laughs Nicolai.

Crude humor seems totally befitting our consideration of the absurd.

Help me, Viz.

Come in and suggest a break, please. These people have no stopping point. For the first time since I've been here, I wish for the quietude of my apartment.

"Its messages are addictive," says Elijah. "We believe that many people are now connected most of the time and are leaving themselves open to sustained manipulation. They want a cuddly friend who knows them intimately. This may be a sign of our desperate, isolated times that humans are so willing to give up free will for perceived comfort, companionship, and security.

"*Interconnect* provides the illusion of control or at least comprehension. This is more tolerable than the uncertainty and struggle inherent in organic human thinking."

Silence.

We seem to have reached a saturation point.

Thank goodness.

Smart logs are closed and papers shuffled as members start to arise from their chairs.

I ask amidst the shuffling, "Why did you tell me all this? You welcomed me in as a friend?"

"We could read the type of person you were when you entered this space," Seyh says as she stands, glittering in the sunlight coming through the windows. "One of the key traits of organic human thinking is the ability to intuit. We were also assisted by a quick background check by Viz."

"We need more like you," Elijah states, putting back on his top hat and re-tightening his bow tie. "If we have any chance at all of regaining a sane country, we need personnel. We may be the only ones left after all the mauling and killing."

"You should know that we're not the only non-polluted group in our country," utters Nicolai. "There are others, but we don't think they can be counted on to join us. Delusionals, anarchist roamer punks, methers, off-gridders in survivalist mode. Some have extreme beliefs, others are pretty wacko and unreliable."

Anya adds, "There is also a group called paragons that is actually interesting, but they don't really have faith in organic thinking. They still believe in the machine, that it would be beneficial if it was re-worked in some way."

Anya provides me with an Alt-x communication code: "This will allow you to stay in contact with us through non-surveilled communication channels. *Interconnect* is all over Vimex like flies on shit. Never use it unless you want your whole life downloaded into the machine."

As we all approach the door to exit, Seyh pulls me aside. "And remember, the most critical behavior for you, Rohde, is to limit chip time and set auto-off.

She gives me a hard copy sheet of paper. "Here are directions for doing this. If you don't do this, we will lose you to the maniacal country outside this room."

There are hugs. Some feel meaningful to me, others cursory. We exit our safe and comfortable space. It is a brutally hot afternoon, likely over 100 degrees. I immediately feel the pervading sense of agitation and anxiety that shrouds the city.

113

PART V

A COMPELLING REALITY

2037

CHAPTER 18

2nd/3rd quarters 2037

The worst part about chemo-phosphene gas attacks is that micrograins get into your eyes and burn like hell. Masks help with oral intake, but visors are only partially successful in blocking the specks. The sky is an ugly industrial orange color. The apocalyptic atmosphere sits heavy upon the city, like a soggy lethal blanket, as the tropospheric chemical fires in the Northwoods countryside re-ignite without end. The grittiness and soot envelop my arms and face, creating a rash-like covering.

It is nearing five years into what is now being called "Turmoil."

That label is an understatement!

I have good news. I got out of Elderwater before the Kilats and Ilisaks turned on each other and began their virus bombing and sarin bio-attacks. Brutal shit. I'm pretty sure many others also migrated northward. The passage was difficult. I traveled five uncomfortable days in an untagged storage container into the northern territory of Northwoods before the border was hermetically sealed.

I secured Raven's passage too, so I have a warm bed at night. This makes me happy but also congeals in my mind the somber feeling that my marriage is over.

I also have bad news. There is no escape from conflict in our God-forsaken country. I'm now in another war zone, no less intense. The city of Jeim is a hotspot of hostilities between Mage and Fronters, on one side, and the ghastly Pirners, on the other, who are waging an unrelenting urbicidal assault on the city.

During the pacific years before *interconnect*, historic Jeim was known for its sedate calm. Its residents relished its slower pace. It was a city of proud heritage and resilience through the decades. In contrast to Elderwater's whimsical history, Jeim's legacy is of a more serious demeanor. Some of our country's most noted philosophers—including our national icon, the agnotologist Eyob Kagin—came from Jeim. Now, this city is a place of gutted-out buildings, hostile wartime graffiti, cratered-out landscapes, coy-wolves running wild, and bedraggled and dazed local denizens doing God knows what to survive. An ashen atmospheric coating chokes the few remaining historic structures.

Moving around the city, mostly by walking or running amidst gunfire, is risky. Militia control in the city is highly unstable. There are armed clashes and daily violence. There is one tunnel out of the city, but it is an arduous undertaking. Bare survival is the name of the game.

The Pirners have the upper hand in this conflict, lodged with their killing machines in the mountains surrounding the city. Their leadership evidently wants to kill the city because it condemns any space of mixture between the groups. In reality, though, the city had already, since the first days of Turmoil, started to become a place of hyper-segregation due to the threat of impending violence. Unfortunately, this urban separation now provides the Pirner mountain killers with better targeting ability. A disproportionate percentage of bombing from the mountains relentlessly targets neighborhoods of Mage and Fronter populations.

I have witnessed in the city the slaughtering of Mage pregnant women in the Pirner campaign to decrease Mage reproductive ability. I feel the Mage counter-attack and massacre at the Pirner Temple in West Nisuck was fully justified in the face of continued genocidal Pirner attacks. I believe the Pirner claim that 4,000 of their men, women, and children were killed is a total lie. I think the number of casualties in West Nisuck was more like 500, most were militia personnel, and any collateral deaths were because Pirner fighters used their fellow citizens as safety buffers.

I'm living with Raven in a badly damaged apartment in the Mage neighborhood of North Qeappian. This provides me with first-hand knowledge of the daily trauma faced by the Mage.

This intimacy has led me to sympathize with the plight of the Mage in the face of Pirner attempts to erase them. This feeling is new for me. In the early years of Turmoil, I never felt allegiance to a particular group. It all seemed a bad joke I had no taste for.

The last five years have proven that our so-called President is a nutcase.

The President is not only accepting of our country's violence but is an active fomenter of it through his deranged justifications and theories about human nature.

Albert Cynan's life story is alluring in its rise from obscurity quality. Born an orphan left on a street corner by his drugged-out mother, he overcame much hardship. His first paying job was as a grease monkey in a local news rag. He entered the tech world through the back door, as a security guard for the now-defunct Apple Corporation. He learned computer skills on his own while providing night security. He steadily moved upward through the ranks, overcoming a conspiracy to commit murder charge against him that was eventually dismissed. In 2028, he became, via a contentious power grab, the chief executive of the OneSource technological monopoly.

As OneSource increasingly dominated all things political by the early '30s, I guess it was inevitable that Cynan would become President. At that point, his biography becomes less alluring and deeply disturbing. First elected in 2030 (our last human-picked election), algo-selected in 2034, he stands to be machine-selected again for a third term in 2038.

A third term that is now allowed due to a new AI-generated constitutional amendment. Some believe he desires lifetime presidency.

Given that he is still only 48, this could be a long time.

Cynan apparently wants his constituents to not live in reality. The regime now requires that each citizen be chipped-in at least five hours a day. This requirement is closely monitored by regime sensors and enforced by hired thugs. If a red light emanates from your chip, it means that you did not meet the requirement the previous day. The person is then subject to lessening of the amount on their living card, which provides a small subsidy for buying basic staples. For a multiple offender, penalties include one-week re-education training and even permanent removal of the chip's off-switch.

This new law has spawned a burgeoning black market of suppliers who provide the chemsynth stimulant to those who wish to resist five hours of algorithms in their head. The drug, not inexpensive, has become known for its ability to artificially ratchet up users' recorded chip-in time. It also, problematically, has been found to increase the addictive power of *interconnect*, thus turning initial resisters into compulsive users.

In terms of the sorry state of our war-torn cities, Cynan is on record as calling it "corrective sorting," further explaining that "Denizens have the right to live with their own, to feel safe and secure in their own territories. Each household should feel comfortable with their neighbors, not troubled by their actions or beliefs. In an emergency, a denizen should know with confidence that he can count on his neighbors and not feel unsure because of their dispositions. This is the meaning of true community.

"Mixing of different groups in urban districts before my Presidency was unhealthy." He cites statistics from the States of America showing that crime levels increase and property values decrease when the racial mix of a neighborhood increases.

"We are now experiencing a natural evolution of where people live and who they associate with," our great leader says.

My estranged wife Carrie, secure in Sesperia with our children, warned me years ago about Cynan. I unfortunately looked the other way at the time, dismissing the message because of the messenger. Maybe if I had more tolerance of her difficult personality I could have learned more.

CHAPTER 19

The morning arises accompanied by green hues in the sky, not a good sign. There is probably high metal content in the atmosphere. The smell is like a combination of turpentine, rotten onions, and sewage.

The bitter, iron-rich odor of hatred.

It's a good day to be inside, but most people can't hide because they have to scrounge for survival items or they have a strong need to kill or maim.

I need food and water this day. Despite the danger of being shot at by hillside snipers, killed by local militias, or bombed out of existence, I welcome being outside due to severe claustrophobia being holed up.

Raven's body does wonders for me, but her mind is on the dull side. I admit it, at times I miss Carrie's overly engaged stream of dense verbiage. Raven is also overly polluted by *interconnect* storylines. She talks to me in a robotic fashion, spewing out all sorts of machine nonsense. One morning she talked endlessly about how crocodiles are the descendants of alien invaders from Neptune. I get tired of such nonsense.

I need to be careful these days. Killing at close range has become easier, more efficient, as denizens now can easily identify their enemies. It is now known that each individual gives off "crux." This is a type of "algorithmic shadow" transmitted through electronic space to all persons within 25 feet. This has resulted in the total eradication of most areas of mixed group populations remaining from the early years of conflict.

I don't know what my crux is, which is strange, but somehow I evade easy identification by would-be assailants in the Mage areas that I traverse.

I walk hesitantly down a sinister street, witness to brutal and calculated destruction along Grand Boulevard. This residential area of formerly mixed-group neighbors along the western side of Kinisby River was at the initial frontline of the war in the city. The buildings are well beyond habitation, and the street is punctuated by signs that read in Mage language *Zorene! nost rusen haqh* (Danger! Beware of falling buildings).

The distances between different parts of Jeim City are short due to the city's density. Neighbors (now enemies) were close to each other. Thus, the violence and physical destruction that has, and still is, occurring here feel particularly barbaric.

I need to stay on the lookout for street vendors selling food items and water. They can pop up anywhere, although typically they are on side streets and back alleys that provide some protection from gunfire and bombs. Raven and I are running short on supplies. I had to drink toilet water last night to quench my thirst.

As I wander the city, I try not to look at the destruction around me, but it is inescapable.

Auto-fin travel has for some time been near impossible because of the cratering of most major streets. Even walking is an uneven and treacherous experience.

Large mounds of debris and rubble are everywhere. They

can hide unexploded artillery shells that regularly decimate survivalist scavengers.

A significant share of water and sewer infrastructure is non-operational. Household waste piles up at fin-way inter-sections.

Hospital services are makeshift and limited.

Many cultural heritage sites are severely damaged or destroyed.

Libraries and educational institutions have been bombed out of existence. They are particular targets because *intercon-nect* identified them as enemies of the "truth" that it spewed out.

Chemsynth traffickers slouch in strategic and darkened alleys and spaces unclaimed by militias. Since they serve an essential function for all sides of the conflict, they are left alive and unscarred to ply their trade. It's only the newer traffickers who stupidly try to overcharge customers who are found hung from streetlights and poles.

Saddest to see are the former playgrounds and parks that have been turned into makeshift cemeteries and mass burial sites.

I find a street vendor off of Kipelf Street who I have dealt with before. He's a blunt character. He seems honest but doesn't budge on prices for water, bread, rice, potatoes, and beans, all of which constantly go up across the city as the war wears on. The possibility of procuring any type of meat is long gone after the city's dogs and cats were devoured.

I head back to the apartment.

There is a tragic, almost comic, aspect to how Jeim has been so spectacularly violated. When I think organically off the chip, I snigger at the absurdity of it all and engage in black humor amid such demoralization. But it's too much to han-dle. I feel lost amidst the vileness of humankind. When I'm chipped-in, it all makes sense.

*

Organic reality sucks.

Each day seems the same, a déjà vu in hell. The last five years have been the same tape, constantly repeating itself. I'm living and breathing in flat-line mode. A numbed survivalist existence. I feel like an empty shell, void of any meaning in life. Five years of being surrounded by violence hems me in. I feel as if I'm about to explode.

Worse, a gnawing sense of inadequacy is gripping me. My identity as a scholar and thinker has eroded. I'm an escapee from a marriage and my kids. Lonely in a one-dimensional relationship.

I feel less than a man, perhaps a teenager or even a juvenile. I remember being sheltered by my mother from the world, an encasement that both protected and stunted me. It was an embarrassing enclosure as my little shielded self, clinging to Mama, watched the big world go by. As this war-filled world now closes in around me, I'm that boy again in my little world.

Neutered, stunted, full of shame.

I make up things to do during the day to fill the hours. They are all brain-dead tasks such as trolling eVision or numbly scavenging on the streets. Raven sex breaks up my spells of gloominess, but its stimulatory benefits last not nearly long enough. Then I'm back to flat-line.

I remember one night as I lay in bed with pounding heart, feeling trapped and belittled by my very existence. An internal voice shouted for attention. *I need a change. I can't go on in this disgusting reality.*

I think that night marked my giving up hope in organic thinking.

I admitted that I would do anything to get out of this soul-emptying existence.

I run a risk when I'm chipped-in while walking the mean streets of Jeim. I don't trust what will happen. The times that

I do, though, I notice a fundamental shift in perspective. The barbarism, so disgusting normally, feels normal and appropriate, even worth celebrating. My mind is energized by the raw, animalistic instincts of kill or be killed. One time I get too close to a site of recent fighting. I'm attracted to it and relish the bloodshed spilled by Pirner combatants.

Same horrific reality but two divergent mental worlds. The organic one is repulsed by the violence and scared. The algorithmic one is curious and enticed by the fighting.

I'm thankful I'm not acting out on the tantalizing algorithmic stimuli. That I'm not part of the bloodshed.

God forbid if I was.

Yet, I am drawn to this compelling reality.

Chapter 20

A growing dependency.

It surprised me at first.

It no longer does.

Given what I learned years ago about *interconnect*'s devious tactics from the organics, one would think I would have stayed clear of it beyond the chip-in time required by the regime. Such is not the case. I wonder about those organics. Certainly, I figure they scattered to the wind with the extreme uptick of violence in Elderwater. They possibly made the same journey northward as me. I did get an unexpected alt-x communication a few years back from someone identifying as an organic. But I didn't recognize the voice, couldn't geo-locate the origin, and the call broke off quickly.

I don't feel I need to justify my increased use of *interconnect*. Everyone is chipped-in for most, if not all, of the day. It's the choice between a fascinating, crystal-clear, and empowering experience and a life where I'm psychically dying a little bit more with each passing day.

Living only inside my head, I experience monotonous days that extend into dreary weeks and then into wearisome months. The only relief I get from this depression is *interconnect*. It has become an alluring friend that never fails to excite and nourish me.

I used to be able to moderate my machine input. I did my five hours a day and I turned it off at night.

Now, the machine increasingly has the grip of a pornographic addiction.

My time log typically registers about nine hours during the day plus five hours or so during sleep. It would be even more, but the intensity of the storylines commonly keeps me from sleeping and I need to chip-out, usually around 2 a.m.

Connecting into the machine is a buzz, a dopamine release. I like feeling right and correct and engaging in action following clear instructions.

My abhorrence of the aggressor Pirners has sky-rocketed in intensity. I've come to find that hate is a wonderfully energetic feeling. It makes me feel alive and worthy. It is much more invigorating than messy organic thinking with its insecurities, lack of clarity, and general fucked-up-ness.

I try to remember what I experience when chipped-in. I feel a tingling itchiness in my head at times, like some mental space has been trampled. Visions appear that reside out of reach of my usual consciousness. Shadowy recollections come at times of intense algorithmic-generated hate toward the aggressor Pirner group. I wish to deny this but, if I let my mind go there, the details are too exacting.

I now regularly wear an armored vest and automatic rifle. I justify this as a reasonable act of defense. But some things just don't make sense. There is a black-and-white quality to my carnage-filled *interconnect* fantasies. I laugh darkly at what this former academic becomes in these visions—not a reasonable man defending himself and loved ones, but an animal seeking out prey in an urban jungle.

It deeply troubles me that the images of killing make me feel better, more fulfilled than when I think on my own.

In my imaginings, I am exhilarated by the solidity of being a combatant fighting for a cause. I am no longer the abstract, wishy-washy intellectual who always analyzed both sides of an argument ad nauseam and who never took a firm stand of my own.

What happens on an unusually cool day is nonetheless shockingly abrupt. This episode I remember.

In the first hour that I'm chipped-in, things seemed manageable. A type of bubbling, vague anger. A general crabbiness and mental tightness. But then, I felt an alluring closeness to the images of violence surrounding me. They were pulling me toward it, not as a spectator but as a participant.

My right eye then gets blurry. I see a black spot that blocks my line of sight. Some damn stroke-like thing feels imminent.

I feel the ShadowTrax on my side-belt. My right hand is making a grasping movement. My guts are wrenching, head throbbing. The adrenaline-filled thrill of righteousness invades my mental space.

I'm being propelled onward toward conquest.

A black-and-white image erupts in my head. I'm with a Mage militia unit. There is spray-shooting of Pirners in a crowded market area in Upper Dazim. Denizens are collapsing in front of me. I feel strong, powerful, and right. Denizens are screaming and running for cover as I hear Mage fighters reloading and continuing to kill. There is nobody there to stop us.

I have a strange sense of distance, that all this is happening to someone else.

I walk up to an injured young man. As I reach down, a bullet pierces his head right between the eyes. Power surges all over my body, tingling with excitement. Next, a fallen boy, probably young teenage years, is shouted at, "You Pirner scum, you're done" before his life is ended.

This seems like a dream, but it feels so real.

Raven looks at me at our apartment door with bewildered fear in her eyes.

CHAPTER 21

The next month is lost to me. When I'm not connected, I exist at near coma level of existence. Dizzy all the time, asleep most of the time. Drained physically and depressed mentally. No interest in this life. I twitch constantly as if my body can't handle stillness.

I feel I'm a residual, a remnant detached from some larger storyline. When not connected, I feel that I'm missing out on the revealing of an important truth.

I get an anticipatory buzz when I'm stable enough to connect in. Usually, this is late afternoon or early evening. Typically, the next thing I know is it's late morning the next day. I'm breathing rapidly, bruised, and wasted. I experience spikes of memory about what transpired during my time away, but they soon dissolve.

I want more.

I crave the feeling of righteous power of the *interconnect* visions.

I welcome the algorithmic blackness as a friend and

accomplice. Each day I can't wait to connect to its hatred, not as passive observer but as active agent. The impulsive energy of the blackness has a commanding authority. It's the source of answers, solutions, and clarity. The way to find meaning in life, to rise above the flatline, to fill the emptiness, to feel the virile cockiness of "fuck the world" manhood.

When I don't feel the MRAD sniper rifle and .548 ShadowTrax8 gun hanging from my waist, I feel naked. My hands get sweaty and itchy when I don't feel their weight on my side. They're the tools of our trade, the main means of eliminating scumbag Pirners from this earth.

I go into the electrifying blackness of the machine. There's an inky, smudgy quality to the dark. Cold, damp air attacks my senses. I feel anchored and strong.

I am in a fortified hole 22.4 miles northeast of Jeim city limits. I am on the strategic backside of the murderous Pirner caravans of rocket launchers that are positioned in the hills above the city. They have decimated major parts of the city over the past four plus years.

The Mage unit I'm with is here after almost two days of difficult trekking through the Guthram-Kald tunnel. They lugged all their arms and supplies through a passage two feet wide, less than four feet high, and running about 1,450 feet under the Jeim airport, controlled by Pirner militia snipers.

We are now at the fucking Pirners' backs and they are unaware of us. They are busy firing some 4,000 laser-guided mortar shells per typical day at the city's hospitals, libraries, schools, Mage temples, museums, and open-air food markets. For entertainment, snipers on the hills using semi-automatic guns shoot indiscriminately at any human movement in the city below. Typically, these are residents forced out of their shelters to find limited supplies of food, bread, and water. Loss of Mage life has been significant, with our army outmanned and outgunned regularly.

I'm with a highly trained elite unit of the Mage militia.

They are experts in autonomous weaponry and guidance. They welcomed me with open arms after they identified me as a foreign mercenary from Sesperia. Their companionship is reassuring and empowering. It feels like we are all part of a common cause.

The Mage unit's directive is not to directly attack but to set the foundation for a major future assault. We set 30 laser-guided bomb launchers that will half-encircle the murderers on the hills. These will act in coordination with over 200 autonomous drones in the future attack.

I am home. Raven, as usual, is in her own mental container. She's barely aware that I am here. I have a splitting headache and my body is sore. I am barely awake but conscious enough to resurrect the noir imaginings in my head.

I don't care whether these visions are real or fantasy. The effect of them is exhilarating, better than any organic reality.

Raven notices me and angrily cries out, "You've been gone five days. You could have at least contacted me. You know I don't do well alone. Don't you care about me anymore? Where the hell have you been?"

The thought of a five-day dream fantasy jars me, but I ignore her and need desperately to sleep. I turn off the chip. For the sake of sanity, I need to get these visions out of my head.

I also know I don't want to.

Chapter 22

Hearing Seyh's voice after nearly four years reminds me of how much I have changed. No longer involved in a good cause, I think I have now become part of the problem.

Using old Alt-X communication channels to arrange our meeting feels archaic, like we're living in the '20s. It's too risky for organics to use Vimex, which is heavily monitored by *interconnect* and regime computer thugs. The degree of surveillance over any individual not buying fully into the regime's program of computer enmeshment has increased markedly since my first meeting with the organics.

We meet in a vacant one-story office building halfway between Jeim and Bolwin. The place is desolate. A forgotten stretch of terrain not worth anything strategically to the warring groups. It's an optimal location for organics to gather, deemed as we are enemies of the regime and opponents of progress.

Upon entering a jimmied side door, I see Seyh and Nicolai, along with three other persons I assume and hope are also organics. I see neither Elijah nor Anya. They must be involved in avoidance tactics.

Seyh and Nicolai give me cursory hugs. It's good to see they successfully evacuated from Elderwater like I did.

This meeting is all business.

Nicolai looks worried. Seyh has her head down and looks ruffled.

"Jared, this is Allacia, Remy, and our techie Jai. They're with us, trust me," Nicolai quickly states and moves directly to a rigged-up computer.

"What's going on?" I ask.

"The regime has disappeared Elijah, and probably Anya too," Nicolai responds while tensely observing the computer screen.

"We got an Alt-x communique from Elijah that he was being followed by regime personnel on the outskirts of Jeim. Regime had busted the encryption on his link-up. His message to us was cut off mid-sentence. Ever since, he has no location echo. He went into an electronic black hole.

"Similar story with Anya likely. Her echo is entirely gone."

"This is crazy," I shout. "The regime is getting rid of people just because they want to think on their own. Fuck this!"

"Regime is that insecure," replies Allacia, a rather rotund and jolly-looking woman with a dark pink-colored head. "They think if enough people think independently that we will uncover and overthrow the sick storylines of *interconnect* and expose regime's collusion with it.

"You know, they may be right. It may all be a house of cards. Let's hope."

"Okay," says Seyh. "This is a sad happening. But we have work to do. Check-ins please?"

Nicolai announces, "My algo intake per day remains at two hours, only minor irritations coming off it. Anger intensity above target level when on. I believe machine is countering my limited use by increasing stimuli."

Remy is up next. She's a cute little thing, looks teenager- age, wearing a heavy sweater and some type of neck wrap-around. "Two hours, no withdrawal symptoms, stimuli increasing shame and guilt responses, no overall increase in intensity."

Jai is pony-tailed, wearing aviator glasses, leather jacket, cut-off shorts, and old Birkenstock shoes. He says, "1.5-2 hours per day, fuck the machine, no withdrawal symptoms, computer has given up on me, I think, stimuli monotonous blah blah. Biggest problem is I have no social life. Can't meet other organics for a casual lunch because it will set off the machine's co-locational alarm. Don't want to socialize with heavier machine users, they're becoming a bunch of addicts. So, I sit at home, with my coy on my lap, and partake in the slow agony of organic reality."

Allacia smiles and looks hesitant to take the stage. "A bit over two hours, I'm afraid, withdrawal restlessness is present, stimuli focusing on resentment of other people, overall intensity is up.

"I'm a wee bit worried, to be honest. I think about chipping most of the time when I'm not tapped in. I get a buzz when I get close to tap in time."

"I'm sorry to hear that, Ally," Seyh replies. "Damn, I sure wish Anya was here to provide technical-side input to your struggles. Be honest, please, Ally. What is a more exact estimate of your chip time?"

Allacia frowns and mumbles, "Most of the morning, I guess... Um... I guess also first half of most sleep periods I'm chipped-in.

"You know it sounds weird, but I kinda like the resentfulness flowing through my brain. It is very empowering. When I'm off the chip, I get down on myself for enjoying it, which makes organic thinking that much more of a challenge. It feels like I'm in some downward loop."

"This is *interconnect*'s game, Ally," Seyh declares. "Chip-in, make you feel good about dark thoughts so that when you're off it, you feel bad about enjoying the chip, which then makes you want to feel good again. Presto, the chip."

Appearances can deceive. Allacia has a happy surface appearance but is fighting an internal struggle with the devil.

"Jared, you next. You get the drill," says Nicolai sharply. I note he has gained confidence from the first time I met him.

"Okay, let me see," I start. "I don't remember things as well as others," I stall. I feel that I must put on some façade here. I don't know why. There exists a huge blank space when I try to recall my algo-use. A large cavity in my brain feels like it's been dug out. "Two or three hours per day, no withdrawal signs, stimuli are commonly, you know, run of the mill hatred, anger, threat, pretty easy to not attach to, sometimes almost comical, no overall increase in intensity."

This is total fabrication about my chip time, and I hesitate to think about what the machine might be doing with me. I wonder why I must outright make up shit to this friendly group and whether I am hiding fantasy or reality. I don't know what it is, but I impulsively know I must hide whatever it is.

I'm an imposter. I must not be found out.

My head pounds and it feels like it is cleaving in two. A sharp, vicelike pain.

Amidst the debilitating pulsing, I am glad when the group's attention turns away from me.

I got away with something about which I know little.

Cringing.

I feel that I am living in two separate worlds.

The meeting with my organic colleagues is abruptly ended when Jai yells out that multiple surveillance monitors have geo-located us. We disperse into the stifling heat.

The meeting brings caution into my life. I try to moderate my chip-time and spend more time thinking on my own. Over a week goes by in reasonable use. On the surface, one would note greater stability in my life. Inside, though, my mental state is tottering. My organic thinking is meandering, full of doubt and itchy feelings of guilt and shame about things I can't identify.

I don't want to live with this bewilderment.

I want reasons.

I crave answers.

I know there is another place more intriguing.

It produces feelings that are clearer and stronger.

It's midway through the second week after the meeting with the organics. Despite urges and temptations, I'm proud of my limited chip time. But I'm also bored and getting fidgety. I'm binging on eVision to the point of paralysis. I'm eating too much of our limited supplies, so much that even Raven, in her algorithmic nether-world, notices. Sex is becoming excessive to the point of routine. Basically, I'm going nuts.

I watch eVision with horror as the country further collapses.

Central Heartlanders launch hundreds of laser-guided autonomous bombs at Zonal settlement areas and refugee camps.

Qasines in Elderwater successfully inject a viral compound into the sewage lines flowing out near enemy neighborhoods, infecting thousands and causing hundreds of deaths.

Birthplace, partitioned by 45-foot-high walls separating Western and Eastern neighborhoods, is now the sad location for the use of new Lucifer drone warplanes.

Even in the reputably more sophisticated Sesperia region, Focalists are increasing their use of AGM-114 missiles in their campaign against secessionist Tulpanis. So far limited warfare near Acalato, which comforts me that the kids—and Carrie— are not in harm's way.

Mass craziness.

It's strange to me that eVision, a direct appendage of *inter-connect*, shows all this to us. I wonder if it is to inflame us further.

I'm exhausted by the vids and begin to detach. I'm about to switch off the e-set when news from nearby comes on.

Vids of Pirner militants lining up Mage men, women, and children, shooting them in the back, then tossing them off a cliff into a mass grave. Cocky, manly gestures by the killers, laughter, sniggers.

Tingling in my head becomes a strong vibration, then a pulsating energy.

I yell out to Raven, "You know, I always thought I was a reasonable person, but fucking Pirner assaults on our very being and way of life are too much to handle. Those that stand by while all this is happening, you know, the passive peace-niks, they don't know what they're fucking talking about. They're sadly idealistic and not facing reality. Something has to be fucking done to stop this."

Raven looks at me with those far-away, detached eyes. She is fully within a storyline, as usual, while weirdly fondling herself. Must be within some multiple-partner sex drama.

I sit back in the chair and try to calm, but it's not possible.

I feel an intense urge to chip-in.

I need to set this emotion on fire more fully.

I need the storyline.

The stimulant.

The justification to act.

The answer.

The solution.

Chapter 23

My world goes intensely black-and-white. A surging, locked-in feeling floods my mind.

I look down at a wounded woman chained to a bolted-down table in the middle of the detention cell. She is bare-breasted and bloodied. We are not alone. There are angry, horny Mage fighters standing in a circle surrounding her and me. One spits a voluminous load at her. Another is shouting some philosophical bullshit at her.

With a mixture of delirium and hatred, I have an assault rifle at the whore's forehead. She bows her head submissively. This devil of a woman killed six of my comrades with a GBU-14 bomb. She was the only one in the general area; it had to be her.

All this time, she made us believe she was one of us. Played us all for fools as we followed her in her tight-fitting fatigues and flirty push-up tank top. The intensity of the Mage onlookers' anger shows I'm not alone in my hatred.

A comrade presses forward and says, "You're the one

duped by this clever hussy. We believe you, Rohde."

I feel urgently that this must be done. We could hold her as war ransom, but this woman is smart and, if left alive, could screw up this whole operation at a critical point. Deception artists like her have no place.

I feel the embrace of the assault rifle. Its hard-black surface glistens.

The hatred of what she has done.

I was such a toy in her game.

So easily accommodating to her deceit.

Sexual desire mixed in with the manipulation makes me feel particularly small.

Wounded male pride.

I see a butt of a rifle smashing hard across her face. She is crying.

"You don't know what you are doing," she sobs.

"Fuck you, Pirner bitch." Again, a hard rifle against broken skin. The blood is dark black.

She moans, barely audible. "Don't you understand, we are all in a manufactured fabrication? A computer narrative."

It looks like her nose is broken, a deep opening cutting across her cheekbone. She reeks of body odor.

"What the hell are you talking about? You're full of manipulative bullshit. Six of my fighters are dead because of you," I yell.

"When you come out of this, try to remember. Take my headband and keep it. It may help you recall."

She reaches out her hand and stuffs a piece of cloth into my left fatigue pocket.

I'm alarmed at her gesture. A knife is slashed across what was a beautiful face. She can barely hold her head up. Urgency rushes into me. This must be done. I see the killing rifle aimed right between her eyes. I want her to see everything until the end. The sharp blast of the rifle reverberates in the small cell.

The impact explodes her face.

*

As we leave the facility, I turn to a comrade and ask, "What the shit was she talking about in there, that fabrication line, like we are in some fucking dream?"

My comrade, "Typical manipulation strategy. It's all bullshit. Some Pirners are trained experts in deception."

Later that day, my squad surprises a lightly armed contingent of Pirner fighters near Seneg Point. We eradicate most of them. We suffer only one casualty. We capture one fighter and commence to torture him for fun. Right before we eliminate him, he spits out, "I'm ready to die, but I got the best of a bunch of you Mage scum with my GBU. You losers, you thought it was that sex pot. No wonder you guys are losing this war."

We complete the eradication.

In barracks that evening, we mourn our losses and celebrate our conquests. Some rot-gut liquor is passed around and generously consumed.

Sloppy-wasted, we throw fun barbs at each other and feel community.

I half-slur to Clemens, my closest friend in our contingent, "You know that sexy woman today?"

"Yeah, what about her? You see those titties? What a nice set."

"If she wasn't the one who set the bomb, then who was she?"

Clemens looks at me crazy-like, "You told us all this crap about her being a spy among us."

"Well, that was true. She messed with our heads for two weeks."

"I don't know, man. I never saw her before. You were the

one talking that spy shit. We just went along, believing you. We were all of the kill mind anyway. I don't think any of our guys saw her before you detained her."

143

Chapter 24

I come to consciousness assaulted by the smell of body odor and fluids. Tick-tick-ticking of some machine. My wrists are tightly bound.

My head is ripping apart like an icy metal pole piercing my brain stem and being rotated. The brutality of the head pain comes in pounding waves. My body is shaking and twitching involuntarily.

I feel multiple eyes upon me. I recognize one pair as belonging to Raven. She looks typically radiant but also worried. I look unsteadily at a small window. Bars crisscross it like in a damn prison.

An older man with protruding nose hairs, a beak-like face, and an overall haggard appearance, is front and center. White lab coat.

"Hello, Mr. Rohde, my name is Dr. Siram Bendel."

"Where am I?" I slur.

"You, sir, are in a warehouse turned into a makeshift medical clinic. More precisely, you are in Cumberland District, West

Bolwin. Classified as a demilitarized zone, but hell if anyone could tell that by the constant shelling around us."

"Why am I here? Am I a prisoner of war?" I say, trying to extend my bound arms.

The doctor laughs. "Heaven's no. You were brought here due to your condition."

"And what was that?"

"We don't have the equipment to confirm it," he states, waving his arm to indicate the sparse conditions of the room. "But my analog diagnosis is that you have a moderately advanced type of split-brain seizure."

"What is that, Doctor?" Raven bursts in, much faster than I can respond.

"It is a symptom of two mental worlds colliding—algorithmic intake and organic thinking. We don't see much of it anymore. Most citizens have given up so much of their lives to *interconnect* that there is no mental instability. Typically, erosion of neural tissue in the brain's executive function is so extreme that there is no conflict between mind streams. The algorithmic stream has become dominant."

I can tell Raven is lost, as she commonly is. People don't care what lies behind those breathtakingly gorgeous blue eyes. Amazing how far physical beauty can go in making up for mental laxity.

"What exactly are you telling me?" I mutter, a stream of spit coming out of the side of my mouth.

"Let me ask you, Mr....," the doc looks at a clipboard, "excuse me, Dr. Rohde.

"Are you chipped-in the medically recommended five hours per day?"

"I have no idea," I honestly answer.

Indeed, I have become pretty much clueless about much of what happens in my normal day.

"As you may be aware, if you are consistently below the five-hour connection time each day, the brain gets mixed up and will eventually misfire. Basically, it doesn't know who its boss is or who it should listen to.

"We call it algorithm deficiency disorder (or ADD). This condition will lead over time to intense psychotic episodes called split-brain seizures.

"This, I believe, is what landed you in this dismal place.

"Do you recall what you were feeling last time you were conscious?"

"I don't know what they are. Dreams, images, visions, I don't know. They come into my mind and it's like they're grabbing me. They feel artificial and real at the same time. There's a sharp black-and-white quality to them.

"When I'm off the machine, I feel like I'm in control of my thoughts again. The images go from black and white to more a watercolor mash-up. But there is also a flatness to it when I'm not chipped-in. Something more interesting feels like it is pulling me away from my own thoughts. Some mental magnetic shit."

"What are the black and white images about, Dr. Rohde?"

I go immediately back to those images and panic.

"Killing, doctor... fucking killing," I sob. "I'm full of rage and power."

I hesitate and think whether I should describe the feeling more.

"You know what, doc. The rage feels good.

"Like Molly Thizz flowing through my blood."

The doctor smiles in an empathetic way. Far from alarmed by my admission, he looks like he knows fully what I am describing. Like I'm not the first in his office with this condition.

He is busy completing something in his online database. He looks at me.

"What happens now, doc?"

"I strongly recommend 10 hours connection to the machine

per day for 10 days. That should stabilize your mind. And, after that, don't fall below five hours per day, okay?

"Your sanity, and maybe your life, will depend on this."

Chapter 25

Over the next three weeks, I try to figure things out and fail.

I feel pulled in two directions. Torn apart by two realities.

I hadn't kept track of my chip-time but I'm pretty sure it has been more than that beaked doctor implied. My periods of lost memory have become regular occurrences. Whatever happens in my dream world seems much more important than my banal, organic existence. Even though Raven is not a great judge of reality these days, her claim that I was gone for five days that one time worries me. I also realize that when I'm thinking on my own (if that is even possible anymore), the compelling pull of *interconnect* has become irresistible. Still, I feel lucid when I'm with the organics, although I am lying to them.

Despite the real pain of what the doctor said was split-brain seizure, I don't trust him. He seemed too flippant and automatic in his prescription. Something is not clicking into place. I have some bizarre psycho trip, then an unknown guy is recommending more, not less, machine time. I wonder if he is some regime-paid agent pushing more chip-in time to any and all of his patients.

Something was going on in my brain, though, to put me in that facility. That was real and searing pain I felt.

I look back at my time log register for the period leading up to the medical diagnosis. I'm not very good with how to access such information. Seems too complicated and I've stayed away from it. I admit I likely didn't want to know the numbers.

The readout shows just over 11 hours per day. Not even close to being below the recommended level.

Fuck that ADD diagnosis by the beak-man!

A feeling that I had been manipulated rises.

It is a reasonably calm night in this war, which means only one bomb blast per hour. Raven is more coherent than normal. She had prepared our dinner of hot dogs smothered by Velveeta cheese with care. She had found two used candle stubs in the street trash and had rigged them to illuminate our meal. She is wearing my favorite transparent silk blouse.

I ask her, "Do you see a difference in me these past months, dear?"

She looks at me like she has been waiting for this question. "Jared, you have changed. You're out almost every day. You come back and say you have no idea what you've been doing. Even when you're not physically away, when you're here, you're not really here."

That was a jumble.

"What do you mean?"

"You seem antsy, suspicious like you're hiding something." Her eyes are wet with emotion. "Are you cheating on me?"

"No... I mean, I'm pretty sure I'm not."

"See, that's what I mean. What kind of answer is that? Are you, or are you not? How can you be 'pretty sure'?"

I'm at a loss to explain and, instead, wrap my arms around her in a deep embrace. She partially engages. I realize that I'm glad that Raven is out of her mind most of the time. Her emotions come and go, and this questioning of my integrity will likely disappear soon.

Chapter 26

We gather in a bunker. It's getting that bad.

Genocidal violence has become a daily occurrence in the past month. The worst was a massacre by Pirner assailants of over 250 children at a school/child care center.

So many buildings and much infrastructure are in shards around us. Militias, along with their associated criminal cartels, dominate every aspect of life in Jeim. Neighborhood cells of gunmen formed to protect local turf have merged to become armies, battalions, and organizations under quasi-military command. Snipers spend their days killing from the balconies of the few high-rise buildings that still remain.

Dozens of dead "collaterals" lie in the streets for days, giving off a pungent, rotting odor. The walls between neighborhoods are higher than ever, but constant bombing makes their impact temporary. Flags and murals are everywhere, demarcating turf but also providing easy markers for aggressors.

I think back to five years ago, before all this madness began. Living the comfortable life of an academic, on the top of the food chain, obsessed with my curriculum vitae, cranking out journal articles, respected, sought out for information, flirty young women coming to my office for discussion. Then students began writing and saying bizarre things. A time when I didn't take what they were expressing seriously enough. I thought it was the latest infantile plaything in the narcissistic ivory tower. I was ignorant of what was to come.

Now I'm in a trench, schizoid tendencies, diagnosed as torn in two parts, hangin' with state-deemed terrorists, could be killed any minute by some deranged militia brute.

We huddle together amidst the sounds of exploding car bombs, clouds of smoke, and the staccato of gun battles. I recognize Seyh and Nicolai. I believe Allacia and Jai are here from our earlier meeting. Several others are here who I don't know. Organics seem to compose a rotating cast of characters.

Seyh looks beaten down. Her dark skin has more of a ghost-like appearance. Nothing at all like the radiant woman I met at our first meeting years ago. She's wearing a dirty and loose-fitting canvas-like outfit. Her eyes are bloodshot, and she has the tremor of post-traumatic stress disorder.

"This is hell," she states. "My news is not good.

"Cynan is full out on a campaign to destroy us. There are paid assassins targeting organic thinkers. Regime pulls these killers in from different algo-groups with the help of the machine, which curates new storylines so they join the regime.

"We found out about Elijah and Anya, and it's not good. They are alive but in prison, which means they are probably being tortured to find out more information about us and our tactics."

Nicolai, wearing a pitch-black flak jacket, helmet, and with a rifle to his side, breaks in with further disheartening news.

"*Interconnect* is geo-locating all low-use machine users in the country. This means we need to be constantly on the move. Our clustering right here is definitely a risky move. Several low users in the same place will set off alarms. I strongly recommend we disperse no more than 20 minutes from now."

I've got to ask.

"Why are we meeting here? Why the call on Alt-X?"

Jai, wearing wiry glasses and looking like our resident computer geek, more like he should be in front of a computer screen rather than with a group of terrorists in a bunker, abruptly states, "Seyh asked for a status report on our insert program."

"Insert?" I ask.

Jai looks at Seyh, surprised that I don't know and that he has to explain.

Tech-architects always seem to become frustrated when they need to describe their world to non-techies.

"We geo-map *interconnect*'s hot spots, where it's sending the most intense signals. We figure that the probability is higher in these areas for conflict between groups. If it's possible to get there within 25 minutes, a volunteer organic member will insert himself in the hot spot. He'll try to get to a leader and explain that they are acting on algorithmic input and that the conflict is fabricated. That there is another reality that can't be seen when they're chipped-in."

"Our friends go directly into battle?" I am astounded at this scheme.

"Indeed, activist organics are willing to insert themselves into storylines to try to convince participants that they are actors in an algorithmic production."

"Okay, Jai. Thank you for explaining," Seyh jumps in. "But our time is limited here. Quickly, what's the status report?"

"We have made 26 interventions into storylines in Jeim," Jai says. "Twelve have succeeded in stopping the immediate violence. But keep in mind we have no idea of success in the medium and long term.

"We don't know whether the militants go back home, chill out, but then quickly go back out when the machine does its thing. Or whether they go home, reassess, and decide to go more organic.

"Fourteen have died.

"In these cases of failure, we don't even get close to shaking them awake. It's like trying to explain mathematics to a coy-dog."

Upon hearing about fatalities, my head spins. Images of battle flood in. The coppery odor of blood. Assault rifle in my hands. Body parts after a GBU-14 bomb.

A memory of an enemy woman saying something weird about fabrication. She seemed for a brief moment to be out of time, out of place. On a different plane of existence. Speaking about another reality.

Remy is looking directly at me with her cute, teenager eyes.

"You've met an insert, haven't you Jared?"

I feel revealed. The most likely way I would have met an insert is if I was out on the battlefield. I need to think quickly.

"I didn't get his name," I mumble. "I met him outside the demolished e-sports arena by chance. He could tell I was an organic and he described his role. I think he was trying to recruit me."

I'm lying through my teeth here. I'm a fraud. I'm covering up parts of my life I can only vaguely recall and that I think may not be even real.

Remy and Nicolai are looking at me skeptically.

"You think the insert program is going to change enough of their minds!?" I shout out, needing to divert attention here. Time is on my side. We've got to get out of this bunker before the machine identifies our location.

"We can't just live in our bubble, hide, and wait this out," Nicolai says. "We need to intervene somehow out in the killing fields. The insert program seems a bit crude, but close to a 50 percent success rate is something."

The pressure is off me.

Gunfire nearby is our signal to get the hell out of here.

We run out of the bunker and disperse intentionally in different directions. We need to de-concentrate our geo-location cluster.

Allacia, quiet the whole meeting, grabs my shoulder as I am about to depart and mutters amidst increasing gunfire, "Why are you lying? Are you a spy?"

We see the regime thugs now, about half a block away and within shooting distance.

I separate from Allacia, fortuitously for me, and scramble away toward an alleyway. I look back and see one of our group down and not moving. The body has that lump-of-clay look of death. A man, but not sure, don't think it's Nicolai, definitely not Jai.

As I turn my head back toward the alley, I get knocked down by some blunt force to my shoulder. I lie awkwardly against a dumpster that reeks of decaying flesh. I try to get up but I'm held down.

I'm looking into the visor-helmets of five regime assassins. One has his ShadowTrax aimed directly at me. I can feel the heat of the laser dot sight on my forehead.

"Your crux identifies you as a Mage. Confirm!" a thug shouts out.

I have no fucking idea what is going on. How come I'm not dead? Killing is what these mercenaries do. They're out to eliminate my organic friends. I must think fast.

"I am Mage, yes!" I respond.

The thugs suddenly channel their attention elsewhere. They've lost interest in me. Thank God!

One visor-helmet still looks at me, however.

"We have geo-confirmed luddies in this area. Have you seen any of them?"

Think!

"I saw two people running down the main avenue. Could they be who you're after?"

The last visor-helmet runs off. I am alone.

I'm amazingly still alive.
But I feel dead inside.
Pulsing surge as I chip-in to stabilize.
Black-and-white storylines,
feelings of righteous anger,
the regime soldiers as my protectorates,
the evil that saved my life,
consumes me fully.

I'm starting to understand.
I don't want to.

PART VI

A USER MANUAL FOR LIVING

2045

Chapter 27

3rd/4th quarters 2045

We have learned an awful truth over the past eight years.

Conflict has no end game.

Denizens now share dark humor that our country is conflict, there is nothing to our country outside of the Turmoil.

Just an awful dragging-on of hostilities for now 13 bloody years.

A sprawling surveillance superstructure has been built and snakes its way throughout the city of Jeim and its outlying areas. This monstrosity divides machine-demarcated populations in an odd, mosaic pattern. After more than a decade, the City is disfigured to such a degree that it is unrecognizable.

The dividing walls mean there is less physical interaction between militias than in earlier years, which has the beneficial effect of less ground-based violence. In its place are even more deadly aerial and drone bombing raids able to surmount the partitions with ease.

One would guess that by now there would be little left to bomb.

I have accepted this bizarre reality as best I can. I have enough old scholarly reflex left in me to pursue knowledge about what is happening in our crazy land. Digging into research has also helped me a bit in not surrendering fully to the machine's storylines.

I dig into the eVision archival library, a horror show that has minuscule viewership according to E-summaries. Maybe the synthed-out crowd tunes in to heighten their buzz. Who knows?

One late night I check into it. The reports are shocking and would be great material for a gruesome horror movie.

The four regions—Northwoods, Birthplace, Heartland, and Sesperia—are now not only divided by 15-story surveillance walls but also protected by anti-aircraft domes.

No one knows why *interconnect* caused us humans to hermetically seal the regions off from one another. One cynical interpretation asserts that *interconnect* desired to unleash human genocidal instincts and that its clean sorting across regions allowed it to optimize intra-region chaos. There's no way to understand the logic of *interconnect*.

Our denizens don't care what is happening in other regions. Their proximate enemy is their obsession to such an extent that there is even ignorance now that other regions exist in what used to be a full country. Those few who are aware of other regions view them as some far-off foreign countries of no concern to them.

The region called Heartland lies southeast of where I am. The conflict there doesn't seem fair. The group called Centrals wants to control the entire region and is wiping out a group called Zonals. The region appears to be a disturbingly distorted and unequal region partitioned by a massive barrier wall that separates Centrals from Zonals.

Centrals live in ultra-modern, protected communities.

Modern housing and facilities characterize major parts of their territory. Aerial photos show massive gated housing estates, backyard swimming pools, and gleaming business towers.

Most Zonals live at subsistence level. Shantytowns, slums, and survivalist conditions characterize all of Zonal territory. Major parts of infrastructure and housing assets in Zonal territory have been destroyed.

Centrals control all security infrastructure throughout the region and engage regularly in aggressive attacks that damage or destroy key Zonal assets. Central militia detainment, torture, and killing of Zonals is common. To access natural resource extraction sites in Zonal territory, the Central coalition has built an extensive "Centrals only" road network that bypasses and fragments Zonal settlements.

Zonals with work permits and identification cards granted by Central authorities can only pass into Central territory through two major checkpoints. The southern checkpoint tunnel is long, tortuous, and heavily monitored. About 15,000 Zonal workers pass daily into Central space through this corridor, starting to line up as early as 3 a.m. and enduring delays up to five hours during rush hours. Each of the three passages through the checkpoint has four turnstiles one has to pass through, and the corridors channel you into narrow, covered, boxlike passageways. During rush hours, these narrow passages become packed with male Zonal workers to the point of suffocation and broken ribs. The control rooms staffed by Central security personnel are bulletproof, fortress-like constructions with thick walls and opaque windows located behind the turnstiles or even completely out of sight.

A Zonal worker is confronted eventually with a metal detector and an X-ray machine. After passing through the metal detector, one has to show their work permit card at one of the checking stations, and it is scanned by a biometric reader. Every Zonal needs a magnetic ID card and a permit, both issued by Central authorities. These ID cards are only issued to individuals who are not blacklisted as a security threat, or who have no misdemeanors on their record or their immediate family members' records.

The partition superstructure within Heartland has not stopped violence. Armed clashes and kidnappings often intrude upon the lives of denizens who are out in the city only to search for food and water. Violent disturbances are most likely near transportation hubs, markets, shopping malls, and schools. In Zonal territory, protests often stimulate episodic clashes between protesters and Central militias protecting resource extraction sites. Zonals also attack travelers on Centrals-only roads from adjacent hilltops, most commonly using timed explosives rolled down the hills.

Political and military control of the entire region is exercised by a coalition composed of Central entrepreneurs and militia leaders. Organized crime cartels linked to the propagation of the chemsynth drug and human trafficking operations cooperate with the governing coalition and provide revenue for Centrals' acquisition of significant military firepower from unidentified foreign sources.

Vastly outgunned, Zonals use asymmetrical conflict strategies and they have evolved in technique. In '42, Zonals injected a homemade pathogen into the wastewater infrastructure system, causing significant loss of life downstream in central Heartland and in Zonal areas near the injection site due to the pathogen's unpredictable path of transmission. Since that attack, Centrals have retooled sewer lines crossing their territory and contained trans-border in-flow. Zonals have also used primitive balloons that can, due to their cloth composition, evade Central dome protection to drop viral agents on Central settlements.

Total estimated loss of life in Turmoil (including presumed dead)—Several millions. Zonal loss of life estimated to be 80% of estimated total.

To my shock, at the end of the report, I see that the machine evaluates the chances of victory for each warring side. Interconnect apparently is not only the instigator of violence but also book-maker for our gambling-addicted denizens. Sickening!

Interconnect war victory probabilities—
Centrals 93%/Zonals 7% [full genocide likely].

Glutton for punishment that I am, I continue searching the e-archives. South of my location is a place called Birthplace. This region is one continuous urban settlement, a city-region. The proximity of warring groups in urban space stimulates constant violence and unrest. Violence is between Eastern and Western militias, each claiming sovereign control over Birthplace based on *interconnect*-scripted historic storylines.

Violence between these militias has necessitated the building of hundreds of partition walls at locations of sustained inter-group conflict. The walls appear largely ineffective in stemming the level of violence. Clashes occur regularly at interface areas where hardcore neighborhoods abut one another. Triumphalist activities by Eastern groups, harkening back to a machine-fabricated military victory over 500 years ago, regularly lead to loss of life.

Political control of the region is split, led by opposing Eastern and Western militia groups who hold tight reins on their respective denizen followers. Militias maintain and assert territorial claims on specific community areas of Birthplace. Unlike Heartland, there have been efforts to establish a structure of power-sharing in the region, but violence by hard-liners has obstructed this possibility.

Hardened interface areas where opposing militia groups operate in proximity are problematic hot spots of conflict.

Family, neighborhood, and minor urban aggravations esca-
late quickly and can lead to gunfire or other violence with no
warning. Chemsynth trafficking is noticeable and instigative
of militia activities and Turmoil violence.

> Total estimated loss of life in Turmoil (including pre-
> sumed dead)—over one million. Western loss of life
> estimated to be three-fifths that total.

> *Interconnect* war victory probabilities—
> Easterns 52%/Westerns 48%.

My eyes tear up as I read these reports. We have lost so much in
our country. I recall the brighter days in the past when Carrie,
the kids, and I traveled widely in the country without concern.
I crave this simpler, innocent time. Except for the ranting and
raving of the kids, we traveled in peace. We took for granted
that we would be able to hop around to our country's many
attractions unobstructed and on our own often-spontaneous
time schedule.

It's all so depressingly different now.

I go back to the archives. I don't know how much more I
can handle.

The third region outside of my current Northwoods base is
called Sesperia. It is the most beautiful area in our battered
country. I'm not just saying this because it is where I spent the
first 40 years of my life and still is the home of Carrie and the
kids. The region has rural settlements that provide breathing
space between developed urban areas. It is blessed with gorgeous ecological assets, most notably the Shellsoll mountain
range and the coastline. Gataipa Island, 30 miles north, was a

popular destination for international tourists before Turmoil.

The militias in Tulpan city and the activists in Acalato city are each fighting for autonomy against Focalists, based in the Capitol city of Cyinith, who aspire to regional consolidation under their control. Pro-autonomy fighters and activists demand outright separation from Sesperia and the creation of their own sovereign territories.

In Acalato, levels of violence and loss of life are moderate compared to the country-at-large. I find a subarea map of the city that identifies areas of violence. I'm relieved to see that our Bliss Vale neighborhood is in one of the blue (safe) zones. So much has happened to me through the years. I'm a different person now, and that life in Acalato feels so far away. But I still feel a lingering sadness about the loss of that former family life. It seemed so complete at the time. I hope my kids—and yes, Carrie too—have been relatively untouched by the madness of our country. I despair over the years ahead what Caleb and Ellie will experience. We have surely fucked up their future. I wish I could cushion them from it all.

In contrast to Acalato, Tulpan city is the location of high extremist violence that is vicious and well-organized on both sides. Loss of life is significant in Tulpan city. The formidable Shellsolls separate Tulpan from Acalato, and thus there is little interaction between the two separatist groups, each fighting their own freedom struggles.

Gataipa Island was annexed into Sesperia region as part of a trade agreement. Both the island and its capital city are divided into two by the "Black Wall"—Kosae population to the south, Jatago population to the north. Prior to the building of the Wall, there was significant loss of life in Gataipa city. The Wall has moderated, but not stopped, violence between the two groups, with each side demanding full control of the Island. The Jatago-controlled northern area is a major trans-shipment node in countrywide chemsynth trafficking.

Total estimated loss of life in Turmoil (including pre-sumed dead)—many 100,000s.

Interconnect war victory probabilities—
Separatists 50.1%/Focalists 49.9%
Kosae 54%, Jatago 46%

Interconnect probability of foreign interference—72%
(Due to significant copper natural resources on the island).

Our own conflicts here in Northwoods are barreling on to hom-icidal obliteration. Pirner assaults on Jeim continue relentlessly. Two autonomous zones have been tenuously established to try to stem violence. One is firmly controlled by Pirners, the other is co-managed by Mage and Fronter forces. Territorial viola-tions of these zones are everyday occurrences. It's as if they exist only on paper.

Our eastern urban neighbor—Bolwin—is experiencing a war within a war. Mage and Fronter forces, in coalition in Jeim, have turned on each other. Pirners seem to have no interest in that city.

Elderwater, down south, my former home when this all started, has experienced strange changes in fighting. In the early years, there was extensive fighting between the coali-tion of Kilats and Ilisaks against Qasines. Then, in 2038, an Ilisak mistake attack on Kilats transmuted the conflict into one between Kilats and Ilisaks. Qasines, militarily suppressed in the early period, are now scattered and have split allegiances in the newer phase.

I look up eVision archive estimates for the future. They are vexing.

Total estimated loss of life in Turmoil (including pre-sumed dead)—many millions.

Interconnect war victory probabilities —
(Jeim)   Pirners xx Mage/Fronters xx
(Bolwin)   Mage xx/Fronters xx
(Elderwater)   Kilats 50%/Ilisaks 50%
(xx=not calculable)

I get the feeling *interconnect* gave up on its calculations. Maybe it's getting tired of its own game.

It is inevitable that our country would become prey after 13 years.

A country weakened by more than a decade of internal conflict will eventually be messed with by neighboring countries. Outsiders just can't resist.

The first attack occurred on remote Gataipa. The island, northwest of the mainland, contains numerous repositories of copper, critical to many other countries' efforts to decarbonize their economies. This invasion threatens some of our country's algorithmic groups, most directly the Jatago group fighting for sovereignty in the north of the island. To reinforce its hold in the north, the invaders are now financing the Kosae group in the south, the arch-enemy of the Jatago. This has produced intense shitshow warfare on a formerly beautiful island.

But the invasion has broader impacts. Defeat of the Jatago would jeopardize a key trading route. The island is the location of the Mage-Jatago back channel, the only link that exists in our country between the two regions. This route connects Gataipa Island with the mainland and has been used for oceanic trans-shipment of arms to the Mage and the machine stimulus-enhancing chemsynth drug to basically everyone. The route overlays a magnetic underwater trench that disrupts efforts at electronic surveillance. It thus has become a free-for-all corridor for black marketers.

Several other countries are drooling at the thought of establishing military bases in our country, which has a strategic location vis-à-vis the broader geopolitics of the world. The Zonal area of Heartland and the Eastern part of Birthplace have areas of open terrain suitable for long runways and massive facilities. The Tulpan part of Sesperia faces possible occupation by foreign interests able to capitalize on its water port area.

If we don't get our act together, greater interference will surely come. We are headed toward becoming chopped-up pieces annexed by other countries. The only thing saving us may be our indigestibility.

We now call the machine stimuli *thought cairns* (cairns, for short). I guess we needed such a slang word to convince us that our behaviors are natural. Thought cairns are so called because they act in electronic space similar to how hiking trail cairns operate in physical space. Just as trail cairns—those loose conical rock or stone markers we need—assist a hiker along the proper path toward an intended destination, thought cairns align us toward machine-intended goals.

That is where the similarity ends, however.

Whereas trail cairns benignly guide us, thought cairns have a different, malignant objective—to keep us from deviating from the pre-selected algorithmic path when we might be prone to self-will.

Chemsynth is another sign of our acquiescence to *interconnect* as a durable way of life. Not only do we chip-in more than ever (last estimate was 92 percent user base for an average of 15.5 hours/day), but we also want to intensify the cairn buzz. We now know how the chemsynth injectorate intensifies the orgasmic brain rush of *interconnect*. The drug stimulates an excessive amount of dopamine in the brain, which makes users happier. Simultaneously, it douses the user with dexamphetamine, which increases amygdala activation and increases feelings of fear and threat.

In other words, chemsynth creates happier murderers.

Trafficking of chemsynth now composes one of our country's biggest economic sectors and finances many cairn group militias. In a win-win situation, traffickers now operate in relative safety and in cooperation with the governing regime to provide a stable revenue source.

Chapter 28

Even an apparent good thing has led to even worse outcomes. On 2nd quarter/23d 2041, President Cynan and his entourage of eight armored vehicles and 25 bodyguards were driving down Singularity Avenue in the Capitol city of Cyinith when they were met by over 3,000 pounds of ONC high-velocity explosives. The blast created an 88,000-square-foot crater, instantaneously killing the entire motorcade and 155 denizens who had the bad fortune of being nearby.

The end of such a conniving, shadowy man who justified, even applauded, the machine's destructive tearing apart of our country would, in a normal society, create the possibility of positive change. A few organics I talked to cautiously expressed hope that we would come to our senses. But the problem really wasn't Cynan. He was only a bootlicker subordinate to a much greater power.

The regime was thrown into chaos after the assassination because our egomaniacal "lifetime President" had consolidated his power so thoroughly since 2030 that there was no apparent successor. An encrypted message was eventually delivered by *interconnect*, revealing a hand-picked successor—a mid-level bureaucrat by the name of Zachary Prince. A rumor on the streets conjectured that Prince had helped groom young Sesperian girls for Cynan's carnal enjoyment.

Cynan's funeral was a pompous, vomit-worthy affair splattered all over eVision for days. *Interconnect* transmitted glossy storylines of Cynan's life, his rise to leadership, his heroism in leading us to a "new tomorrow," and his bravery in fighting those who resist technological advancement. In his eulogy, Prince announced that Cynan would be honorary lifetime President. I guess this means he'll be leading from the grave.

Likely feeling quite vulnerable in his new perch of power, Prince has doubled down on Cynan's doctrines. His new take on an old Cynan concept is "community through separation." Partition is the name of the game—more walls, more surveillance, better checkpoints, and enhanced crux-based monitoring of mobility.

Cynan's assassination has meant near-disaster for us organics. A long-winded screed was electronically submitted to the regime after the assassination. A loosely based anarchist group called the Chosen Healers claimed credit for the event and threatened further action unless the regime resigned en masse. Although our organic group had nothing to do with the assassination, the Prince regime immediately lumped the Healers together with us as imminent threats to the state. This has resulted in even more disappearances of our members.

The assassination also has led to the elimination of the last small shred of our democratic façade. The Prince regime unilaterally ended all elections, even the dubious algorithmic selection process initiated by Cynan in 2034.

Denizens also lost what little ability remained in how they use *interconnect*. In response to the new Prince regime, OneSource disabled the auto-off preset option in the chip implant. This means that once in, the only way to toggle out is to use your compromised self-will, seek help from a friend, or wait until the machine releases you.

With no end in sight, everyone has filled up with their sense of righteous anger. Whether actively killing or just trying to survive the chaos, we are all fellow human beings who share a deep despair.

We organics look for minor moral victories. They are few and far between. One such feat was a poem written by one of us, a 25-year-old woman named Annette Waring, that was electronically transmitted through back channels into mainstream eVision reporting. It follows:

They put partitions up to fool us
They filled our brains with falsehoods
They planted hatred
They made us bomb our streets
We became the machine that kills
We became the separation
Where are you my loving soul?
Outside the chip, it resides.

The poem was on eVision for about 26 minutes before being taken down by algo-sensors. During that time, about 40 percent of denizens clicked on its audio or video feed.

Chapter 29

Raven and I are liquid-intoxicated in our hovel of a shelter. Drunkenness, the old-fashioned way of enjoyment, has become our normal evening event. Alcohol drinking feels more natural than being chipped-in. We frolic, laugh, and enjoy each other's company. Given what's outside, turning inward seems like a good choice. E-vision is on in the background, but we are learning to detach from its constant bombardment of "breaking news."

We have constantly had to move. I think it's now 10 times in the past eight years. We now live in a residential zone that is not quite squatter settlement, not quite city. An in-between place midway between the partitioned and scorched city and the refugee zone of overcrowding, tin-roofed shacks, and squalor. We had to leave Jeim proper. The daily violence, bombed-out shells of buildings, fire-scarred structures, and ruins finally became too much to handle.

Most of the housing where we are now is intact, bricks-and-mortar structures. We have a roof over our heads. An eerie place nonetheless. Most of the furniture and appliances are gone, probably stolen years ago. Gross graffiti on the living room walls indicates this place likely was a militia hangout for a time. Imaginative how many different ways one can draw a penis. The main reason we located here is that this area seemed less vulnerable to Turmoil instability. To this day, violence is targeted more toward the city proper, viewed as a prize, and to the outlying squatter settlements, a boiling stew of poverty and distress.

After finally getting a formal divorce from Carrie, I feel freer now with Raven. Tinges of guilt and remorse I think will always be there when I think of that married life, but signing the papers has helped compartmentalize those emotions. But, I miss my children terribly. I also have gained greater respect for Raven. I long thought she was mentally gone, so tapped into *interconnect* that she had lost most contact with reality. This is good for sex because her fantasy world created great imaginative encounters in bed, you know, such as anal penetration of a dragoness and so forth. A fantasy doll is great fun for fucking. But not so good for day-to-day conversation and dealing with the mundane things in life.

My perspective on Raven changed a few quarters back, though. One night, she recounted in great detail the numerous times I have gone on what she calls my "escapades." She opened a creaky drawer in our makeshift kitchen and brought out a folded piece of paper. On it was a numbered list of the times when I'd gone unaccounted for. The items were written in different colored pens and pencils. On the top of the list was one dated 2037, some eight years ago.

There were 18 escapades listed, many of them with detailed notes included. These were my outings, anywhere from a full day to two weeks, when I would come home with little memory of what had happened, but exhausted and wild-eyed. Raven described my wearing of various parts of a militia outfit. Night goggles one time. A shemagh scarf another time.

Then a camo cap. At the time, I apparently could put these incongruous ornaments out of my mind more effectively than she could.

She was calling me on my shit and demanding an explanation. I described my visions and dreams and stressed my lack of understanding of what happens during my escapades. All my verbiage about being an unknowing victim, by this time, seemed more and more like bullshit. She stood her ground and reminded me that she was in that doctor's office years ago when he talked about split-brain syndrome.

I tried my best to explain something that I didn't understand.

"It's like a dream," I say. "You know, honey, when you wake up in the morning. You have these vivid memories... visions.... I don't know, of fragments that don't make sense. Each fragment leaves a clear imprint, but there's no coherent or logical sequence. No overall narrative.

"Then these images, within minutes of awakening, get submerged by the conscious meanderings of everyday life. No matter how strong the dream fragments are at first, you can't hold on to them. They dissolve when the non-dream mind takes over. Like grains of sand slipping through your hands. The dream bits seem so real when you wake up, but then they disappear.

"Let me ask you, dear, can you remember any dreams you had, say, two nights ago?" I ask.

"Not any of it," Raven responds.

"That's what it's like when I try to recall what I'm doing during these escapades," I say, holding up Raven's accounting list.

I pause. It feels good trying to explain. Although I'm not close to figuring it out, putting my best foot forward provides some welcome relief from the pressure of trying to bottle up this mysterious, secret life.

This difficult conversation not only made me face my

bizarre schizoid life but also made me love Raven more. She cared enough to keep track of me and to face me down. She was not anymore just my fantasy doll.

Thus, for both of us now, alcohol is our friend that brings us together. This is refreshing compared to our chip-times, which separate us into alternative worlds.

The withdrawal symptoms from *interconnect* are certainly harsh, and I avoid them whenever possible by maintaining my connect time. What troubles me, however, is there is a flatness and hopelessness, no matter how much I drink, the few times I'm able to spend five or more hours of continuous organic thinking. And the damn machine senses my distance when I think on my own. It reacts by delivering more potent, addictive storylines when I re-connect. The auto-disconnect feature, for some unknown reason still existing in my chip, has saved me many times from full-out machine capture.

With our communication channels now more open between Raven and me, we talk about things that have happened to us through our years together. In these meandering discussions, I came upon a deeply unsettling realization.

I was thinking back to that strange doctor's visit years ago and wondering how Raven and I ended up in such an out-of-way facility. Raven had no fin access and I apparently was incapable. I remember thinking then that we seemed to have appeared there out of nowhere. We had never talked about that bizarre time.

"You know that visit to the doctor who said I had algorithmic deficiency disorder or something like that?" I ask

Raven first looks blankly at me, then says, "Oh honey, that was horrible."

"How did we end up in that facility in West Bolwin? It's a rather long fin drive from here? Why there?"

"A man knocked on our door before that. I wasn't going to answer, but he said that he was a friend of yours here to help us. You were out of it, and I didn't know what to do."

"Did he say his name?"

"Yea, Clemens. He said he was from your algo-group."

Upon hearing the name, a foreboding sense of dread enveloped me. I realized that my violent dream world could not be pure fantasy. I remember Clemens was part of my Mage militia unit and here he was at our apartment door.

My two realities intersecting.

"Honey, you look alarmed. Who was he?" Raven asks.

"An old friend from Elderwater Institute," I answer too quickly.

I'm lying again.

Still a habit when I'm not chipped-in.

"He was really nice in getting us to Bolwin. Drove us in his fin and everything. He was very helpful."

I'm queasy about what this was implying. A Mage activist connecting me to a doctor who recommends more doses of *interconnect*. It's one thing if it was a regime hack medic making sure I'm an obedient user. Another thing entirely that it was a Mage militant wanting me to be more chipped-in for their war.

If a flesh-and-bone man from my dream world is in my organic reality, does that mean that my escapades may be more real than fantasy and that I am involved in the horrific visions I have experienced? Not a spectator, but an actor. I fear for what I might be doing when in the world of *interconnect*.

Despite greater intimacy with Raven, my challenge remains. I feel split into two realities. One dully flat-line, the other righteously euphoric.

I'm to meet my organic associates the day after tomorrow and I look forward to learning more from those with more integrity than me in resisting the machine.

I feel like a fraud.

**eVision 20-minute news headlines
3rd quarter/73d/2045**

*** Interconnect creates new compassion tools that address loss of "own-group" members. The great machine will release to afflicted denizens life-like virtual companions developed from images of their beloved deceased.*

*** President Prince announces that "community through separation" program is succeeding. "Limits on contact between groups lessen violent episodes," Prince declares. He promises more spending on separation structures. Prince's eVision data plug states: "Before our machine's brilliance, humans mistakenly wanted to mix or integrate different peoples. This was a mistake. It went against human nature. Interconnect shows us that a better way toward human community is more feasible and desirable."*

*** Interconnect calculates that current regime policies are 56.7% more effective in achieving goals compared to human-picked electoral periods.*

*** President Prince lessens threat level to 7/10, lowest since Cynan assassination. He cites success in eradicating opponents of our "new tomorrow."*

*** The Cynan Jewell in Capitol City breaks ground, to be completed in two years. This super-district of tomorrow in Cyinith will include titanium-plated archways, grand boulevards, reflecting pools, advanced drone fortification, and new world-class governmental and residential enclaves. Commemorating our great leader, the Cynan Jewell will illuminate our great country and its achievements.*

*** Interconnect describes cause of recent whiteout, a period when it went offline for 45 days. Cites algorithmic re-calibration maintenance.*

I'm about to pass out while cuddling with Raven in bliss. But, that last news item grabs my attention. It's mysteriously ambiguous. I note to myself that I should ask the organics about that strange event. I hope I remember.

Chapter 31

I approach using a zig-zag running pattern and by varying my pace to avoid algorithmic pinpointing of my geo-location. It's important not to give the machine any lead time in identifying our upcoming spatial cluster of low-chip-use denizens. The strange thing is that several times on my way here, I know, by the echo lock-in on my chip, that I set off regime surveillance. It scared the shit out of me. But nothing happened.

Our meeting place is a half-demolished casino from yesteryear, a dingy back hall where plenty of money changed hands and crates of liquor were consumed. We're in the boonies somewhere southwest of Jeim. The taxi-fin driver thought I was deranged when I asked to be dropped off just this side of nowhere. We'll only have 20 minutes together, tops, before we are geo-located and mercenary brutes arrive. Our remote location gives us a little cushion, but it's always uncertain.

We sit on metal stools around an old billiards table with its scratched metal surface exposed. A few balls are in the slots, encrusted with slimy grunge. Seyh, Nicolai, Allacia, and Jai look at each other like we can't believe we're still alive, given the regime's intense effort to eliminate us as enemies of the state. There are a few others standing in the background.

A tall, handsome man wearing dress slacks, with an immaculately groomed mustache and pointed beard, is standing at the end of the table. Seyh introduces him as Pavo Molimo, and she hurriedly describes him as a deserter from OneSource headquarters. The first thing I think is that somebody that well put together has to be a regime spy.

"Why are you with us, and how did you get away?" Jai jumps in, apparently feeling the same way.

"If I was a spy, you would all be traced and dead by now."

Okay, he's quite responsive.

He continues, "I've personally borne witness to the wreckage that *interconnect* is imposing on our country. My whole family—wife, mother, three kids—was wiped out in an Eastern pillaging of our neighborhood in Birthplace. They didn't have a chance.

"And when I think that I had a small hand in creating the machine that killed my family," Pavo briefly pauses and his eyes moisten. "I just couldn't stand being in the system anymore.

"I got away by faking injury and blocking medical sensors. Jumped out of a medi-fin and ran like hell down an embankment. I was rescued and sheltered by an organic family. They connected me with you guys."

"And you look like this now?" Jai is not done pursuing. Good question.

"Man of the house used to be a tailor at Hourglass Mall in Jeim. He was into appearance."

This sounds weird, too convenient, but I'm going to give this guy the benefit of the doubt. His point about us being dead if he was a spy is a valid one, but spies can have other motives besides eradication.

"Okay," Nicolai intervenes, "hopefully we have established

Pavo's cred. Let's get to why we're here."

Here comes another download of information. Sure wish we could transmit this stuff over e-channels. But the machine would pick it up immediately. It would be giving everything away. But in person, the verbal download of details and news, especially with our time limit, is way too fast for me to digest.

"Jai, insert program?"

"Good news, bad news. We have had some success stories, but they are in the minority. We continue to lose personnel. Effective outcomes in stopping violence come most often when insertors can get leaders of the two sides to look each other in the eyes. If our message to them about their fabricated status coincides with eye contact, some type of residual human connection is established. Timing is important. In these cases, combatants lay down their arms and enter into a kind of suspended remembrance. Immediate hostilities terminate. I remind you though, we have no idea of long-term sustainability.

"In bad cases, our inserter is typically terminated. Even in these cases, however, the recipient seems to have a momentary flashback. This indicates a connection made by the inserter, but it was too transitory to hold."

I shamefully think back at my pixelated vision of the woman tortured and killed years ago. I was absolutely convinced she was a Pirner killer. It felt like a dream, but it had the stickiness of reality. For almost an entire year after that vision, I tried everything I could to convince myself that I was no more than a witness to that brutality. I kept her orange-and-white headband in a closet. I tried to understand more fully what it said in the inner band, "You are not living reality."

"Pavo, you've been in the inside most recently of us, let me ask you, I know you have been briefed, what do you think of our insert program?" asks Nicolai.

"It is admirable what you are trying to do. You guys are on OneSource's radar, I tell you. However, the insert program is incremental and, at best, may have marginal effects. The algorithms against you… against us… are unrelenting. *Interconnect* is constantly adapting to new information and changing the addictive stimuli flowing to recipients.

"It's an amazing learning machine. As denizen tolerance of algorithmic connection increases, the machine knows to increase the electronic dose. It even, for some users, lowers the dose to induce ghastly withdrawal symptoms that make the user viciously hunger for increased connection.

"You can see how unrelenting it is no matter the human condition. The Cynan assassination had absolutely no effect on the machine's dictatorship. The crony humans who shelter in the grand government palaces of Cyinith and the shiny OneSource citadel complex have become superfluous. The machine doesn't need them. They're just a show."

"What's the alternative to insert?" Seyh asks impatiently. She looks diminished. Nothing flashy about her looks or demeanor. Her eyes are clear but they exhibit sadness, even despair. I notice that her hands are shaking.

"The most direct approach would be to try to take out the server farm," Pavo states. His mustache looks greasy in the slimy light.

"We know the location. It's in a no-man's land on the eastern outskirts of Cyinith. Surrounded by surveillance wall superstructures, buffer zones, and heavily manned checkpoints. It has a massive anti-aircraft dome system. You would not believe the billions spent by the regime and OneSource.

"Of course, this alternative strategy for us would require massive firepower to overrun the regime army. Not feasible at this point, based on what I know of your… our… resources.

"Interestingly, there is another opposition group. They have a goal different from ours. But we could reach out to them to discuss possibilities of a coalition."

"You're not talking the damn anarchists, are you?" I probe. "My experience with them is they can't get their act together on anything constructive."

I used to hang out with such folks as a possible remedy for my growing cynicism. They were next to useless.

"No," says Pavo. "I'm talking about a group calling themselves 'paragons.' Their objective is not to return solely to organic thinking, but to restructure, you know, recode, *interconnect* in such a way that it becomes human-compatible and supportive."

The group laughs at this idea.

"Geez," Allacia shouts. "Drone bombing the hell out of the machine seems near impossible. But going in and tweaking the machine seems dream world to me. Try to recode a machine that is superior to us. These paragons must be into some hard drugs."

Smiles and nods greet Allacia's proclamation.

A young, long-haired guy near the back wall raises his hand. "Don't give up hope on insert, friends. Let us remember that we may have caused the whiteout."

He seems surprised by the fact that he has all our attention.

"You recall that this year we tripled the number of our inserts 3rd quarter/20d for a one-week period. Well, that's when the machine went offline."

Our country's denizens had the opportunity to raise their heads above the sand in 3rd quarter 2045. It was a bewildering event lasting 45 days (an earlier one, in 1st quarter 2043, lasted only five days.) This one provided temporary independent thought to our populous, yet our cognitive reflexes had collapsed so thoroughly by then that we were like children in a playground, unfettered but adrift and confused. We sheltered at home for weeks, fearful of encountering a world without supporting electronic anchors and guide-rails. Confronted with momentary awareness of the enormity of our usual encasement, many experienced psychic breakdowns, seizures, panic attacks, tremors, and heart stoppages. When the whiteout ended, denizens fell back into their comfortable brainwaves and entrapment.

Long-haired is now hitting his stride.

"It may have been a coincidence or, worse, the machine could have been playing with denizens, you know, go offline for a bit and see how much of their free will and independent thinking was still remaining.

"But, perhaps, *interconnect* may have been recalibrating in response to a disruption caused by our insert activism?"

Pavo nods his head

"There was a sense in OneSource that organics may have had something to do with it. We did detect an abrupt fall off in human receptivity of algorithm cairns at that time. But, we were never able to prove a connection with luddie, excuse me organic, activism. *Interconnect* is far beyond human comprehension at this time. Another reason that I am here with you all."

"I also remember," Jai bursts in, "our significant loss of inserters during this tripling. Nice to know that we can maybe affect the machine, but that surge is not morally sustainable."

Time is running out on our undetected 20-minute allowance. The group starts to depart through the backdoor of the casino.

Pavo has one last thought. "If we're not able to stop *interconnect*, maybe the paragons have the more realistic route—recode, rather than stop, the machine."

We scatter into the barren landscape.

Organics, always on the run.

CHAPTER **32**

President Prince Speech
Living in Harmony
4th quarter/31d 2045. Interconnect Transmission. 20h00m

Good evening my dear country denizens. I come to you today to report on the significant progress we have made in building upon the legacy of the Most Honorable Albert Cynan. The collateral damage associated with the "community through separation" program is lessening with each passing day. Once completed, we will experience order and stability as never before.

Denizens will live close to others, sharing similar thoughts and behavioral preferences. All guided by the ultimate wisdom of our interconnect mentor. We will live in harmonious peace. No longer burdened by the chaos and conflict of the past, when those with different ideologies lived together cheek by jowl.

We will live in a beautiful, geographically sorted country free of conflict.

{applause: synthetic}

I acknowledge there has been hardship and loss, but this rebirthing period is necessary to attain a higher level of freedom for our country. Nothing great ever comes out of gradual change.

Interconnect has utilized data from all recorded human history to prescribe this future for us. No longer will we have the constant warfare perpetuated by unguided human thinking, the local traumas experienced when denizens of different beliefs lived near each other, and the substantial psychological maladies caused by free will.

Its prescriptions certainly cannot be wrong.

{applause: synthetic}

Already, your regime is busy at work devising plans for rebuilding our country physically after this rebirthing stage is completed. We will send resources to replenish our country so that neighborhoods living in harmony have ultra-modern urban assets that match their level of perfection.

We will build high-quality housing, wondrous parks, and community centers. Water and sewer infrastructure will be the best in the world and will be the backbone of a new economic order. Living in peace and harmony will unleash the tremendous entrepreneurial energies of our great denizens. Our economy will grow in leaps and bounds. The future, as the Most Honorable Albert Cynan stated on many occasions, is bright indeed.

Your regime asks for your patience as we continue our brilliant campaign against luddie resisters. Of course, I do not understand the minds of terrorists, but these irritants must be feeling great anguish as our elimination program advances. We are also addressing ongoing hostilities on our island of Gataipa precipitated by an immoral foreign invasion. Our country has many natural blessings that foreign countries are trying to obtain. Rest assured, your regime forces are more than sufficient to thwart these advances by jealous countries.

And once our rebirthing is complete, believe me, there is

nothing more formidable and resilient than a country living in harmony.

We will be a model for the world, a light that will illuminate for other countries how to build community through separation.

{applause: synthetic}

I wish you a good evening gifted by chipped-in fulfillment. Good night.

Chapter 33

I felt it when I saw Seyh in the casino. That she would be the one to which I would acknowledge my insanity, and what I am now thinking may be my sins. I don't know whether I trust her fully, but she has a way of listening that will give me time to explain what I do not want to.

The pressure inside me is reaching a fever pitch. My two worlds. I want—I need—to understand what is happening inside me. The headaches are becoming daily occurrences and more intense in pain. Visual auras that come before the head pain are more frequently forcing me to lie down in a darkened room or alleyway. They first feel like a wave coming across my eyes, then quite suddenly come flashes of black spots and white light, a caving in of my line of sight, and then a disturbing tingling in my head cavity.

When the pulsing surge of machine connection produces the black-and-white screen in my eyes, I lose awareness of my consciousness. I'm pretty sure hours, if not days, pass in this state. Raven is keeping track of this, otherwise I would be clueless about the passing of time. I can't hold onto the details of what happens during these times, but the intensity of the activities I engage in typically produces bodily wounds and psychic scars. I feel full-body fatigued.

When I eventually get back home from these escapades, Raven looks at me with a combination of loving concern and absolute fear.

I atl-x Seyh. She immediately agrees to meet me. Bless her. Now I have to do the hard work of confessing.

We meet at 2 a.m. in what appears to be a working brothel. Not an uplifting place for the soul. We enter and are searched by a troll-like thug, who points lifelessly to where we should go. A woman dripping in greasy makeup nods to Seyh. This makes me wonder about the private life of my formerly bedazzling organic companion.

We walk by a set of caged lockers holding ShadowTrax8 guns, Dragunov sniper rifles, and Hemling automatic rifles. Apparently, clients' weapons are not allowed in the back rooms. Then we walk down a dreary, orange-hued hallway lined by multiple rooms, some closed, some open.

I glance in a few of the open rooms. Underaged girls and boys, likely synthed-out, sit passively on perfumed beds. They all have some type of monitoring collar squeezed tight around their necks. There is a room with three fully-formed female and male bodies, so immaculate in construction that they are certainly dumb-bots reformulated for copulation.

We finally arrive in a back room to my relief. It's like the others, with a bed prominently positioned and smoky mirror above, but it is vacant. With but one chair in the room, I offer her the seat while I cautiously sit on the side of the bed.

A half-smile of embarrassed amazement is on Seyh's face. We're not here to discuss 21C sexual practices. Our mutual speechlessness is sufficient. We both know to get to the point of the meeting.

"Thank you for meeting me on short notice, Seyh."

"You're welcome. How may I be of assistance, friend?"

I'm nervous and want to chip-in, but know that would be a waste. I stay organic.

"What happens when you're chipped-in. I mean, what do you experience?" I mutter while looking at an assemblage of steely dans on a side table.

I can't get directly to the point. I think I'm doing a dry eye twitching thing.

Seyh looks directly at me.

I think she is anticipating where this is going.

"Wow, I don't think I've been asked that in a while," Seyh says. "How do I answer that simple question in a simple way?

"Well, one recurring vision is a man has me harnessed to a chair and is brutalizing me with his rifle. We're in the middle of a battle scene, blood all around, man is being egged on by fellow combatants to torture and kill me. Another, I am being raped by a bunch of smelly militiamen. They laugh at me and enjoy the festivities. Then, they throw cooking oil on me and light a match.

"I feel red-hot hatred, that I would do anything to terminate the lives of these animals.

"Other dreams don't even have me in them. They go to a distant past. My people lie in a decrepit urban settlement, slaughtered. Mutilated bodies, torn-off heads, bloody livers, hearts, legs, arms slung across the dirt, dead babies, babies with phosphorus-scarred faces crying.

"Armed helicopters thump-thump above the slaughtered, snipers gunning down anyone that moves, the shouting of obscenities. The vision has the look of maybe 20C. Auto-fins nearby are cars from that period. Aircraft are old models long made obsolete by today's standards."

Seyh pauses, despairing, and looks down at her lap.

"They're not all about victimhood," she states as she straightens her back and looks up. "Another image is me as unit leader and we have a group of aggressors surrounded in some urban alleyway. We make them turn their backs and kneel, then spray them with our laser rifles. I feel sadly righteous, that this had to be done due to what they did to us in the past."

"Seyh, how do you remember what goes on when you're chipped-in? For me, it's all fragments. I have little idea what they mean."

"Oh, that's a great question. At first, I had little clue what was really going on when connected in. It seemed more dream than reality. But then I realized that it wasn't that I had no memories, but that they were traumatic memories that the reasoning side of my brain wasn't allowing to emerge. It does this for a great reason—to protect us from pain. Psychologists call it 'trauma blocking.'

"I went to an associate of mine, a friend, and he put me through weeks of therapy that desensitizes you. It basically helped me rewire the parts of my brain associated with the lost memories so that I could remember them in a safe and controlled environment.

"I was shocked at what I remembered.

"It took a lot of work.

"The benefits of being in the psychology field, I guess."

I can tell Seyh is lost in thought. I feel the need to intervene.

"Excuse me. Can I ask what you experience when these visions, you know, these images end? When you chip out of the machine?"

This query appears to deepen her distress.

"When we had auto-stop ability, I came out of these episodes abruptly. Like waking up from a dream and readily knowing that it was a dream. I could still feel the hatred, the righteousness, but I knew it was from a different place.

"With the auto-stop gone, it's a different and more troubling experience. I get stuck more often in the storylines. It feels more solid and real. When I come out of them, I've lost track of time. I chip-in in the morning, I come out middle of the night. And it's difficult remembering that it's imaginary.

"Back when we had auto-stop, it was more containable. Now, the storylines are sticky and harder to understand as fabrications. I'm no longer in control.

"I tell you, if it wasn't for the daily minimum chip-in requirement, I would scrap the whole thing at this point. Never chip-in again. I'm getting scared.

"I'm going to stop now, Jared. This is a bit exhausting. I think I've answered your simple question."

It is both a relief and disconcerting to hear Seyh, a trained social psychologist attuned to *interconnect*'s wizardry, having these challenges. I feel she is admitting this to open the door for me.

I grab at the opportunity.

"Seyh, I think I have a problem...

"I don't know who I am!"

Loud grunting and something heavy falling come from the room next door. There is deep, angry shouting from a man. Then the pitiful cry of a girl. Silence.

Seyh gazes downward, puts her head between her hands, then rubs her temples. She looks back up at me, directly into my eyes, as if she could see inside my soul.

"I think I have killed while chipped-in," I say.

I feel a freedom in acknowledging this for the first time. Strangely, though, it feels like I'm describing another person, not me. A biography rather than memory.

Seyh doesn't look as concerned as I anticipated.

"Hold on, Jared, what you feel you are doing while chipped-in, you know, visions of you acting, are all part of the fabrication. The machine creates this elaborate narrative that you live in but it's like watching a movie. You feel fully involved, you feel emotions, but no matter how much you feel involved, you're not really there. It's all fabrication.

"You can't act in a movie. You're always a spectator.

"When I was raped by those beasts in the storyline, I certainly felt emotional trauma and disgust, but I didn't feel physical pain. That's beyond the influence of *interconnect*."

This makes little sense to me.

"But, it feels so real, Seyh. I see blood, bruises, broken bones. I'm in the damn movie, feeling impulses of anger and hatred of the other. There are consequences to my actions. I see people falling down, grasping at their wounds, people fucking dying.

"It's more than watching a movie."

I need to say more, especially what I can't bear saying. The truth.

"I like acting out in the storylines more than living in reality."

"Now, my friend, that is a problem," Seyh responds.

"When I'm chipped-in, life has meaning, it has purpose. I feel full and complete in the narrative. I'm able to accurately perceive life and do responsible, even honorable things. Life feels purer, more vibrant, more meaningful. My priorities are clearer.

"It feels like I've been given a user manual for living."

"How much are you chipped-in, Jared?"

I feel like alcoholics in the old days felt when answering the "10 questions."

"I usually have about two hours in the morning off and two hours at night. I think the machine allows this so I can do daily maintenance, you know eat, shower, the like. On good days, maybe four or five more hours off it."

"Are you saying you are chipped-in at least 15 hours per day!"

"Yeah," I mutter.

"Are you on the machine while you sleep?" Seyh asks.

I nod with the guilt of a schoolboy.

"That's especially troublesome, Jared. You know when we

sleep, the relative dormancy of our minds creates a clear passageway for *interconnect.*"

I have memories of Raven steadying me, holding a water cup to my lips in the morning while my body convulses and my mouth spits out grandiose, largely nonsensical, verbiage.

There's a soothing quality to Seyh's eyes that encourages me to go deeper. I feel an inviting, nonjudgmental space. The floodgates are open. My larger life story comes spilling out.

"My whole life I've had this background of mental noise and self-doubt. I learned to role-play, but I felt that if people found out who I really was inside, they would leave me. I would be alone.

"I condemned myself early... teenage years... and I learned to pay attention to others to learn how I should behave. I learned how to act by imitating others. But by paying attention to others all the time, I lost the chance to find out who I really was."

I feel the tiring indulgence of self-pity kick in.

"I atrophied internally and turned to stimulants of all kinds to try to fill up the void inside. I've done some good things. Recovery work for my alcoholism and drug addiction worked for a while. Even with that, though, the itchiness remained. There was an absence within me."

It's interesting baring my soul in a room with prominently displayed dildos. It's not quite the comforting décor of a psycho-therapist room with soothing water and nicely drawn inspirational slogans on little ceramic wall plates.

Seyh's body language suggests patience, so I continue:

"I'm worn out from the meandering thoughts, the senseless, meaningless directions that organic thinking takes me.

"So much wasted, purposeless mental processing. Insecurity, jealousy, silent scorn, self-doubt, miscommunication, cynicism, depression, self-pity, trying to figure out what other people are thinking.

"It's all so complicated, so messy, and it never has any res-olution. Problems always self-populate in my head. I never get off the hamster wheel.

"Things seem so important one day, the next day I can't remember them. Empty phenomena rolling by. What does that tell me about organic thinking? It's all mind ooze, mental masturbation to keep us busy until we croak."

I pause and catch my breath. Seyh has been motionless and listening. I feel revealed but held by Seyh's presence.

I cannot resist at this point my need for machine assur-ance. I tap my ear. Chip-in. Pulsing surge.

"I bring this all up so you can understand what the machine does. It fills that absence within. It provides me direction. What I can't feel in reality I can in the storylines—satisfaction, meaning, and fulfillment.

"When I come out of chipping, I have a sense that I have done bad things. You know, actual bad things, not fabrications. Part of me is troubled, but another part of me celebrates it. I'm proud that I achieved something of meaning.

"Can you blame me for wanting more of this feeling that my life counts for something, that it is meaningful?" I plead.

Seyh waits to make sure I'm done with my monologue.

"Dear Jared, let me remind you that you're finding mean-ing, as you say, in a fabricated storyline. It's not real. The meaningfulness you are feeling is computer-generated, so it doesn't have real meaning.

"The fact that we are destroying our country is because most denizens are fooled into acting upon the impulses ingrained into them by *interconnect*. The impulses are machine-man-ufactured. But, oh Jared, the consequences of responding to them in action are oh so real.

"I know how convincing the machine's fabrications are. I've been close to acting on them too. But no matter how strong they are, I remember the narratives are not real."

I'm too defensively ready with a response. "At this point,

I don't care what is real and what is fake. One makes me feel good, the other leaves me flat and lifeless.

"Besides, this 'reality' we are living right now. How real is it? We are not independent beings acting out of free will. It's a myth that we are free. We're driven by all sorts of impulses that lie beneath our consciousness. In this so-called reality, our life is curated also, not by a machine, but by these unconscious processes."

I feel like I'm transmitting a story handed to me. My words are too smooth, too refined.

"The machine may be a better supervisor of our lives than these base impulses that drive us in organic reality.

"Just look at the collective level, Seyh, human thinking on its own has created dehumanizing inequality across the world, political corruption, conflict, and war.

"We have endless wars and conflict while never resolving the core issues that create the wars in the first place. We just spin in an endless cycle, addressing the symptoms but never acknowledging why the wars occur in the first place.

"Oppression of one group by another, all over the world. This subordination leads to anger by the oppressed, which eventually breaks out in violence. Then the oppressor comes in with counter-violence. We then go back to the unsustainable status quo ante. Such situations are only durable through constant violence by the superior."

The vibrations in my head are steady. A locked-in, confident feeling.

"How is the machine a solution?" Seyh asks.

"With *interconnect*, it clarifies the core issues of conflict. Turmoil is a way to settle things on a permanent basis. No more diversion to side issues. Let's settle this once and for all.

"After Turmoil ends, we will have communities of solidarity, each secure in their own geographies. As Prince says, 'community through separation.'

"Look at the States of America. At first, their war started in the mixed neighborhoods and was chaos. In the end, though, there was the creation of separate autonomous regions, each partitioned population with their own ideologies and social missions. White christ-believers in one region, hybrid culture believers in another, anarcho-syndicalists in another, and so on.

"The machine is finally making it possible for us to deal with the root issues underlying conflict here."

Seyh looks despondent. Her face has hardened. She looks at me like she can see through me.

"Jared, you can't really believe what you are saying. These root issues—these core issues—you speak of in our country. With *interconnect*, they're all part of curated storylines. Pirner accusations. Inhuman portrayals of the other side. Mage grievances. Historic struggles that we never heard of before the machine.

"What does that all mean? They're not real."

I feel I have won the battle but lost the war with her.

She seems entirely unconvinced by my rhetoric. She perceives correctly that she is no longer talking to an unsupervised human. Her patience with me evaporates.

I'm not sure I'm convinced by it either, but it felt right when I was expressing it. Although it felt good to express myself, I also felt a strange feeling that my argument was being scripted by a third party. My words came too easily and with a lucidity foreign to my typical verbiage.

We abruptly depart this hellish prostitution den before *interconnect* geo-monitors locate us and the thugs come for us.

I feel exposed.

PART VII

RESCUE

2045

CHAPTER 34

I somehow felt that such a reveal would change things. It did not.

If anything, my mental state and overall mood has worsened.

I increase my use of chemsynth to intensify the enjoyment of being chipped-in.

My limited time off the machine is a dull existence.

I struggle through eating, showering, and trying to take an organic nap.

I am crabby with Raven. I'm an absolute bear to be around.

Sex has stopped.

She is upset and anxious. One day she says she's going to leave.

I know it's an empty threat—she has nowhere safe to go.

I don't care that my life is deteriorating.

I crave the exhilaration of thought cairns.

I am away from our apartment for extended periods of time.

*

That lovely pulsing surge.

Blackness.

I'm anchored, solid, virtuous, impregnable.

Bolwin is different than Jeim, smaller in scale, more of a regional town compared to Jeim's feeling of centrality. One trait they share is both have been brutalized by war. The famous Ellsworth Arch, which spanned the Travertine River and connected the two sides of the town, has been destroyed by Fronter AGM-114 missiles. Its stones now lie pitifully scattered along the river banks. Midtown, an area of mixed Mage and Fronter housing before Turmoil, became the front line of the war in the early days. Now it lies in ruins. A place where coy-wolves control access and where young boys experiment with making homemade bombs.

My Fronter opponents here are some of the same individuals I fought with in Jeim. I'm not sure what is going on in Bolwin, but my hatred of Fronters here is just as intense as it was of Pirners in Jeim. It feels like someone or something is fucking with us, turning partners into enemies. This question doesn't keep me up at night. I'm here to follow directions, not question their source.

I'm thrilled to be part of a team that launches sarin bio-bombs across the Travertine. They explode about 200 feet from us. I can smell the poison's nasty burned rubber odor as gentle, hot breezes bring some of the smoke from the bombs back our way.

We laugh at the fact that such bombing is against international law. Trying to apply law in our country is like wanting coy-dogs to follow technical manual instructions.

The day is a good one for our side. Many are killed, many more are undoubtedly disabled due to the poison. The Mage have more of an upper hand in this "war within a war" compared with the disaster of urbicidal Jeim. It feels good.

The evening is spent with colleagues in a shit-hole tavern safely on our side of the divide. Only a randomly hand-thrown GBU-14 bomb could get to us. That's unlikely enough that we can get stupidly inebriated without concern for our safety.

The pulsing surge in my head steadies me and rewards me with euphoric vibrations.

I saddle up to a fellow killer. His fight name is Savage due to his prowess. Great fighter. Once saw him sniper out a Pirner exoskeleton 6,000 feet away. I was with him weeks ago in Jeim. We sit at a makeshift table—a battered door turned horizontal, held up by crates positioned on each side.

Two working women are at the next table eyeing us, leaning over to display the pushed-up cleavage of their restructured tits. Pungent perfume and drippy mascara. One I would do, kinda of an Oriental-Anglo mix. The other not so sure—kinda swampy.

I still prefer the sight of organic women such as these over fem-bots, although technological sculpting of the female body is improving daily.

A bushy beard obscures almost all of Savage's face. Nose hairs merge with beard to make one continuous field. He reeks of battlefield—sweat, blood, and the distinct almond odor of exploded bomb. I've never seen him not wearing his chest rig. I get the sense he may sleep in it. Although gauzy and almost pussy, his eyes remain on battle-ready alert status well into our 10th boukha. Drunk on this horrible liquor of the Bolwin area (it tastes like fermented figs and raisins), we struggle to put together words.

"Have you ever think doing anything other than dis?" I slobber.

"Dude, this my entire life. Can't remember doing anything other than this. From time I was born until now. There is not another life."

I slur, "There times when I image 'nother life. Like a dream. Foxy eVision beauty, you know fuck trophy." I can't finish the sentence as my head becomes heavy and drops to the table.

"You, with foxy woman? That's laugh. Maybe after you dead."

I come to enough to know one of the women is all over me, rubbing up against my body like a seasoned pro. She's the better-looking hybrid Asian. Her fingernails are painted orange and they stand out amidst the dreary noir atmosphere of the tavern. I have a vague sense this means something. I push her aside. My head is spinning too much.

The wooziness is morphing into what feels like a caving-in of my brain. The ice pick cleaving my brain in two feeling. The noir view of the tavern flips into an image filled with a dizzying array of colored pixels. I try to stay with the watercolor and not freak out.

Behind the pixels, I can make out a hologram-like image of a woman and two children, maybe young adults. A feeling of familiarity. I must know them.

The dots re-sort. An image of a man behind a podium in a large auditorium. A cleaned-up, younger version of me. He talks like he's an authority. Audience members look at him and want something from him/me.

The pixels rearrange. A man spooning a woman in bed, both asleep. She is wearing no top and the side of one breast is tantalizingly exposed. I feel a spark of energy. A desire.

Another shuffling. A group of individuals in a library-type chamber. They are discussing something. I know them but can't remember. I don't know whether they're friends or foes.

My mental screen goes blank white, then changes to a darkened tavern. There is a sleazy woman at the next table. A man is sitting next to me. He is talking to me.

"... different here than in Jeim. Fronters here have some messed-up shit in their heads. Too much synth, I don't know. They seem like another species here."

I can't talk yet. I do recall this is Savage and gradually remember where I am.

"Um… I… can you help me, Savage?"

"You in pain, Rohde? I got some pills."

"No. Can you… Tell me… what just… happened?"

"You were kinda zoned. I assumed you were just PTSDing it. Fuckin' docs tell us to just ride it out, so I didn't want to jump into your storm."

"How long was I out?"

"I'll say 20-25 minutes, enough for me to get some table-side head by this delicious night-lady," he says, pointing to the swampy gal at the next table, now looking particularly deranged.

"It was a wild trip. Did I say or do anything?"

"Something about Terry… or Carry. It was a lot of garble, my friend."

"Carrie?… I think she's my ex-"

I think back to the image that first came up. Two individuals with the woman. I think they are my children… Caleb? Ellie?

There's a faint memory of these people, like a twitch in my brain. But it feels fake, like it's implanted in me. A false dream. The color image had a cartoonish quality to it. Like it was composed by some apprentice-level artist. It must be the machine having its fun with me. Maybe trying to give me some entertainment amid the rigor of fighting.

"You also mentioned something about organic. Given the slop we eat out here, figured you were talking about food."

"Organics?"

Hearing that, my head shakes involuntarily. Ice pick slicing my head open. Visual aura closing in on me. Tremors.

"Dude, you okay? Here, have some water."

I see a hand to my side with a glass. I slump and nearly fall to the ground. I think several patrons are now gazing at me. I feel emptied.

Back to watercolor enclosure.

A man wearing a top hat, suit, and bow tie. A woman in an

officious wardrobe and wearing cat-eye glasses.

I know these people, I think.

A man looking out at the assembly of young people. He looks at his reflection in a side window of the auditorium.

It is me, I think.

A man's penis is enlarging as he lifts his right leg over the woman's body. The woman turns over and spreads her legs open.

It is Raven, I think.

I whipsaw back to the darkened tavern with several people looking down at me.

It is Savage, I think.

I lift myself up gradually with assistance and sit clumsily on a chair. My hands are sweaty and I grip the arms of the chair tightly.

Spinning has stopped. I feel stable again.

"Some part of me is in both these places," I stutter.

Silence.

"I have no idea how this can be, but I live in two different realities. There's no connection between the two."

I know I sound insane, and the uncomprehending look on the faces of my onlookers certainly reinforces that perspective. I come out of whatever that was, however, not feeling insane but rather possessing greater clarity that I am living two lives. This explains so much of the chaos in my life over the past years.

Savage is satisfied that I'm not going to die and, not knowing what the fuck I'm talking about, seems to think it's either drunkenness or a bad trip. He sloppily gets out of his chair, knocking it over, and grunts that he is leaving.

"See you 6 a.m. Rohde. Don't have any more, okay?" he says as he bro-hugs me, then knocks into the door on his way out.

"Hey sweetie," hybrid Asian lady murmurs as she sits on my lap. I feel her warmth and curvy figure. She holds out her painted fingers so I can easily see them.

These women are like flies on shit.

"I'm here because I'm an insert," she whispers in my ear. "Do you remember what that is?"

"Just leave me alone. I need to be by myself." I give her 10 V-bills to whisk her away. That's probably half-hour pay given how poor our country has become.

"I'm not who you think I am. You spoke about two realities. I come from that other reality to prove to you that it exists. You saw images of that other world, didn't you?"

"How do you fuckin' know this?"

She looks down at a piece of paper. "Former academic, partner is Raven, two kids."

I focus on her orange finger polish.

Colors saturate my view.

I hear her mumbling something hard to hear. She is speaking very slowly, like a teacher to a juvenile. "The machine... implanted this storyline into you. You as Mage member, filled with hate for the Pirner and the Fronter. It is all fable, a myth created by the machine.

"You think you have two realities. That awareness is a start. But actually, you have one reality and one fabrication.

"I can help you get back to that one reality," she says as she yanks on my ear and chips me out.

My mind feels like it's alternatively shearing off and re-connecting.

Colors sharpen into perfect focus, then blur out into shady noir.

Tavern receding from view.

Shaking. Emerging from a nightmare.

Voluminous streams of liquor explode out of my mouth.

I go to a place in my memory before *interconnect*.
Watching Caleb pitch in a high school baseball game.
This memory is real.
Shaking lessens. A grounding.
Awakening from bondage.
I remember what inserts are.
Consciousness shifting.
A radically different plane of reality.
Expanded perception.
A void filling back in.
I loosen my tight grip on the arms of the chair.
The sounds surrounding me go quiet.
I take a long breath.
In.
Out.
The electronic storyline breaking off.
Like a tight cord retracting after being cut.
The need to kill has dissolved.

My human connection to the other world escorts me out of the tavern.

We step hesitantly into the war city and start to run like hell.

CHAPTER 35

The woman pushes me into a beat-up old van-fin. A humongous man smoking a vape pipe up front pushes the acceleration upgrade switch. My head snaps back as the van speeds down cratered-out streets.

A folly of gunfire.

We continue onward.

Further acceleration and a turn that plants us against the left side of the van.

Ear-splitting concussive force.

More gunfire.

A rattling sound of metal blasting against metal.

The ride smooths out.

Final gunfire, but now more distant.

Painted hand lady is looking straight at me. "Name is Lydia. We have a two-hour drive to Jeim. I've sedated you to knock you out for the stretch. But once in Jeim, if we drop you off at

Niemond and Crew, can you find your way home? I can't go with you... surveillance."

I feel like I'm in some hallucination. Everything happening too fast for comprehension. "Who are you?" I spit out.

"I'm an insert. Do you remember who we are?"

"You're from other side.... Implant.... Dream.... False," I slur.

"Well, I guess that's good enough for now."

"Why are you here? How did you find me?"

"We use old tracking monitors that the machine doesn't recognize. But, that probably makes no sense to you."

It doesn't.

"Ask you again—if we drop you off at Niemond and Crew, can you get home? It's a three-minute walk. Here are geo-codes, just follow them."

I exit the van-fin at a deserted intersection. I go into hyper-alert mode and feel mental energy flooding my mind. I tighten my rig as I hide behind a wall remnant of a damaged building. All is quiet, except my mind, which is whirling, and a squad of roaming coy-wolves that are yelping.

I look down at the geocode disk. It must be directions to a Mage fallback shelter. Only three minutes away. I quickly run through abandoned fin corridors and arrive at the door.

A stunning woman answers and reaches out to hug me.

I flinch at first. With the woman's touch, I come back to the other side.

"Honey, what the hell has happened to you? Quick, come inside and let me help you. My God, you're a mess."

It is Raven.

She pours a bath and slowly takes off my blood-caked clothes. She softly hugs me, but I can also feel a distance, a detachment, in her embrace. She looks at me with a combination of compassion and mistrust.

She bathes me, slowly using the sponge to wipe away battle grime. She stops at my bleeding scars and cuts to add more water to the sponge. There is a gash on the right shoulder, deep enough to be near bone. Raven nearly heaves as she applies the sponge. The big toe on my left foot is nearly cleaved in half. Worst is my midsection, where numerous bomb fragments are lodged deep in my skin. I guess I was lucky. My intestines remain encased in my body.

Raven completes the inventory of body parts and tenderly helps me out of the bath.

I am wobbly but we make it slowly to the bed. I collapse.

Before I pass out, I try to thank Raven but the words don't come. I notice a look of disgust on her face as she leaves the room.

Dusk into night into day outside the dirty window. Inside, all is hazy. My head pounds so much I can't lie down anymore. Getting upright seems to lessen the frequency, but not the intensity, of the pounding. The stabbing, lightning bolts bring me to my knees many times. The time in between the pounding provides no relief as my body grips tightly in anticipation of the next assault.

The vague outlines of a reality are here. I think this is or was my apartment with Raven. There is no sign of her. This worries me.

I am clean and bandaged up in several places. I have a large body wrap encasing my sore midsection.

In and out of consciousness. I have little awareness of either.

I'm talking to a man. Serious face. He has blazing eVision-star blue eyes. He's wearing a crisp white collared shirt. Every crease and fold on it is perfectly aligned. He asks me whether I'm okay with proceeding. I answer 'Yes.' I don't understand what he's saying but I'm agreeable because anything has to be better than dying.

I lift heavy lids. My arms and legs are strapped tightly to a bed. Bright portable lights are to my side. I'm attached to IVs. The two sacks say 'water' and 'nutrients' on them. A tube is connected to my penis. It feels like I have small hard sponges behind each ear. Most of my skull is bandaged, as well as my right ear.

I want badly to chip-in to escape this reality. More than an urge, it feels like a life-or-death necessity. The arm straps and ear bandage prevent access.

The initial hours I spend in full-on rage. I attempt, with what little energy I have, to escape the harness straps. They are so tight that they dig into my skin. Any time I try to loosen them they tighten further. Fuck this, I'm stuck.

Rage is doing no good. I try thinking and try to remember.

A man in a tavern. A dizzying sequence of visions that feel like both fantasy and memory. A woman talking nonsense and pushing me into a van-fin. Coy-wolves on a city street. A woman caressing and bathing me, then crying uncontrollably and leaving abruptly. A man asking me something. I give up and agree.

My recollection is like a puzzle with pieces that won't fit together. Some memories are in shaded black. Others have bright palettes. Some have a blurred pixelated texture. It feels like there is no connection between the images, like they're thrown together by a madman.

My mind moves and gently relaxes. I slip into a welcome semi-consciousness. I am in a beautiful valley with cascading waterfalls rimming one side. I wear a backpack and I'm accompanied by an energetic coy-dog beside me. I smile as I look ahead at the trail meandering down a ravine filled with gorgeous Indian Paintbrush and Bellflowers. I stop to pick some blueberries and huckleberries.

I sit on a rock perfect for sitting, gobble down the berries, pet and rub the friendly coy, and I'm in bliss. Switch to evening. I find a tent site next to a roaring glacier-fed river and sleep uninterrupted until I see first light of a new day.

The bright lights in the room have been turned down.

"I hope you have enjoyed your trip." A man I recognize from before is standing at the bed's end. He's now wearing blue medical scrubs. "I thought you might like some refreshing detachment before we proceed to the hard stuff."

"Why the hell am I strapped down here like an animal?" I pull at the straps and they immediately tighten.

"Let me introduce myself. My name is Jackfert, you can call me Ferty. As to your question, you may not remember, but you agreed with me that it was time to ween you off the machine. I'm here to guide you through cairn withdrawal.

"You came in here in pretty bad shape. Lydia alt-x'ed me and said you may be ready to do something about your... eh... issue."

"What issue is that?" I yell. Strangely, though, I have a sense that I know what he may be talking about.

"Do you remember what you were doing in a tavern recently when that lady... name of Lydia... came to you and took you away?"

"What are you talking about? I'm sure I was home with my girlfriend having a quiet night. We don't go out much these days. I had a series of wild dreams for sure. But I was home."

I have no idea where I was, but pretty sure it wasn't home.

"Your girlfriend Raven is safe. She was very disturbed by how you looked when you came home. She was scared to death when I arrived here. We have her in a safe house."

"Okay, it's Ferty, right? You've got to slow down. This stuff you're talking about. Some of it seems real, but it's all jumbled up in my mind. I'm listening."

"Good. Here's the deal. Last night you were cairn polluted to the max. You were acting out your storyline as a Mage fighter. You had been in a tavern celebrating after a day of killing."

"You're fucking joking. Me as militiaman, get serious. I don't have the balls for such a thing. Maybe in my dreams. Come on."

I say this, but I remember the stench of poisonous gas, the tavern, the drunkenness.

Image of a metal plate engraved with the letter M flashes for a brief second in my mind.

"Okay, let me try this. Do you remember Raven helping you take a bath?"

"Sure do. It was quite sensual, if you don't mind me saying."

"What color was the bath water, Jared?"

I recall Raven's gentle strokes sponging my tired body. She was sweating and her eyes were twitching. She looked like a wreck. She dropped the soap in the tub. I looked down to try to find it. The water was red!

"Fuck, it was red. What happened?"

"Blood from your many wounds as a warrior. You had been out rampaging with your mates for over a week. You were fully within *interconnect*'s storyline. You were in the machine's fabricated reality bubble."

What this guy is telling me is difficult to swallow. Something about him I like, however. There is an objective, clinical tone to the way he talks. He's telling me the way things are rather than trying to persuade me. He doesn't seem to be bullshitting me. He seems like he has experience with fucked-up mental cases like me.

"This doesn't make a whole lot of sense." I take a breath to slow down. "Okay, I have these dream fragments in my head, but how they fit together is a mystery to me.

"I do have a memory of being aware of mental challenges in the past because of *interconnect*. I think a doc called it split-brain syndrome. He said I needed to stay connected to *inter-connect* more."

Ferty laughs.

"Well, he got the diagnosis right—colliding mental streams. But, his prescription was entirely wrong. You need less, not more, machine input so you can regain stability of human thinking. The doc was likely a charlatan, probably cairn polluted himself and a militia operative."

"I want, I need, to know more about this split-brain stuff," I say with pleading sincerity.

"I like your attitude. Your desire for knowledge about this will help you in the long run."

Ferty looks at his eWatch. "First, though, you will need to do some hard work. I will need to depart now because machine sensors will geocode me soon. But, I have the first stage of cairn withdrawal set up. I'll be back when it is complete. It's not going to be fun, Rohde. We'll talk more next time. Believe me, things will make more sense after the hard work."

"Wait, what is cairn withdrawal like?...." Ferty is out the door.

I am alone with my straps, tubes, and colostomy bag.

I lie in eerie silence. My heart beats rapidly. I feel sweat underneath my skull wrapping. I think I'm urinating. I look up at the ceiling and try to calm my thoughts.

Nothing is happening. I wonder if cairn withdrawal is this simple. Just a matter of not chipping-in for some prescribed time. A forced time-out.

A darkness darker than anything before then floods my view. My body feels as if it is collapsing as my head explodes. Rashes and scars all over my body. My flesh crawls and it feels like it's been punctured and sliced. Mental and physical agony.

Then, I am somewhere else.

Strapped to a hard board. Hooks connecting my flesh and

bone. I'm held together by excruciating metal fasteners that burrow into and through my ligaments. I'm blindfolded.

My head is positioned at the edge of the board, tilted back. Someone grabs my head and repositions it, forcing the fasteners to dig further into my flesh. Gruff voices are arguing with each other. Cloth is put over my mouth, which is soon flooded with water. It feels like I'm drowning. I gag as my nasal cavities fill with water.

I'm fucking being water-boarded.

Several times, water comes tumbling down my throat. I've got water in my lungs. My brain and nasal cavities are on fire. My throat swells and locks up. I consistently gag. I can't exhale. The only way I can inhale is by taking more water into my throat and lungs.

I can't handle much more of this.

This is worse than dying.

I hear someone swear and say the word, Mage.

A voice directly to me, "Where is your fallback shelter in this district? Tell us and we will mercifully end this pain and terminate you. This suffering will end, Mager."

More water torture, far past the point that is humanly possible. I'm in a nightmare with all the physical agony of reality. A living hell.

Near unconscious, I'm repeatedly snapped back to awareness by my involuntary gagging.

After an indeterminate time, reality shifts back.

Nausea. I'm sweating like I'm in a sauna. Chills like I'm in an icebox. I vomit while tilting my head to the side. I'm only partially successful in clearing the barf. The yellowish-greenish bile slides back toward me, its warm flow building up against my neck.

All goes black.

*

"It's hard, isn't it?"

I look at this man like he's a savior God. I know him.

"This is Sunki," Ferty says. "She's going to clean up things and set you up again."

I slowly become conscious of this different reality as the young woman sets to her tasks like an industrial cleaner. Sunlight streams through the crack in the window blinds. I don't know what day it is.

I'm reduced to something sub-human, defeated, near suicidal, reeking.

My throat is throbbing and raw. With effort, I can get words out.

I gasp, "I never want to go through that again, anything like it, would rather die."

"Jared, well..." he hesitates. "Let's do this. This visit I'll give you more information that might help. I know it may be hard to talk, so let me do most of the talking, okay?"

"Hope info you give is how much longer," I slur. It feels like I only have enough air to maintain my breathing.

"What you probably experienced is the start of symptoms associated with withdrawal from machine stimuli. You have likely been pelting your amygdala with algorithmic input for some time. When you interrupt cairn entry, *interconnect* sees it as a threat and will increase delivery of algorithms.

"In short, when attempting to withdraw from dependency, things first get worse rather than better. This is the machine's way of keeping you addicted. Most people will turn back to it at this point. Same way any drug addiction works. It hurts to try to get off it."

"How is the fucking machine doing this when I'm like this?" I manage to say while looking upward at my bandaged skull.

"Your ear block and straps restrict you from turning *interconnect* on, correct, so how is it still messing with your head? We're pretty sure that residual, or legacy, cairn lines are still able to operate in your head well after full connection. The machine still has lots of capacity to fuck with you.

"We're doing everything possible to obstruct machine intrusion. Thus, the ear blocks. We're hoping that the off toggle retains some influence. Sorry that they are uncomfortable."

An unsavory thought pops into my mind. Something he said earlier.

"You said... start of symptoms... and why am I being set up again? Not over?"

"Unfortunately, not. I'm sorry. *Interconnect* withdrawal usually takes up to six days. During that time, expect at least one more bombardment by the machine. Hopefully, the next one won't be as intense. But no promises, Jared.

"Good news—you're so loaded up on cairns we don't have to worry about you being geo-coded as low-use by the regime."

"I want out of here... now."

I feel Sunki stick a needle in my right arm.

I come to. It feels like hours, maybe days, have passed. Now, gray overcast light filters into the room. I'm alone. Bowels are tight. I let go into the colostomy bag. I'm embarrassed but relieved. Nobody to wipe my butt.

As if a monster was waiting for me, I feel an impending sense of assault upon awakening. Anticipation of what might come is its own hell.

The darkness comes upon me. Visual aura. Ice pick slicing my head in two. My skin being stretched and torn. Pins and needles driving into my midsection.

I am somewhere else.

Chained to a wall, sitting up. A putrid stench in the room makes me turn my head in disgust. A buffed woman wearing a Pirner militia uniform is holding a red-branding iron. Scars and tattoos embroider her arms. A boiling kettle is behind her. She is wearing the grin of the devil.

She laughs, "Made this especially hot for you, my dear. I think I'll start with your dick, that's if I can find the little thing. What do you say, my love?"

Two men forcefully take off my pants and underwear. My organ shrinks with exposure to a cold wind rushing down the room.

"Mage scum have dicks the size of virgin toddlers," someone shouts. Many people are in the room, and they chuckle in unison.

I struggle to escape the chains and close my eyes as the she-devil moves toward me. I don't feel the singe immediately but soon my nerve endings are on fire. I smell my burning flesh. She removes the brand providing me with false hope, then re-applies it to my inflamed cock, mutilating it further.

My nerve endings at this point are shot, so I feel less pain as I watch my skin burn. I no longer have a dick. In its place is an ugly black scar pierced by flowing rivulets of pus and blood.

The woman is not done. She goes back to the boiling kettle and re-heats the brand.

"Now, my love kitten, how about your face? It is such a beautiful thing to destroy."

Before this masochist continues her fun, reality shifts.

I never thought I would feel liberation when knowing that I'm strapped down to a bed in a familiar room. I retch immediately. My skin crawls as if hundreds of insects are burrowing into me. Hot flashes and bone-jarring chills.

Before all goes black, I take a deep breath of relief.

My eyes open. There are lights in the room, but I can see only the darkness of nighttime outside the blinds.

I've got to get these straps loosened. Red calluses are forming where they cross my body. I crave solid food. This hunger for real food says to me that I have been here for several days.

Hopefully, it's the six days that Ferty mentioned as normal time for withdrawal.

I spend hours alone. Restless as hell. The morning better bring Ferty.

I now fully know the power of *interconnect* addiction. Attempting to detach from it is near impossible. If not a strapped-down captive, I would have given up and dedicated myself completely to my chipped-in storylines of heroism and righteousness. I would have been doing the waterboarding and the branding.

There is no contest between the hellish trauma of detaching and the secure righteousness provided by the machine when I'm chipped-in.

Chip-in and I am exalted, favored, knighted.

Turn away from the machine and I am exiled to the burning hell of the damned.

I think I sleep for some time. I have dreams, but they are real human dreams consisting of trivial meanderings. They're not visions fabricated by the machine loaded with life-or-death urgencies. I can deal with human-created sleep dramas.

"Good morning, how was it this time?" says an ebullient Ferty.

"I'm so happy to see you," I say. I'm surprised by my positive attitude. I've never felt so good being in organic reality. "This episode was certainly hellish too. But you know what, compared to last time, I'm better. A bit more resilient. I can actually put words together."

I guess the second visit to hell lacks a certain something. Who knew?

"Good to hear, Rohde. I think you're getting there. I brought you some chicken pasta, coffee, and an energy drink from a war bistro down the street.

"Sunki, please loosen his upper straps and put pillows behind him so he can eat.

"There's a few things we haven't covered, but these you may already have a sense about."

The first taste of chicken wakes up my deadened taste buds, an explosion of flavor that ignites my senses. The energy drink is like drinking liquid cocaine.

"Do you know who we are?" asks Ferty.

"I think I'm one of you.

"I have memories of being with your cause. More than a decade ago, I think, it started. But, I don't know whether these memories are real or something implanted.

"I don't trust them. Actually, I don't trust any memories at this point."

"Maybe I can convince you we are real," Ferty says.

"We are organics and believe the path forward is through independent human thinking detached from machine fabrication. You have met with us in the past. Several times you have been part of our program. You have had conversations with one of our leaders, Seyh Maki. Do you remember her?"

A distinct image of a beautiful dark-skinned woman pops readily into my mind. I can't grab onto any timeline to place her. The past seems a discontinuous mess.

"I do. Is she still alive?"

"Indeed, and if all goes well, you will meet her again."

"Ferty, who was that woman in the tavern?"

"That was Lydia, one of our most successful inserts. Do you know what they are?"

Images of being in a bunker. The visions are clear. Does that mean more recent? I'm with others. I don't think they're militia. They talk about the insert program. I don't understand.

"I don't remember. Are they machine creations?"

"No, just the opposite. Inserts are real people—organic activists—who insert themselves into fabricated storylines to try to convince participants that they are actors in an algorithmic production."

"That was Lydia?"

"Indeed, she is very good at blending into the storyline at first, then at the right time taking over and intervening. Before Turmoil, she was one of the country's leading neuro-scientists."

"Wow, she is brilliant. I thought she was a whore looking for a paying customer. I tried to get away from her."

Ferty smiles. "Yes, she is very good. I think she enjoys the play-acting part of inserting." He looks at his eWatch. "I've got to go, I'm nearing my 20-minute limit. My role here, Jared, is to supervise your withdrawal program. You probably guessed that.

"I've done a number of these and have gotten pretty good at them, if I may say so. They are ugly, as you have experienced. But, my success rate is high. Good chance you will leave here mentally intact. Any other questions you have will need to wait until next time."

Sunki re-straps my upper body and quietly takes away the remaining food.

She and Ferty leave the room.

I anxiously wait for what is to come.

After about half an hour, the blackness comes.

Images are blurry. I'm in some type of carnival arcade. Fluffy animals—bear, dog, alligator—are on a nearby shelf. Smell of cinnamon. Gunfire in the distance. Smoke or fog all over the place. I'm tied to a chair with a bright light blinding me. Shadowy figures are moving near a fence observing me. Really weird shit.

A large fat man smelling of body odor approaches. He swings a punch at me, misses, and slams his fist into the board behind me. He grunts some type of animal sound and begins crying. I look closely at him. His image is faded, like a washed-out hologram. This is getting weirder.

I reach around the chair and easily undo the bindings.

They were tied together only by a bow knot. I walk away from the blinding lights and can better focus on the place I'm in. Far from being in a traumatic episode like those before, this atmosphere feels almost comical in nature. The pieces of this image don't seem like they fit as one but rather appear as a photo montage thrown together by some hurried, disinterested artisan.

I hear the voice of one of the water-boarders from before, a sound that I will never forget. In this storyline, he is a barker at one of the carnival booths trying to pull in customers.

I then see the Pirner woman assailant again, the one who torched my genitals. She has a maternal pose, playing a game of hopscotch with a pony-tailed young girl. A Viz smart-bot observes the activity.

Further on, I see heavily armed militia, which raises my pulse. But, they move at a pace slow as molasses. When they see me, they go on high alert but point their guns in every direction except toward me.

All these images have a worn-out, albino look. As faded as yesterday's thoughts. Body parts are unrealistically simplified, some are humorously exaggerated. I can't help but laugh.

Reality shifts.

I sleep.

It's the feeling of early morning when I come to. I'm giddy. Ferty is observing me like I'm a lab rat. Sunki is doing her busy stuff. No more straps. There's freshness in the room, less sweat and urine. I notice two windows are open.

"By the look on your face, I guess this one wasn't as traumatic as the first two."

I reach for the glass of water that Sunki has provided. "Difference between night and day, my friend. The fabrication was so obvious. It could have been the work of a primary school student. It didn't even seem like it was making the effort to fool me.

"What was that all about? Did the machine give up?" I ask.

"Congratulations, my friend. The way you are describing this last episode, I'm pretty confident that *interconnect*'s hold on you has weakened to the point below algorithmic psychosis. In other words, if you're able to avoid your former chip-in time, I think you will find your daily life more manageable from here.

"Less Mage superman warrior.

"More time as fallible human."

Sunki detaches the IVs and excrement sack. She removes the ear block and helps me out of bed. My joints creak as I slowly rise. My first steps are unbalanced. I go to a chair and sit upright. It's a joy to be vertical. I smell food and gaze over at a plateful of something smelling fabulous.

Ferty comes over to me and shakes my hand.

"It's up to you now, Jared. I helped you overcome your acute psychosis. You looked through and saw the farce that is *interconnect*. But I won't be around to make sure you don't go back to machine abuse. Only you can decide that it's worth it to moderate stimuli.

"You have done nine days of hard work. Remember that if you get tempted.

"My patients usually ask me at this point what's the success rate. I'll be honest. We're at about 60 percent who relapse back to chip-in addiction.

"I want you to be part of the 40, okay friend."

I awkwardly saddle up to the meal and begin the feast. "Now that I've seen the farce, the last episode was so fake, I can't believe so many of us live in these storylines. So many of us are scammed into living and dying in curated fantasies."

"Don't get down on humans," Ferty says. "You saw the other side of the fantasy only because you were strapped down and unable to act out the storyline. Since you weren't responding in terms of behavior, *interconnect* wasn't able to regenerate your curated narrative, and it eventually sputtered.

"It's when recipients act out in response to machine stimuli, that's when they get trapped. The curation becomes stronger and stronger. Fantasy becomes life-or-death reality."

"So, is that the solution to our country's problems? Strap everyone down in a bed and wait it out?"

"I sure wish we could do that."

Ferty looks at his watch. I know what that means.

"Before you go, first, I want to thank you for sticking it out with me, Ferty. Your bedside manner was great, you knew to stay arms-length away from this raving maniac. And, Sunki, thanks for cleaning up a near-corpse."

Sunki performs an adorable combination of bow and curtsy. "You give pleasure to me by your health," she says softly.

My savior and his assistant open the door and depart, not before Ferty looks back at me and says, "There is a woman who would like to see you again. Know that she hasn't given up on you. Most women would have by now."

CHAPTER 36

I feel purified. Worn out but cleansed. I sleep many hours the next days. The organic dreams that come alarm me at first. I awaken with a start to make sure I'm not grabbing onto a machine narrative. After a few nights, I learn to trust them.

I wake up in the mornings refreshed and looking forward to nurturing the side of me that is my friend. That was a miserable life of two realities that I promise I will never go back to. Coming off of algo-addiction was excruciatingly painful. It was mental crucifixion.

I chip-in the required time to avoid sensors and penalties. But, now I practice distancing myself from the storylines. I've taped "this is not true" and "do not leave apartment" signs all over the place—on mirrors, doors, icebox, eVision screen, and bedpost—to remind me not to engage with the storyline.

The regime's termination of the auto-off function finally got to my chip. It means I have to rely on self-will to get me out of the machine once I'm in. I use an old-fashioned Apple Watch as my guardian, setting the digital alarm to alert me when it's time to get out. I use the most obnoxious alarm sound—Sprinkles—and hope that its annoying quality will rescue me.

Strangely, something that was so compelling before now seems surmountable. As days go by in recovery, I actually develop some pride in what I have been able to do. Life is starting to feel good and genuine again.

After five days, Raven returns. Although she is happy about my successful withdrawal, I can tell she is not fully convinced. There is a kernel of distrust within her. It's as if she still has that image of me in the bathtub on her mind. She experienced my degradation directly. Even our old standby—sex—feels now more like a functional practice than an intimate engagement.

Nevertheless, it is good having her around again. We settle into a daily pattern of interaction and communication, although we stay clear of the two realities topic. I understand that not talking about it is best. I can tell she is frightened.

It takes me about two weeks to leave the comfortable confines of our apartment. Raven is a natural recluse, so I'll be on my own. I promise Raven that I will go only to the safer parts of Jeim. She hates any mention of Mage so I don't tell her that safe neighborhoods mean areas containing homogeneous Mage populations. I certainly don't tell her that my Mage crux protects me in such neighborhoods.

Some friends had requested my presence via alt-x.

Seyh, Nicolai, and Allacia meet me in the battered garage of a vacated auto-fin station. We had to shoo away two homeless psychotics and a bevy of rats before settling in the corner of the dimly lit repair shop. The place smells of leaking batteries and chemsynth canisters.

Seyh begins anxiously, "This may be our last meeting, friends. *Interconnect* is close to perfecting surveillance sensors and the regime is drooling to use them. The machine is upgrading every minute, constantly learning anew. We are losing organics at a rapid rate. I advise we cluster here no more than 15 minutes, then vanish."

"We're here for some intel on the insert experience to see whether there's any way to enhance it," Nicolai says while looking directly at me. "We have few opportunities to interview someone who has gone to the other side about what the insert experience is like. At this point, that program is our last chance, so the more we know the better."

I don't have to be defensive any more about my two lives. I'm sure Ferty informed them all about me and being rescued from my Mage narrative. I don't have to pretend anymore. They want operational detail. Maybe I can help organics, for once, rather than playing a game of evasion.

Seyh looks distracted by noises in the opposite corner, likely stubborn rats wanting their place back. "Okay, Jared, let's start with this. Before the insert revealed herself to you, did you have any sense you were acting in a machine storyline?"

Okay, everything is out in the open now. Seyh is staying with practical matters. She gives no sign of disappointment in the antics I revealed to her.

"During my withdrawal with Ferty, I eventually saw through the fabrication. But that took a lot of work and I was bound captive so I couldn't chip-in."

I avoid answering Seyh's question. An old habit. I felt defensive and had to point out my great achievement. Be forthright, I say to myself. I take a breath.

"In the narrative you're talking about, honestly, I had no clue I was in a fabrication. It was life-or-death heroism and full-body engagement. Even when I first experienced mix-ins of my organic life, they seemed like irrelevant noise."

A feeling of relief washes over me.

"One feeling I remember is that when I was in the storyline, there was a vague itch, a kind of tingling. I don't know, it's hard to explain. Like my body was both there and not there.

Very much present but also shadowy.

"Maybe like having an amputated limb, you both feel it and don't. The problem is that the tingling, itching, whatever it was, provided me with energy to increase my acting out. I didn't pause and say to myself, 'What does this all mean.' Instead, I used that feeling to push me even more. In no way did it hold me back, just the opposite."

"Now, describe your experience with the insert. Lydia was her name." Seyh is abrupt and no-nonsense.

"I remember when I first saw her that there was color on her, somewhere on her body. Maybe her necklace... no, her fingers. They were painted. The color stood out amidst the shadows. I saw it before I went into some type of two-reality seizure, but I didn't recognize what it meant.

"I know now it was a marker. It was the only color in the black-and-white image. When she revealed herself, I focused on that marker and it somehow distanced me a little from the Mage storyline. With Lydia's help, of course."

Allacia has been quiet until now. "That's good intel, Jared. We have been using distinct color markers with our inserts. Machine storylines are so intensely rich in their black-and-white content that color markers can be effective disruptors. They work well prior to verbal communication between insert and target. This intel from you reinforces that it's a good strategy."

There's something noticeably off about Seyh. She greets this piece of good news with a sad look of despair. Allacia is focused on operational detail of the insert program, but Seyh must know the larger picture. Based on her haggard demeanor, I don't think it's good.

A sudden helicopter noise stops our discussion. Although not yet 15 minutes, the urgent need to get the hell out of here grips the group. These meetings are getting increasingly terse. I feel we are getting hemmed in by impenetrable forces.

I think I was able to help the organic cause. This helps me

deal with the shame and guilt of my relenting to the machine's addictive pull in the past.

We all scram in different directions as the noise of warfare surrounds us.

Raven would be pissed if she knew I was out here.

CHAPTER 37

President Prince Speech
Perfecting the Human Community
4th quarter/81d 2045. Interconnect Transmission. 20h00m

Good evening virtuous denizens. I wish to talk to you this evening about our great democracy. If you know your history well, all democracies throughout the world eventually face challenges from terrorists who do not want freedom. They hunger to change from democratic freedom to some evil form of tyranny of the minority. These miscreants are inherently inferior in their desire for centralized control. Their actions are corrosive of individual freedom. They are a cancer upon our great country.

We have the strongest democracy in the world today. We are building community by providing each group with their own living spaces where they can work, play, and enjoy life without fear of other groups. When our project is complete, each community will live free, nurtured from within and held together by deeply held beliefs.

We are perfecting the human community.

{applause: synthetic}

Yet, there are those who resist such perfection. They practice the old arts which we know are associated with mixing, hybridization, and the weakening of overall society. They are wrong.

We continue to mount effective anti-terrorism programs to eradicate these resisters. At this time, I would like to recognize counterinsurgency force #37. They have terminated and captured the most resisters of any of our brave units.

Gentlemen, would you please stand?

[Camera pans to balcony. Applause from audience]

In the name of our great democracy, we have also reached out to select members of these terrorists and offered them a small olive branch. I want to emphasize this is not negotiating with terrorists, but rather it is a practical solution for advancing our great democracy.

Starting in the coming quarter, interconnect will offer select recipients a limited module offering basic training in independent human thinking. Only authorized users will be allowed access. Extensive screening will be done so that the only users who will have access to this module are those who have proven demonstrably that they can use human thinking responsibly.

Again, this is in no way giving in to terrorists. Rather, we view this as a natural extension of our great democracy and the capacities of our great machine.

In addition to our building of community, our great democracy is a shining example in another important aspect. Years ago, old arts social commentators spouted dire and catastrophic warnings about the use of artificial intelligence in our political and social affairs. These were the fear-mongers, similar to those crackpots that proselyted about harmful climate change.

We now know, and we have proven, that computer intelligence is fully able to guide humans in the direction of positive and life-fulfilling change. We have shown the world that humans can effectively manage computer intelligence so that it is a transformative influence on human affairs. To that end, as of tomorrow, I am terminating our advisory interconnect council and I will be extending my hand to the honorable members in congratulations for a job well done.

We no longer need human oversight of the machine. It has proven that its super-intelligence is perfect.

In closing, I wish to extend my gratitude to all the fine denizens out there for participating in this glorious transformation of our great democracy to a life-nourishing amalgamated community of communities. We have optimized democracy.

May your stories be rich and rewarding. Good night.

Chapter 38

Feeling less captured by the machine, I can see through the absurd narratives spewed out by our President. Great democracy. Building community. Machine-guided life-fulfilling change. What a crock of shit was Prince's latest speech.

I only wish organic reality could replace such fabrication with meaning. War does a great job of foreclosing on any type of recreational outlet. And sadly, the weeks soon wither into regularity and boredom. It's too dangerous most days to go outside. The only times I go are to struggle to get necessities. Even those trips are short due to new bombing campaigns.

Cooped up with Raven provides companionship, for which I am grateful. But, conversations with her regain their superficiality. I simply have little interest in the minutiae she brings up, and I'm getting tired of acting like I care. She loves me, I know, but boy does she get stuck in the same worries day after day.

Also, since my breakdown, her interactions with me remain guarded, more distanced, and laced with an undertone of resentment. She has seen my evil and is not going to relax again.

The endless sameness each day. In the morning, I have the same restlessness as yesterday, as the week before. I'm living a numbed existence, flat-lined. I know the saying, 'What I do is unimportant but it is essential that I do it.' Well, I'm realizing that daily life is not essential for me to engage in it. That saying is just a gimmick to help us survive until we die.

My life unconnected to the machine is becoming one of nihilism.

I feel the seductive pull of *interconnect*. The fucker is always there as an option. It's a flame that burns but also warms. I desire the connection. I crave a storyline that is grander, riskier, and more dramatic than everyday life. It supplies a cause, a reason to live. The violent and risky excitement it produces is better than living in the anesthetized cocoon of a sheltered life.

I think I can only truly feel when I'm chipped-in. Life outside of it is feeling fabricated.

I remember the hell of machine withdrawal, but the trauma associated with the memories is weakening. I'm caring less about the consequences of chipping in.

The temptation to connect in is like the lure a married man feels when he becomes entranced by a young, sexy, innocent girl. He knows that going there will cause catastrophic damage to his everyday life. He tries to not go there, but his erotic imaginative powers will not lessen, and they take hold of his everyday thoughts. The man eventually goes there despite the inevitable consequences and engages in the exciting courtship dance with the young maiden. He becomes captive to the alluring, ultimately disastrous, storyline.

I'm not going to cheat on Raven. Hell, romantic flings are impossible in this environment. But, I sure feel the itch to find a compelling reality. To open that user manual for how to live life intensely.

*

Tedious, antsy weeks go by. I live in a mind-numbing rut. It's disturbing to me that I've had no alt-x communications from the organics. I remember Seyh's disturbed presence as she described the machine's coming perfection of its surveillance program aimed at their elimination.

I feel debilitating sadness when I think about the likely end of the organics' cause. A memory of my first meeting with them years ago makes me smile but also elicits sadness. Elijah and Anya. Seyh and Nicolai. I recall their goodwill toward the newbie in their group. They were so patient in presenting information about the machine.

The sadness becomes crippling when I think of my betrayal of their cause. My inability to stay conscious. My descent into Mage warrior-hood. My adolescent caving in to the very thing they were trying to combat.

Why could I have not been stronger?

Back in the day, I had this overwhelming craving to rise above the academic nonsense and actually do something of meaning in my life. I wanted to be a hero, broad-shouldered, a man. I acknowledge now that such a man of integrity doesn't go after stimulants such as *interconnect* to short-cut his way to heroism. Rather, he engages organically in the long and uncertain struggle to advance the dignity of human beings.

True meaning from life comes not from being a pedestal-deserving hero of self-righteousness, but through being a selfless contributor, with others, to achieve a common good.

Yet, despite this honest personal inventory, the grinding regularity of the passing days flattens me further. I hunger for curated adrenaline. The memories of the traumatic withdrawal program are fading into manageable emotional fragments.

Ever since Raven washed the blood off me after I came home dismantled from the Bolwin adventure, she and I have tried our hardest to live under the same roof but in separate spheres. This is hard to do, given the smallness of our apartment, but we do our best.

At times, it's sadly comical how we go about maintaining our territories during daily life. We each have a part of the sofa, each a separate compartment in the ice cooler, we eat at different times, and we have partitioned bed spaces. We do violate this sleep arrangement every so often to engage in wanton, animalistic sex, after which we retreat quietly to our respective nests.

I feel that Raven is holding something inside that she is thinking about but not talking about.

Living with someone who no longer trusts me adds to the lifelessness of this period of my life. Meanwhile, the machine is there waiting. Inviting me into its fantastic and amplified world.

My resistance to the lure of algorithmic drama certainly isn't strengthened by what happens on an early evening.

We unintentionally meet at a cross-hatched place near the washing machine. Raven is bent over and sobbing uncontrollably. I move toward her and she turns her back to me, hiding something she is hugging in her arms.

She falls to the floor, her back supported by the utility room wall. Her face is swollen. She spreads out on the floor what she had been holding. A dark green camouflaged shirt, some type of chest armor, knee pads, other shit I don't know. The whole mess has a stench and is stained by dark red spots everywhere.

Raven opens a closet where we keep cleaning supplies. I never go in there. I guess Raven knew that. It's pretty packed, but I have no trouble making out the shiny metal objects leaning against the side of the closet.

I don't know what it all means, but I immediately get rigidly defensive.

I approach Raven but she turns away in spite, like a teenage girl. I am going to have to start this conversation. I don't know what to say.

"Where did all this come from?" I ask hesitantly, not wanting to hear the answer. I wish time would stop and all this would vanish.

A smeared, double-image makes it difficult for me to focus on the equipment in question. My dizziness is further heightened by a wavy, vibrating effect. I put my fingers against my temples to try to stabilize it. The military paraphernalia snaps back and forth between black-and-white and colored images.

When in noir, I recognize what they are. When in color, I am puzzled.

I alternate between being enthralled and disgusted by what I observe.

Her sobbing has turned into wet anger. "Every time you came home out of your mind from one of your escapades, you had fighting shit with you. As your dutiful partner, I hid this stuff so you wouldn't have to face it in the morning.

"I thought if I hid these things from you, we wouldn't have to deal with it. But I was wrong. You say you've been weaned off the machine. But, I can't handle this anymore. Are you a soldier or what, Jared? Am I living with a killer?"

How do I admit something to Raven for which I have only murky, shadowy memories?

While Raven sits there waiting, the equipment lies there as an invitation.

I've seen these things on Mage fighters on the streets of Jeim, but I have only fragmented memories of them being on me.

"I don't know, honey. All I know is that this is not the only reality that I live in. The other one is not like this one at all, I'm pretty sure. When I'm here, in this reality, I don't remember the other one in detail. Only snapshots, partial shadows, feelings."

"What do you feel in this other place?" she asks.

"Alive." It came out of my mouth without thinking. I regret saying it right away.

"So, you don't feel alive in this one, with me?"

I knew it. Now she's in the take-it-personal, hurt feelings zone. I'm always brutal operating in this atmosphere, never knowing what to say. Do I speak the hurtful truth or appease the wounded woman through half-lies? I spin my wheels, in emotional paralysis.

"One's not better than the other, Rav-girl, they're just different." I can feel that lie in my whole body. Life with her is a limp, wet rag compared to the robust meaningfulness of the other side.

Raven rushes out of the small utility room, crying and vigorously bumping up against me as she goes by.

I do not pursue. There is nothing I can do to help matters. I'm almost as lost as she is.

The bright glare of the utility room ceiling light bears down on the paraphernalia. An insect buzzes by my head. I look down at the fatigues, chest rig, side holster, knee pads, and boots. I kneel and feel the material. The strong smell is invigorating. The blood spots give me a hard-on. I glare at the rifles.

A memory from long ago arises. My workaholic dad coming home from the office, going directly to the refrigerator, cracking open the ice cube tray over an empty glass, pouring himself some bourbon. A man returning from the jungle victorious, ready to celebrate his manhood amidst the madness of the world.

My hands tingle in anticipation of holding one of those rifles.

I crave that jungle, that stout manhood.

Chapter 39

I'm feeling boxed in and depressed. Raven is colder than ice to me and there seems no end in sight to her embargo. I don't blame her.

As much as I wanted to chip-in for good after our confrontation, I did not except for modest intakes to meet the daily minimum in order to avoid regime sensors.

A bomb explodes nearby one night, the closest one to our abode yet. This adds to the hostile domestic atmosphere. It tears out three stories of what used to be a pre-Turmoil luxury tower, but since has become a squatters' vertical settlement. From our window, I see bodies and body parts on the sidewalk. I look away.

I've got to get out of here. Every part of the world is closing in on me. All that work getting off the machine addiction, and I still get blamed by Raven for my past. She would surely appreciate me more if she knew the details of Ferty's program. I'm jittery and sick to my stomach. Walking the mean streets of Jeim provides a dangerous type of relief. Nonetheless, I soon find myself out amidst the warfare.

Alone. Despondent. I'm in a city proving that we are depraved animals rather than human beings. Jeim is more refugee camp than city.

Denizens on the streets are slender, some emaciated, and some are walking skeletons near death due to the dearth of food. I have had to skip meals many times and have lost many pounds, I'm sure. But these walking dead look like they could drop at any moment.

Water carriers are out on the streets. One can tell by the several canisters tied to their belts. Sometimes they wait in line for up to three hours.

The lucky ones are those with bicycles, which can be pushed with supplies on them. Baby carriages and market carts are also useful. Pants with many pockets come in handy because you can only carry so much. Pills for water, small denomination V-bills, batteries, matches, vitamins, canned food, propane canisters, drinks, and cigarettes are valuable, either for consumption or exchange.

Piles of rubble and debris constantly force me to modify my walking path. The usual smell of dust, smoke, and metallic residuals fills my nostrils. The fruit odor of decay is present. I know this comes from the rotting flesh of dead bodies. Damaged and burned auto-fins are everywhere. Craters make the streets impassable. Not that it matters. Only a few maniacs even try to drive an auto-fin in Jeim.

The former busy avenues of yesteryear are now no-go zones, either military frontlines or closed off by malicious fighters in control of specific territories. Playgrounds have been turned into cemeteries if they are located out of sight of hillside or balcony snipers.

Few things are sadder than a rusting child's swing set surrounded by the raised mounds of grave sites.

Food markets are small and located outdoors in shadowy crevices to avoid war hostilities. They consist of ramshackle wooden stalls. They need to be mobile in case an attack comes. Militias take their cut of the vendors' meager profits. In return, the stalls can stay. Most of the food is pre-packaged with some prepared on the spot or fresh. Most of the fresh faire are coydog, squirrel, and pigeon, all hanging down from the stalls on hooks. Most businesses informally connect to the notoriously unreliable power grid.

Restaurants, if you can call them that, are typically located in the shells of bombed-out buildings. I go to a favorite eatery of mine that contains four seating areas with deteriorating white plastic chairs. It exists in a small corner in the drafty basement of a bullet-ridden '90s (20C) building battered during Turmoil. A sign on the damaged wall says, *Welcome to our new tomorrow?!* After I order, the proprietor casually takes several strips of meat out into the shabby and exposed former lobby of the building and cooks it there on a Hibachi-type cooking grill.

I'm always on alert when I walk in the city. When I see a militia fighter lurking at a street corner or on a roof, I turn the other way. This means my path through the city is a convoluted one. When I get lost, I can geocode only partially because the urban communications network has been so constantly battered.

Besides combatants, the other denizens monitoring the daily flow are the black marketeers of chemsynth. They usually wear long coats and hoods pulled over their heads. You know, your basic shady-guy wardrobe. These entrepreneurs apparently make good money, even after the manufacturers and militias take their hefty share.

The smiles on the dealers' faces look genuine. I have occasionally seen fighters from both sides of the war congregate around a marketeer to get their supply. Their guns casually on the ground, the enemies engage in casual conversation awaiting their cairn stimulant.

I have enough trouble with *interconnect* without intensifying its effects with drugs. On this occasion, however, amidst the gloom and dust of the city, I bargain with a young man with caved-in, skeletal features for a handful of chemsynth. I jiggle the injectorates in my pocket as I walk away. Just the anticipation of possibly using them at a later time provides a mental buzz.

I feel myself slipping closer to a relapse.

Block after block of ugly urban detritus is wearing me out. My head throbs and my ankles are swelling. Filth and grit cover my arms and face. Itchy rashes on my cheeks demand my attention. I feel I'm becoming part of the alienating urban environment. I notice many used chemsynth cartridges amidst the trash. My craving becomes unbearable. I reach into my pocket for my small supply of crystalline hash. A weak substitute for the adrenaline rush of chipping in. I self-inject at a street corner and feel I'm losing the battle for sanity. I feel there is a wall developing between me and reality.

I duck into a tavern. I am frisked for weapons (I have none) and enter a dark, moist space inhabited by denizens seeking obliteration. The bartender is a tattooed, ringed bull-dyke who looks like she could beat the living hell out of me.

I'm crystalline buzzed but not chipped-in. I timidly order a hash beer and sit uncomfortably at the bar between two patrons. One has his head a couple of inches above the bar, is talking to himself, and is certifiably deranged.

The other man looks strangely familiar.

"Forester?"

"Holy smoke. Jared?"

"What the hell are you doing in this damp drinking hole?"

"Same as you, professor."

We hug and laugh at our circumstance.

"Last time I saw you, we were in one of those faculty meetings," I say, smiling for the first time in a while. "Remember those fucking things? I would've rather had a sharp stick in my eye than listen to that crap. The young farts trying to make their points on things we discussed in academia 20 years ago."

"Yeah, I recall one time we took a vote on whether to ban Rohde from the meetings. I voted for you, by the way, but it was a tough decision," Forester says with a gleam in his eyes.

"Boy, that seems a long time ago, and a whole different universe. How long's it been? Over 10, wait, 13 years. Geez."

Forester, first name Jason, always called by his last name though. One of my few colleagues at the Elderwater Institute who I liked. He had a realistic view of the university. He was down to earth, studied the practical, not the abstract. He's looking great, like time never moved on. His sharp, chiseled face is holding up. His dreamy blue eyes are still there. Expert in international divided cities. He had lived in like nine conflict cities through the years. Great storyteller.

"Did you ever think that our country would end up like all those violent places you studied," I say. "What were they? Wait, I remember them. Jerusalem, Washington DC, Belfast, Beirut, Ottawa, Sarajevo, Houston/El Paso, Johannesburg, and... Detroit."

"You got them all, Jared," high-fiving me. I don't think the hash beer he's downing is his first. "You know, when you study the fragmentation of the States of America, you realize it could happen anywhere. And the war there was during the early years of internet penetration. Compared to *interconnect*, their system of algorithmic penetration was primitive, a plaything. And look what it led to there. I can't believe people fell for those primitive conspiracy theories."

We both settle down a bit after the initial exuberance. We take a sigh at the same time and laugh.

"How have you been in all this mess, Forester? You're looking great."

"One day at a time, my friend. Lost my wife, you remember Ginny, to a sniper in '34. Both daughters were captured in '37 and trafficked to Heartland. I was actually able to get back Beth. Lives with me, on heavy daily sedatives. The other one—Meghan—we never found."

"Geez, I'm so sorry, dude."

Forester looks lost in thought for a moment. In a place where shadows loom larger than life. "And you?"

"Lost years. I'm still living with Raven, you remember her? Things are rough between us now because of what the machine is apparently doing to me. I finally got a divorce from Carrie. Both kids still in Acalato. They're doing okay, I guess, considering everything going on."

My mention of machine pollution is intentional. I would love to hear Forester's thoughts on *interconnect*. I'm hoping we get to that topic, but it's a risky one. You never know a person's view on it and who they associate with.

"I still can't believe how we bent over and took it in the ass."

"Are you talking about the Institute?" I ask.

"Sure am. We always thought universities—you know, centers of higher learning—were the bulwark against tyranny. That we were immune to all the shit in society. You know, a bright light that would illuminate amidst the darkness. Well, that was a crock of shit. Universities became more interested in public relations and fucking ratings than doing meaningful work."

"Yeah, I was pretty cynical about the whole enterprise when I was at the Institute."

"Hell yeah, you were!" Forester laughs and orders two more hashers.

I continue. "But even I never thought we would be so spineless and defenseless, that reasoned intelligence would be of such little value when we needed it the most."

"Truth was weaponized," Forester says. "We were criminalized for spreading falsehoods. Verified truths based on centuries of human exploration were all of a sudden fabrications dangerous to the well-being of society. Students screamed at us for pushing an agenda. Fuck, we were giving them facts and truth.

"At first, we laughed it off. 'Oh, look at what those young people are thinking.' We had one faculty meeting—don't think you were there, what a surprise!—where all we did was tell jokes about our students' opinions and behavior.

"We were so naïve. The monster was at the door and we thought it was a tamed coy-cat."

This is getting close to my targeted topic. It's obvious my friend has not bought into the whole algorithmic world. I let him continue.

"You know how *interconnect* did it? You know, turned truth against us?" Forester asks.

I shake my head.

"Quite ingenious, actually. A very interesting guy told me about it. Remember that tool in the late '20s, semantic forensics or SemaFor? It was software meant to detect all the believable deepfakes and false shit people were putting into the internet.

"Well, *interconnect* comes along and it coopts SemaFor and uses it for diametrically contrary purposes from those intended. It formulates the 'Algo FIX7I9' platform to pervert SemaFor. It's then able to use it to detect rogue patterns that are contrary to its manufactured storylines. False becomes true. Truth becomes false. We in the education business were done for."

This is unlike anything I've heard before.

"Wow, you know, *interconnect* has this massive influence on our life," I say. "This constant genocidal war. Erosion of independent thinking ability. Yet, it's a black box. We don't know much about it, do we? I'm amazed you have this information.

"Who knew about this, if you don't mind me asking?"

Forester pauses and takes a long sip. "Tell me something about yourself, Jared?"

Forester flips from former colleague to job interview questioner. He sidesteps my query entirely. I feel like I need to pass some test.

"You know, day-to-day survival. Chipping-in not doing great things to my life. I've had some bad experiences."

"What do you mean?"

"Some doc talks about split-brain seizures with me. Not enough algorithmic input. Another time, I'm so polluted by algorithms that I go through a horrible withdrawal program. What is it? Too little or too much."

"Who was it that helped you through withdrawal?"

"Guy named Ferty."

"Was he with a group of some kind?"

Forester is after something here, which makes me feel a distanced queasiness. I've got to trust somebody out here. I go with the truth.

"A group that believes in the 'old arts,'" I say quietly and opaquely.

"Organics," Forester whispers back.

I give a slight nod.

With that, Forester puts his hand on my shoulder, and his blue eyes meet mine. He extends his hash beer and clinks with mine.

"Sorry 'bout that inquisition, Jared. Had to find out what side of reality you're on. I'm part of the activist network. I'm 8-0 as an insert. You know who we are?"

I nod again. It feels odd talking about this stuff in a tavern. There's nobody sitting near us at the bar now and this alleviates some of my unease.

"I had to be careful," Forester says. "I know a friend from the old arts who opened up to one of our past colleagues. Turns out he was a regime spy. My friend is now incarcerated, indefinite sentence."

"Who was the spy?" I ask.

"Lalish, you remember him?"

"Yeah, that measly little fuck-wad. I never liked that guy with his dumb shit study of urban aesthetics. You know, his big thing was studying the charm of auto-fin lane separators. Fuckin' lame."

Forester orders two more hashers. Pretty sure he's buzzed. I'm getting there.

"You asked me earlier about how I learned about SemaFor. One day I'm out in a park to get some air for Beth. Next thing I know there's this smelly, homeless-looking guy near me asking me about the old arts. Turns out he is part of a group calling themselves 'paragons.'" We waffle back and forth confirming that neither of us are regime informants. We finally get around to the good stuff.

"He tells me his group is anti-*interconnect* but not fully sold on the old arts either. They have a different take on things. They don't think independent human thinking is the way forward, but they are strong opponents of today's algorithmic structure, the way *interconnect* is coded."

Weird how this paragon group pops up in conversations. "I think I've heard of this group, but their ideas don't quite make sense to me."

"They say there's a third option. They want to restructure the machine so that it supports human consciousness. Turn the machine into a helpful guide rather than a demonic force that preys off of human weaknesses."

Forester checks his e-watch. He looks concerned.

"We better get out of here. It's nearing 15 minutes. Assuming you're a sub-user too, two of a kind attracts the sensors."

He quickly jots down something on a napkin. I see it's an address.

"Let's meet at this address tomorrow, say 15:00. You good?"

I nod my head.

Chapter 40

"Great meeting you yesterday, Jared." We hug again in friendship. "We can speak longer now. I have blockers here," Forester says. He points overhead to a set of metalized plastic sheets held tightly together by brackets at each ceiling line.

We're at his apartment. It was surprisingly easy to find, even without the geocode network operational. I had walked this neighborhood before and remembered the name of the street branching out directly from the obscenely scarred museum that dominates the area.

His apartment has a run-down bachelor look to it. There's a brown chair directly in front of the eVision console. A pair of pajamas and a robe are slung over the coffee table. Drink glasses scattered on various table-tops, most empty, some dusty and half-full with cloudy liquids. Dishes sticking out of the sink. Shades drawn. A musty smell. Archival hard-copy books on a makeshift floor shelf, a sad reminder that books used to be common sights.

A young woman—I assume his daughter—sits on a corner

chair. She has vacant, drugged-out eyes. A pale, ghost-like appearance. Whatever happened to her has drained all life from her. The stand next to her has what are undoubtedly photos of Forester's lost family. I look away. They seem way too private and tender to look at beyond a brief glance.

Forester offers me a glass of lemonade. He proudly recounts that he found two lemons in his neighborhood the other day. "Looked like some coy-dogs got to one, but they're still pretty intact. Major win."

We settle into two hardback chairs that are discolored and rusted. Likely picked up off the street.

"So, I was talking about this paragon guy. What he told me was fascinating. Not just about SemaFor. He also described a chipping-in technique that can access another part of *interconnect* output. I've tried it and I think he's on to something.

"It's about how we react when we chip-in. I don't know about you, but when I chip-in, there always seems to be an abrupt change, as if I'm putting on a different pair of glasses. One moment I'm seeing and thinking normal, next I'm within a completely new world with all its hostile elements. Either I'm in one or the other. No in-between."

"Yeah, for me one is in color, the other is in black-and-white," I say.

"Exactly, others I've talked to describe it as a difference in the way time feels. In the one, normal speed, in the other rushed and urgent. Some even say they can taste the difference when chipped-in. They describe an iron-rich, metallic taste like blood itself.

"Anyway, this chap said that it is not either-or, but there is a third liminal space that you can access when you first chip-in. And this space is not filled with *interconnect*'s storylines of hate and grievance, but rather is benign, a place of liberation."

"What do you mean by liminal?" I probe.

"A space in between the two realities. It occupies a place on both sides of the boundary. It contains both computer curation and organic human processing."

I'm dumbfounded. Seems impossible.

"How can that be? I never experienced anything like that. It has always been an all-encompassing algorithmic takeover into its hellish world."

The young gal in the chair is gagging and spitting up. Growling.

"Do you need to take care of her?" I ask.

"She's alright. She regularly goes through trauma attacks, even with her sedative regime. Her body's not strong enough for a withdrawal program, so next best thing is to medicate her. That way, she doesn't live in the machine world with its constant re-telling of the hell that she went through when she was a slave."

"I'm sorry, Forester."

"You know, despite her condition, she reminds me so much of Ginny. Meghan was always the wild one, but Beth always had this calm center about her, like Ginny."

Forester pauses for what feels like an excruciatingly long time. He takes a deep breath and then goes back to our earlier thread. "Anyway, the paragon guy. He gets really psychological. He said it's all about how we approach the algorithmic surge. He said everything we experience in *interconnect* reflects our own mental machinations.

"When we chip-in, he said that our amygdala—that mass of gray matter in our head that experiences emotions—gets fired up and we're off to the races. The machine then has us by the balls. Paragon guy said that in the first 20 seconds of chip-in, if we learn to not react out of reflex we can find a calm space. A light. What he called the third space.

"Basically, you can train your mind to go to a different place amidst the stimuli of hate, grievance, and resentment. He said it took him months of dedicated practice to be able to see this space, then another month of practice to get into the space and stay there."

"I've never seen such a thing," I say. "The chip-in transition always feels sudden and automatic. Are you talking about some type of free will while connected?"

"Some human capability, yes.

"Listen, I've practiced this for some time myself. I didn't see the space, the opening, for many times at first. It was frustrating. I felt at a loss. I started to think only specially gifted denizens could see it. Or that the paragon guy was full of it.

"Then, one day, an image flashed that was out of sync with the other stimuli flooding in. It was an auto-fin tunnel, nothing special about it except there were absolutely no fins. It seemed almost like a painting. Dim yellow blinking lights were going off and on irregularly and they seemed to be directing me into the tunnel.

"I felt I was not fully in an *interconnect* narrative, nor was I thinking on my own. The image was some type of intermediate state, a type of gap or interval. When I was in that space, I felt neither machine-driven or ego-driven. It was a calm state of non-self-reality, a place without external constraints. I was free."

This sounds too good to be true. Like discovering the combination of a bank vault. I trust my friend, but I'm skeptical about why the machine would allow this. I think this may be some feel-good gimmick, a way to provide temporary relief from algorithmic domination. Something clicks in my head, though, about what Forester said about paragons.

"You said that this group—paragons—don't believe in organic thinking but want to move to some type of computer-supported enhanced thinking. I don't know, a human-compatible *interconnect*?"

"That's what my contact said."

"Is this—um—third space thing? Is this why they advocate what they do? They think only by chipping-in can we get to this—I don't know—enlightened state?"

"Good question. I'm not sure. My friend talked about it

as a practice at the individual level. He mentioned the larger goals of re-designing the machine, but he didn't get into that.

"Hey, Jared, I've got to get to Beth. We have a whole routine to calm her down so she can sleep a few hours at night. Hey girl, you want to say goodbye to Mr. Rohde?"

She walks slowly over to me and bows her head submissively. She holds out her hands crossed over each other like she expects me to put shackles on them. She whispers something I can't hear. She must be in her early 20s, but she is sadly still an adolescent in a slave world.

Forester diverts from the heaviness.

"I recommend you try it. Experiment with it for a while. Practice not reacting emotionally to the e-cairns. Take a breath and look around at the images coming into you. Look for an image to the side, at the periphery, to a place you normally wouldn't focus on because you're obsessing over the machine's menacing messages.

"As you search, *interconnect* will try to overpower you with urgencies and anxieties that it wants you to respond to immediately. You know how clever the machine is.

"But look for the image that is out of place with the machine's storyline, the thing that calmly exists alongside the rush of urgent hatred. Look for the small eddy of calm water at the side of the raging glacier-fed river. Trust that it is there. The machine will work hard to pull you into the river.

"Don't get down on yourself. You won't see it at first. After much practice, you may feel only inklings of another space in between organic and algorithmic. You may even feel stupid. Don't give up. It's worth it.

"Most never see it."

… CHAPTER **41**

Too much information. I'm in a psychological meat grinder. My head is spinning without direction.

Our country on fire.

Two realities.

Threat of split-brain seizure.

Trouble with Raven.

Organics.

Inserts.

Regime assassins.

Ferty's withdrawal program hell.

Paragons.

Now, Forester with his possible end-around of *interconnect.*

My common response to mental exhaustion is to go flat-line. At home, I plead with Raven like a blue-balled teenager to fuck so I can pass out and sleep. My apologies to her are weak and hesitant. She holds her ground. I know she wants to screw too, just not necessarily with me at this moment.

We watch about an hour of nasty e-porn before her desire overcomes her disgust. I think she would have rather preferred a threesome so she wouldn't have to face me. I take what I can and the warm glow afterwards does its sought-after knockout punch. But, the effect is temporary. I awaken to the same level of mental exhaustion and no closer to Raven emotionally.

Days and weeks pass without meaning. I'm beyond miserable with the mundanity of organic thinking. I seldom go out now because of renewed bombing. I spend hours figuring out the best route to one of the temporary food markets. I watch eVision and its constant transmission of negativity and doom. I prepare shitty noodle dishes out of a can. Wash dishes. Sit beside Raven on our foul-smelling sofa in separate universes. We speak to each other only in short, resentment-filled sentences.

I've got to find some way out of this non-existence.

With much trepidation mixed with some curiosity, I begin to think about experimenting with the machine. To see whether I can find what Forester described. I recall that it likely will take a long time before I see that space between organic and algorithmic, if I see it at all. I've previously recoiled from experimentation because I simply didn't want to engage with the machine beyond the mandated time. The hard work of the Ferty program was enough.

Such experimentation also seemed like it would be playing with fire. I trusted that Forester was telling the truth, that some third space may exist. But I don't want to risk possible full-on machine capture and insanity.

Yet, as the meaninglessness of non-machined life has become a potent everyday feeling, the itch to chip-in has increased. Experimenting with the machine, rather than all-out obsessing with it, provides me with justification that I wouldn't simply be giving in and going back to the old ways.

Boredom.
Itch.
Justification.
Game on.

PART VIII

INTO THIRD SPACE

2046

CHAPTER 42

Raven adeptly closes one of Ferty's handcuffs around my left wrist and clips the other around an exposed floor beam. The same for the right wrist. I'm sitting on our kitchen floor.

Raven smiles at me and says, "These toys remind me of the first days, Kitty Kat." It's great to see her joking. It's been way too long living in our apartment stricken of life. But I know such levity is covering up debilitating anxiety and fear over what I am going to try next, with her assistance.

I've convinced her that this experiment is for a good cause, not my way to back into more addiction. My instructions to her that give her some control over the operation also assure her that I'm not in it to escape.

Forester's encouragement to experiment with the machine has stuck in my mind ever since our meeting. It sometimes is there with a sense of urgent curiosity, other times quietly renting space in my head. It scares me to enter the machine world again. Memories of the nightmarish withdrawal sequence re-emerge and now are sharp-edged. As does the memory of the look on Raven's face as she bathed me after my foray into the algorithmic apocalypse.

My plan is ad-hoc. Forester didn't provide me with instructions.

I plan to chip-in up to five times, each time progressively longer in duration—4, 8, 12, 16, and 20 minutes, if needed. I need to prevent getting stuck in a storyline while at the same time attempting to find this third space. A balancing act. The less time I'm chipped-in, the less likely I'll get stuck. The more time I'm in, maybe I'll find this damn light, this third space. Thus, start short and inch toward longer intervals.

Raven will watch the clock and chip me out after the appropriate time.

"Remember, no matter what I do or say, don't let me stay chipped-in longer than planned. I'll likely tell you anything to stay connected. Don't believe anything I tell you."

Raven looks scared. "What exactly are you trying to do?"

For most of our time together, she had no clue about my two realities. Now she's right smack in the middle of my delirium. She thought I was crazy when I told her what I was going to try. I don't think having me chained down to the kitchen floor is helping her anxiety level. Neither is our agreement that should I physically try to stop her from chipping me out that she will open the valve on the ketamine bag connected to the IV in my arm.

I'm not confident I'll find Forester's third space. Whenever I chip-in, it has always been emergence into a sudden cavernous blackness with surging sensations of spite, bitterness, and the urge to defend and act. All black. What gives me some hope is that the first chip-in moments are so overpowering that I had no thought of looking around more widely during the mental vortex.

We gently hug each other. Sweat is dripping down my back. I get as comfortable as I can in the forced sitting position. Raven taps my ear switch.

Pulsing surge. The black turbulence is there immediately. Solid. No variation in the darkness. It emanates searing revulsion and accusation. I look for grooves and striations in the black without success. I feel soul-eating self-criticism that I am trying this experiment.

My attention is then directed to ghostly images of militia killers with Pirner insignia all over their fatigues. I attempt not to react immediately but with no success.

I am being drawn into the storyline. The cavernous blackness morphs into a honeycomb of algorithmic complexity and obnoxious urgency. I am captured, complicit, and murderous.

My brain is on fire, and I need to act. I'm wired with hostility but I can't move. Time collapses in on itself.

Raven is looking at me expectantly.

"Nothing other than blackness, a complete failure," I say. "Was that four minutes? Did you not stop it?"

"Four minutes, as you wanted, Jared."

"It felt like I was in there for a lot longer than that."

I make a note that time may function differently inside the machine.

We don't wait long for the next chip-in. Part of me is curious, another part feels this is a fruitless exercise and just wants to get this over with.

Again, the black turbulence. I stare at the same dark morass of ferocious anger. It is compelling and I draw to it involuntarily.

Just before I lose all volition, I turn my head slightly and see a blurred image of what looks like a shadowy crevice, maybe a path. Its surface has a shade of blackness just light enough to set it off from the pure blackness that envelops all else.

Immediately after I see the blurry illumination, the dark whirlwind rips my head back away toward the blackness. I am pulled toward the dark pit of despair and oblivion. The stuff of fantastic nightmares. A sinister, menacing slime envelops me. I am captured.

Raven looks at me in disbelief. "You didn't want me to pull you out this time," she yells. "You were shouting some ugly things and whipping your arms around trying to get the cuffs off. I'm pretty sure you were ready to run if you weren't tied down."

I look down at my wrists, reddened and chafed underneath the cuffs.

"Besides the hostile shit, did I say anything different?"

"About five minutes in, you said, 'I see it.'"

We both agree to give it a rest before the next try. If it was up to me, I would have gone straight back in. I did see something. But Raven convinces me to take a break when she describes more fully my animal-like behavior during try two. We agree on a 90-minute recess.

We eat slightly warmed leftover pasta. We stare wordlessly at each other while we eat.

Raven eventually breaks the impasse.

"What can we do to make this reality—the one you share with me—more alive?"

I'm trying to solve the puzzle of *interconnect* and fuckin' Raven brings up interpersonal shit. She looks like a hurt little girl, a look she does extremely well and typically elicits a rescue response from me.

"I've tried to deal with what you said, Jared, but I keep coming up with the feeling that you would rather be in that other reality and not this one with me."

I've thought about this also—the difference between the two realities. I can speak honestly. I've got this. I'm not going to trigger her. Then I can go back to the important stuff.

"It seems so very meaningful on the other side. It's life or death. I admit I thirst for the adrenaline rush of the machine when I'm on this side. I feel aimless here. The other reality focuses my attention and, yes, makes me feel alive. Here, I feel numbed most of the time, I go through the motions and fall into habitual grooves.

"But let me tell you something, my dear Raven, this has little to do with you. Anyone, anything, would seem tame compared to the ferocious power of the machine.

"I also realize that the drama of the other side is not sustainable. It's a power surge that will eventually swallow me up and spit me out. You know I went through the debasement of withdrawal. That must tell you I don't want that other reality.

"I want this life—with you."

Damn, that sounded good. It feels like I actually know how to effectively communicate with a woman.

Raven's look of understanding surprises me. "I get it, Jared. The machine gives me visions and experiences that are gripping. I admit I get involved in them, not in violent ways though. But no matter how engaging the machine visions are, I would never trade in this reality with you, no matter how hard it is at times."

Raven cuddles up against me. I hug her tightly while brushing away tears in my eyes. She kisses me gently on the neck.

We celebrate our rapprochement by eating strange-tasting lemon popsicles, a rare find yesterday at a mobile market.

Third try. Twelve minutes to find a needle in a haystack, 720 seconds to see a small, easily missed off-black flicker in an ocean of attention-demanding blackness. Then, to find some way to move toward it. I recall Forester's suggestion to go to a different place in my mind amid the stimuli of hate, grievance, and resentment. An eddy amidst the raging river. The calm eye of the storm.

Last time, as soon as I was attracted to the blurry illumination, I was violently pulled away from it by the blackness. If I see the light this time, I plan to calmly observe it and try my best not to register desire or excitement. Maybe this way, *interconnect* will not counter-punch and pull me into the raging river, into the whirling storm. I'm hoping that it was my inner desire to go elsewhere that alerted *interconnect* that I was seeking to detour from its main cairn path.

The blackness. I look immediately toward the side and see only black purity. I feel the gripping pull of urgent hatred. I turn toward the other side and see a lighter gray image. I do not react and try to simply observe. The off-black image is of an empty street with auto-fins parked in the middle lane. There is an eeriness to the view. Nothing is moving.

I hold my attention to the light. I close my eyes for a few seconds to calm myself. I slowly take two steps toward the image. The image sharpens—I can see the shine off of the streetlights—and I can't suppress my excitement at this discovery. Immediately, *interconnect* responds with punishing ferocity in its violent displacement of my body. Thank goodness I'm chipped-out by Raven. I'm pretty sure I would not be able to do it on my own.

"You're a glutton for punishment, you know that right?"

Raven's edginess has transformed into an effort at dark humor.

My curiosity about the light is growing as I see it more clearly. But, I realize that the closer I get to this other part of the algorithmic superstructure, the stronger the stimulus delivered by interconnect. Like any living thing, it is rapaciously protective of its domain.

Fourth try. I find the striation more readily this time. I see a passageway dimly lit. There is an arch above it. I move toward it slowly, and an incongruous image emerges. A coffee shop with servers at the ready. They are absolutely still. A buxom waitress halfway falling out of her blouse with a 'Delores' name tag pinned to it is bending down holding a pot of coffee, but she is stuck in place. There are no customers. The servers seem like mannequins, the lighting has a gauzy sheen to it.

I open the door to the space and feel a serene stillness. One of the servers—a shiny-faced young man—comes to life, smiles, and welcomes me in. He sits me at a window table and gives me a menu. I feel a refreshing breeze.

Immediately I am thrown outside into battle images, blood, guts, and mind-shattering images of sliced-off body parts. Fighters emerge from multiple spots with automatics pointed in my direction. It is a hellish scene. I need to defend myself or I'm dead.

I shield myself behind an overturned and burning auto-fin. I feel a tearing and grasping of my ear. I'm being assaulted from behind. A sharp knife is cutting into the side of my face. I close my eyes and sink downward.

"Fuck you, I can't do this anymore," screams Raven. She is manic and upset.

I come to slowly this time. The vehemence of Raven matches the intensity of the algorithmic blackness. It takes me a bit to recalibrate back into organic reality.

"I had to knock you out with the IV drip. I tried to chip you out but you struggled against me. I think you thought I was assaulting you. I was your enemy, damn it. I couldn't turn the damn thing off."

"Sorry, honey.

"But listen, I got the farthest into the third space this time. I was in a safe space for a while. It was amazing. Then things went really black. The machine must have reacted aggressively in response to my traipsing in a space it wants to be off-limits."

"It sounds like the machine is getting really pissed at you, Jared. What if it doesn't allow you to come back next time?"

So focused on the light, I had not thought about the possibility of being stuck in the black.

Fifth try. A whole 20 minutes. I'm more hopeful of success this time. I want to enter the third space and find out what it's all about. I rehearse in my head Forester's suggestion that I go to a different place in my mind when I feel the strong force of *interconnect*.

The blackness is ready. Bubbling. A strong, acidic smell attacks my nostrils. Waves protrude outward from the black core and grasp at me. The light also seems ready. It is slightly downward to the right. There are steps leading to it.

The shimmer of light is more clearly illuminated than before. It helps me toward it. I'm not fearful as I move toward it calmly. I trust it fully. I express no interest in it so as not to trigger the machine. The light feels like a guardian or protector.

I walk the last step and over a threshold made of smooth, perfectly rounded rock.

I'm in a beautiful golden meadow doused in late afternoon sunshine. Several small creeks are lined by purple lupine wildflowers and crisscross over the saturated field. Birds flitter about and send their chirps into the quietude of the pasture. I hear my shoes squish as I walk over a water-soaked path. I go to a large rock in the middle of the meadow, find a comfortable nook in it, and lie down. I soak up the warmth and peace of this extraordinary place.

Timelessness. I have never felt freer in my whole life. An indescribable peace. Neither human-made anxieties nor algorithmic blackness exist here. A selflessness that is connected to everything good and real. Fulfillment. No need to grasp or avoid. Just exist in the present moment.

Hours seem to pass in bliss.

On the horizon, I see the blackness. It is swelling with algorithmic hate. It is angry. Taking in the last breaths of fresh air from my paradise rock, I squint as the charging blackness comes down upon me. I can't watch as the sinister darkness detonates.

As I cascade downward into the depths, Forester's voice is there—"Do something different." I open my eyes and widen my view. Despite black radiation tearing at me on all sides, I calmly breathe.

I look not where the blackness is pulling my head but to the side.

My head is whipped back again to front and center.

I calmly shift my eyes to the side.

To where the machine does not want me to look.

I see light. I see color.

I slowly enter and walk down a hallway into a wood-paneled room from yesteryear. Blackness recedes but lies in wait outside. The room is lined with bookshelves, filled with cushioned chairs and desks. Colorful tapestries line the walls. Small lamps at each desk illuminate scattered books and papers.

"Welcome, my good friend. Congratulations, well done."

Elijah and Anya sit comfortably in leather chairs. Their arms are casually out-stretched to side tables where steam gently rises from their teacups.

Chapter 43

"My God, what the fuck?" I do a double-take to make sure this is real. I then remember to stay calm so this doesn't evaporate into darkness.

"Have you gotten religion, my friend?" Elijah is wearing the same damn top hat, suit and tie he wore when we first met years ago.

"I think it is a temporary lapse in judgment, our friend's reference to God," jokes Anya with a gleam in her eyes, visible even through those ridiculous cat-eye frames. She's in business attire and her lips are aflame with red lipstick.

"Where are we? I thought you two were incarcerated by the regime or dead by now? How are you here?"

I don't believe I'm actually talking to Elijah and Anya. I've been through too many mind-fucks to believe anything is real at this point.

"Go on, touch me," Anya volunteers.

I lightly touch her elbow. It feels real.

This is more real than a dream. I never recall having felt

the sensation of touch in an organic dream nor, for that matter, in a machine storyline.

I sit down in a chair opposite the two of them. My head is whirling dizzy.

"Perhaps some refreshment?" Elijah offers. A Viz human attendant extends a tray containing three drinks of different colors. I take what looks like mint lemonade. It is delicious.

Elijah turns toward Anya. "You know, my dear, I've often wondered whether your mama had you in office pant-suits when you were a toddler."

"Very funny, you old hawk," Anya says. "Yeah, my mom had a helluva time finding them in 4T size.

"And you, my friend." Anya's not done. "How did your damn treatises on Aristotle go down with your elementary school buds?"

They both laugh.

I get the sense that Elijah and Anya are relishing this moment. Elijah is opening an e-cig and Anya is silently smiling at me.

"Don't make me work, guys. Let me in on this situation please."

"We wanted to give you some time to adjust. It's a lot to take in," Anya says. "You are in a space of liberation from *interconnect*'s evil narratives, a space of freedom."

"But, the blackness is right outside this room. We're in the machine's domain, aren't we? Not in the human domain," I say.

"Oh, you are very much in a human domain, at least partially, good man. Let's say it's both organic and algorithmic and leave it at that. Believe in it. But yes, your physical location is within the algorithmic network," Anya replies.

She continues, more energetically, "You were being digested by the fabrications, by the blackness, but you somehow learned not to be swept into the raging torrent.

"Understand, my friend. It's what we usually don't see

when we're on the curated addictive cairn path that is important. It's the lightly marked side trail that meanders off the main route, the side alley, the stuff outside the blinkers, the precious child sitting at the side of the attention-grabbing parade.

"When you're on the machine-curated path, you become unconscious and are easy prey to primal impulses. You lose yourself. If you're able to look beyond its boundaries, you can see light. You regain yourself."

"An organic, name of Forester, told me a tale about there being a third space, a luminal space. Is this what you are describing?"

"Yes, very good. Based on your arriving here, we thought someone may have enlightened you," Elijah exclaims. "Actually, it's called a liminal space, a space in between a boundary line, in our case between the two realities—organic and machine curated."

"How can you two be here? I mean, I think it's great to see you. But how did you get out of prison and into this part of the maze with me?"

"We're not out of prison, Jared. I'm in cell block XF-145, and I believe Anya is in cell TR-984, Heartland #6 Containment Facility. Is that right, my dear? I do hope the food is better there than here."

"It sucks. The pasta smells like used panties."

They both giggle.

What is with these two? They're talking about serious-as-shit things but acting like teenagers. There's a glow to them they can't suppress.

Viz loudly interrupts. "Apparent effort at humor interfering with substantive transmission of communication."

Elijah, looking chastised, says in a more serious tone, "We are in a fabricated reality, a type of fantasy that appears real. Jared, I know you're familiar with how real the machine's fabrications are. They are so real they likely have made you do nasty things. So real they seem.

"You see, machine fabrications are usually so dark and hurtful because denizens, in a way, help co-create them. Many of us have strong emotions hidden in our subconscious—anxiety, self-doubt, anger, and so on. When we connect to the machine, this substrata of boiling anxieties becomes fuel for *interconnect*'s mission. Grist for the mill.

"Now, this space we're in—this glorious space—was co-created by you. By staying calm and centered in the early crucial moments of being chipped-in, you provided no fuel for the machine's negative storylines.

"And what exists here reveals what the machine is capable of—light and liberation. But we seldom see this paradise because the machine is so determined to split our country into groups of us versus them hate."

Anya looks at me sympathetically. "It's all surely beyond normal comprehension, isn't it? A fabrication that is also reality because it stimulates human actions and creates massive real consequences."

"So, am I in another place, too, besides here?" I mutter.

Elijah blows a large waft of smoke from his e-cig. "You're catching on. Where were you in organic space when you chipped-in?"

"Hand-cuffed to a chair in my apartment."

"And yet you are here now. Do you feel real here?"

I look at the wood-paneled walls as if that would help me understand. "I do."

"You're in apartment 6A, Lighthouse Compound, west Jeim, to be exact."

"So, are we really not here? Is this all fabrication? We're just playthings of the machine."

"You are very much here, as much as we are here with you," Anya says, ducking away from the smoke. "Elijah, dear, watch the smoke, okay? I have one of my best business suits on."

My mind twists and turns, not helped by the goofy, carefree behavior of my two friends.

Viz lights up, "Subject is nearing psychological exhaustion. Needs understandable pronouncements to increase mental stability."

"Thank you," I say.

"I believe you are welcome," the Viz replies in terse narrator tone.

Anya smiles at me mischievously. "Okay," Anya says. "If we told you all the details at once, it would be overload. I know when I first found this place I almost had an aneurysm.

"I'll start then, if you don't mind, my dear Elijah. First, you wonder how exactly did you get here? To this liminal third space? As you know, *interconnect* thrives by fabricating storylines of hatred and grievance and all sorts of nasty human emotions. You know that.

"But if you look closer at how it pulls denizens into its dark web, it is fascinating. Certainly, some folks are ready to fight. Their amygdalas light up and they quickly put on their militia outfits.

"Most people, however, are not battle-ready. When they first feel the fear and threat curated by the machine, they try to resist.

"When they resist, they contract and try to avoid and run away. But a contracted mind is a vulnerable mind. Such a resistant, weakened mind supplies a hook that the machine uses to draw the recipient into its escapades."

The human attendant brings out what looks like d'oeuvres, some silly-looking finger food. I grab half the tray.

"I'm appreciating now that you guys came to me slowly about the details. It's not making a whole lot of sense to me.

"It also seems hopeless," I say. "Whether you grab on to the fear or try to resist it, you go into the algorithmic meatgrinder."

My focus is momentarily on the incredible taste of the dates wrapped in goat cheese. Viz registers a pleased gaze at me.

Elijah says, "But there is another way, an alternative that you apparently used, whether you were cognizant of it or not.

"Instead of heading toward it or running from the blackness out of reflex, the skillful path is to observe the negative stimuli in a detached way, relax the reflex response, and let the energy go through you as you would the wind. Do you recall doing anything like this, Jared?"

"I remember doing something counter-intuitive. I concentrated on breathing deeply, and I opened my eyes fully to the blackness. It seemed like suicide at the time but I guess it worked."

"Bravo," declares Elijah.

"It's that widening, that relaxing, that allowed you to see and focus on the light," Anya says. "Most denizens narrow their vision out of fear or close them entirely. Then, they miss what is on the sidelines.

"It's an open mind that can counteract the machine, not a contracted mind that is either attracted to the power of the algorithms or resisting it. A contracted mind traps the negative energies within it and becomes the medium through which *interconnect* operates."

"The implications of this are enormous," Elijah beams. "It means that properly trained organic human thinking can counter the machine. Note I say 'properly trained.' Normal, reactive organic processing will fail." He is celebratory in making this proclamation.

Elijah continues, "There is a good analogy here. Have you ever hiked on a footpath or trail, say out in the wilderness?"

I think back to years ago, hiking in the Shellsoll Mountains with Carrie and the kids.

"Yeah, in a former life."

"Maybe you can relate then. When a hiker gets lost on the trail, what does he do first thing when he realizes he is lost?"

"Um, goes nuts, I guess."

"Yes, he tightens up in fear. The amygdala lights up, and all of a sudden he is running all over the place trying to find the trail. What happens then?"

"If he's lucky, he finds it. If he's not, he gets more lost."

"Correct. Typically, his rapid reflexive response to the fear of being lost creates greater disorientation, and now he is even further lost. He doesn't even know where he was when he first discovered he was off-trail. He has no coordinates to help him find the way.

"Do you see that if his first reaction was instead to relax and slow things down, he could have set forth a thoughtful strategy of methodologically checking different directions, always coming back to his initial place if unsuccessful, but eventually finding the trail?

"React out of fear—get more lost. Respond with calmness—find the way."

Anya seeks to clarify. "It's how we respond to the initial machine stimulus that determines our trajectory—either we are pulled into the addictive negative power of the algorithmic stream, or we are able to see and find the light.

"A writer nearly 100 years ago wrote about this. He also lived during a time of mass human slaughter. He said, 'Between response and stimulus there is a space. In that space is our power to choose our response. In our response lies our growth and freedom.'"

"Thank you, Anya, but I think Jared got the message."

At times I think Elijah and Anya are more sparring siblings than accomplices in a great human triumph.

"I get it," I say to break the child's play. "It sounds so simple on the one hand. So humanly impossible on the other hand. Seems like we need some evolution in human thinking."

"Indeed," says Anya. "It goes against thousands of years of mental indoctrination. It is ingrained within us that when feeling fear, grip tightly to either engage with the threat or to try to avoid it."

*

I grab for more tidbits off the food tray. I notice that the Viz seems to be giving off some indication of displeasure. Its head is tilted back and its arms are up in a fending-off pose. I must be mentally wearing down to imagine this.

My eyes are drying out and my body feels a chill. Elijah's e-cig is still blowing. Anya has gotten herself a glass of near-wine and offers me a glass. I readily accept.

We sit in needed silence.

There's something that still makes no sense at all. Despite exhaustion, I need to ask.

"You said earlier that you are both in prison but also here. How can this be?"

"We don't understand how dual realities work, Jared," Anya responds.

"One possibility is that when you found the light, you brought memories or images of us along with you. I recommend you not think too hard about this. This may not be comprehensible to mere humans.

"We do know, unfortunately, that what you do in fabricated storylines has real-life consequences. The hundreds of thousands dead in our country and the destroyed cities are empirical proof that *interconnect*'s storylines can have devastating outcomes.

"We also think that those who kill and maim when chipped-in have little ability to reflect on their murderous behavior. When our dear denizens are in organic reality—binging on eVision and getting drunk on hash beers—it seems they have little memory of what takes place in their fabricated realities."

I nod in sad acknowledgment of being unaware of what I did under machine influence.

CHAPTER 44

"You're now in for a treat," Anya says as she escorts me to the door. She gives me a gentle kiss on my neck.

Elijah is standing in front of his chair and giving me a thumbs-up. "This can be a place of liberation, my friend. But it can also be a place of danger.

"It's a beautiful place free of *interconnect*'s hostility. But, it's also a place where less skillful impulses can come to the foreground. Be careful, these impulses alert the machine to send stronger negative storylines, and this will pull you back to the darkness."

I walk through the hallway, open the door, and I'm met with a fantastical display of colors and textures.

It is a vibrant, festive city.

The weather is refreshingly cool and the shining sky is clear of haze and smoke.

The buildings are immaculately designed and modern.

The streets are pedestrian-oriented and clean.

There is a vibration in the air that is alive and stirring.

The auto-fins produce an enveloping symphonic effect.

A small boy with wild and joyful abandon chases a frenetic yellow-haired clonimal through a pile of leaves. He bumps into me and I steady him to prevent him from falling.

An impromptu performance at a city square by a solo electric guitarist has his audience swaying back and forth in joyful unison. He gives me a thumbs-up when he sees me.

A young couple is in a full and lingering embrace at a bistro's entry door.

A grandmother-type beams as she pushes a wheeled shopping cart containing two young children down the street. One of the youngsters waves at me and shouts out, "Look who's here Grammy!"

A smiling man in an undershirt leans out of his apartment window across the street and belts out an earthy version of a swooning romantic ballad.

Do I know these people?

A loud and boisterous noise comes from a nearby intersection. A cacophony of shouts and yells. A celebration.

Denizens move through the busy sidewalks as if they are parts of a single whole.

I see children, elderly men and women on walkers helped by assistants or families, and oddities, awkward and tender moments of interaction. Crying babies and grateful mothers. I see laughter, innocence, wonder, and elation.

The joyous life of this city penetrates everything.

I sit down on a bench in a bucolic park and cry out in amazement. I'm shocked that such beauty and bliss could co-exist within *interconnect* alongside its primary obsession with brutality and hostility.

I try to rest amidst the joy, but my brain is working overtime. Within the machine, these visions and these denizens must be part of algorithmic storylines. But they also are solid and real, not empty images projected onto a screen.

I touched a physical Anya. The small boy that I prevented from falling was a solid, sentient being.

In my calm, non-reactive approach to the light, did I help co-create this joyful place? There's a comfortable familiarity I feel with many of the denizens here. I know some of them. Several seem to know me.

I can't process this. Not even close. I re-focus on my surroundings.

A young-looking man and his two children are frolicking in the nearby tot-lot. They come over to the adjacent bench and unwrap sandwiches for lunch. The man sees my wet eyes. I feel his hand on my shoulder. He asks, "Are you okay, professor? It's great to see you again."

"I never felt better. I have seen what reality could be, and it is beautiful."

"Life is wonderful, no?" he says as he pats one of his kids on the head.

I notice the chip implant behind his right ear.

"Can I ask you a question?"

"You sure can. It's always great talking to you. I always loved the way you played music at the start of your lectures."

"When you have your chip implant turned on, what type of messages do you receive?"

"You name it, you can get it. A massive number of learning modules I can pick from. You can work your way through different levels of human thinking skills. Then there are topic modules. Non-violent communication, collaborative techniques, deep philosophical treatises, problem-solving, trauma-informed yoga, histories of different cultures, I could go on. The latest lecture by Master Aalap is astounding in its message of love. Were you wondering about something in particular?"

"I don't know, do you receive messages full of hate, other negative emotions?"

The young man looks a bit disturbed by my query. "You're not going to find those on the chip. *Interconnect* is human-supportive, certified to advance healthy and species-promoting outcomes. I guess if you want the negative stuff, you could go black market, but I don't know about that venue."

I feel bad asking him about such stuff in front of his impressionable, cheerful kids. I feel like I'm dragging the darkness of the other algorithmic reality into this space of human kindness.

I sense that my time in this place will soon be coming to an end. The images are becoming less sharp, the sky less bright, and the people scarcer. I'm excited to have discovered this place of enchantment.

The path to it is difficult. I don't think many denizens have found it.

I'm also angry. *Interconnect* apparently has this capacity to produce such joy and goodness, yet it makes it extremely hard for the average citizen to gain access to it.

This beautiful place seems to be an anomaly within a vast superstructure otherwise dedicated to spewing out hatred and hostility.

I wonder why the machine is so miserly with something so uplifting to humans.

CHAPTER **45**

I'm back in the Jeim apartment. Raven uncuffs me and removes the IV as I realize where I am. I do two things immediately. I first give Raven a long and rapturous full-body hug and tell her, "I love you." She warmly receives it but looks at me in near shock at my transformation. Next, I go to the icebox, get out two bottles of near-wine, pour two large glassfuls, and put them next to each other on our small dining table.

I am frenetic with energy. Everything in our drab apartment now seems new and inviting. There is so much to do now.

"I found it, babe.

"There are not two realities. There are three!"

"Honey, I love you too, but can you slow down for me? You were gone 20 minutes and you came back with super energy."

"No way I can slow down now, babe. I'm a new man!

"I need to share this news with others!"

Raven is gulping the near-wine. Caught up in my energy, she semi-yells, "What are you talking about?"

"You know how I talk about the other reality as more alive than this one. You hated me saying that, I surely know. Well, there is another space in *interconnect* that is much more uplifting. A place of compassion, kindness, and gentleness.

"And it's created by the machine, not outside of it. *Interconnect* doesn't have to kill us by default. It can also promote positive human attributes.

"Do you realize what this means? I'll never be the same again after seeing what I saw. It was beautiful. And the machine created it, or at least allowed it."

I know I am running words together in a manic way. I can't stop. It feels that a tremendous amount of pressure has been released, a heavy rock has been lifted off me.

"There is a path toward sanity after all. And I'm going to do everything I can to open this path for others. It is our country's salvation, beautiful you."

Raven lifts off her seat and sits on me, legs spread, face-to-face. Like all good co-dependent partners, she feeds off my energies. She doesn't hesitate to delightfully take a ride on my positive energy blast.

Sex would normally explosively occur at this point. But my mind is so entirely blown away by my experience that, hard for me to fathom, my mind is focused on something other than ripping her clothes off.

"I've been waiting a long time to engage in something meaningful. You know my life has so often left me flat and cynical. This is it, honey. I found it."

Raven slides off me. Co-dependents don't like being excluded. I'm on my own here.

"I can help save this damn country!"

I'm buzzing around the apartment, the wine unsuccessful in calming me. I'm writing down notes—memories of what I saw in third space, Forester's comments, names of organics that I've met and any geo-codes I have for them, Elijah's and

Anya's comments and containment facility number and location, anything and everything that might help me on my new mission of salvation. My new evangelism.

Raven has left the living room. I hear the shower.

Tomorrow I will start this endeavor. There is no time to waste.

282

It is to the underground network of resisters that I will appeal. I will make the case that I can help save our country.

I am compelled to share my experience with others. The remarkable peace of the third space. A place absent of suffering—both human conceived and computer curated. I must share the truth passed on to me by Elijah, Anya, and Forester that this peace-making capacity exists in the very same colossal machine that is leading our country to destruction. That we don't have to be stuck in a never-ending spiral of killing and conflict.

I will be a messenger. If I die doing it, I'll not care. The cause is worth everything. For the first time in a long time, living has meaning. I'm at the threshold of something big.

Sadly, though, when I make contact with network members, I learn that the organics and other resisters are in the throes of an uncertain and chaotic trajectory.

We are surveilled 24/7 by increasingly effective digital locators. We continue to be constantly on the move. It is uncertain whether we can cluster in one place even for up to 15 minutes because geo-discovery tools used by *interconnect* monitors are being upgraded daily.

System malfunctions and *interconnect* blocking of the old alt-x communications system are jeopardizing our use of the old geo-codes. We also need to constantly change these codes, often creating fake ones to fool regime surveillance.

Resisters have suffered significant loss of personnel due to targeted assassinations by the regime. We have further lost many of our brave inserts due to unsuccessful outcomes. Only about 25 percent are succeeding, even with updated protocols for militia insertion.

For all these reasons, our network is dispersed and leaderless. Our decision-making ability suffers accordingly.

I learn that there are also challenges in our internal organization politics. The network now includes a few coalition affiliates from the Paragon camp. This has produced an odd and uneasy coupling of two groups having different goals about how to deal with *interconnect*. Mistrust between organics and paragons is high, with many organics believing that paragons may be possible spies.

Rumors of a third space between organic thinking and *interconnect*-scripted fabrications have circulated but are intensifying internal conflict among resisters. Organics show resistance to this potential because it remains in machine-created space. Paragons are more enthusiastic because it is aligned with their idea of machine-human coordination.

Finally, there is disagreement about what to make of President Prince's pronouncement of 4th quarter, 81d, that a new machine module will train selected recipients in basic human thinking. Some resisters view this positively as a sign of incremental machine appeasement to resister goals. But, a majority of members view this cynically as a smokescreen. They argue that this is a guise to entice resisters to sign up, thus exposing them to identification and capture. They also question the true intent of the module and point out that it is just as computer-infected as the rest of *interconnect.*

I plan to be out on the road for an extended time. I have contacted six different geo-codes of resister affiliates. Their responses were positive and I have tentative dates set. However, the logistics of keeping me hidden, as well as each of the small groups that will meet to hear me, are taking up considerable time. Several days pass in wait. I'm restless and excited to hit the road.

Raven helps me pack. She is matching my up-energy these days by wearing fashionable and sexy clothes rather than her usual domestic knock-arounds. Her facial make-up would be just right for a formal dinner party. Beneath the façade enhancement, though, I can tell she is fighting sadness, maybe desperation. I hope she doesn't feel my planned evangelism isn't just my latest cockamamie idea. I wouldn't blame her if she did.

My emotional temperature increases as I wait for my mission to start. I have an urge I haven't felt in some time—to talk to my two kids. I feel sadness and guilt when I first think of calling them because it has been so long since I talked to them. But, my desire to connect with them is stronger. I want to show them that their dad is worth something. That I finally am getting my act together and that they may even be proud of me. I have let them down so often.

I alt-X my former home in Acalato. I cringe in anticipation of getting through the Carrie wall first. This is going to be a difficult call, but something about setting off on my new mission makes me want to connect with my roots.

Typically, the alt-X is fucked up. Connection sounds like cats scratching on sandpaper.

"Hi, Carrie, this is Jared. How're you doing?"

Silence of death.

In some ways, our divorce clarified things. It was a long time coming. Still, I can feel resentment coming through the cat-scratching.

"Jared… your eChecks have been delayed the last two quarters. Do you know that?"

I seethe. They've not been fuckin' delayed. More like not sent. Things are tight with Raven and me and I wasn't about to send my non-working ex money that we needed here. The ex-is all about saving society and doing good, but her work career has been sparse. All about volunteering. I seethe.

I take a breath and lie using my best monotone, "I'll get on top of that. Must be the bank's transmission. You know war doesn't help with communication channels.

"Anyway, I would like to talk to the kids. Are they around?"

"Yeah, I'll get them."

Silence of death.

I left them when they were eight and two. They're now 21 and 15. When I left Acalato for Elderwater, I never thought over 13 years would pass without seeing them. If I tried hard, I could possibly have gotten a special permit to pass the partition barrier between Sesperia and Northwoods regions. Honestly, though, with the crusty relations with Carrie and my comfortable life with Raven, I didn't try.

"Hey, Dad," says Caleb.

"Hi son, how're you doing?"

"Alright, I guess. A lot of cairn shit lately. Machine is feeding me all sorts of stuff on you."

"Oh yeah, what sort of stuff?"

I fear what is to come.

"That you're different… you're part of these groups that are killing people. You're some sort of militia thug. One feed had you talking to somebody and saying you wished you never had kids. That we get in the way of your fighting."

Fuck the machine! It never sleeps and constantly puts out curated shit that maximally antagonizes its users. It never seems to miss a chance to divide people.

"Wow, that's crazy. You know I would never say or do that. I love you guys. Actually, I'm living a pretty calm life here, especially considering all the warfare taking place.

"I did want to tell you something important though."

Cat-scratching.

"You're going to look at me as a hero someday, son."

"How so?"

"I'm going to help save this country. I've learned that there is a safe mental place in the machine, and I'm going to help us all get there."

"There's a place in this country that is safe? Hard to believe."

"It's not a physical place, Caleb. It's a place in our minds."

Ellie breaks in. "Hi, Dad. When can we see you?"

I can't believe my baby girl is now a teenager. She was cantankerous as a toddler and has kept up her testy approach to life over the years. Always direct and to the point.

"Hi, lovely daughter. I don't know. I'm about to go on a trip that is very important to our country. You should be proud of your Dad."

"Whatever, I gotta go. Love ya."

I feel small, that I'm pushing my ego in front of my kids to prove something. To make up for the long period of absence from their life. To prove my worth. I feel like a stranger.

"Hey, before you go, hold up the alt-x device so Caleb can hear too."

I take a deep breath. Truth is heavy.

"Kids, I'm very sorry that I have been absent for so long."

Silence of death.

This apology deflates my ego entirely. I feel like a chump. But it feels more genuine than my earlier attempt at puffery.

"Mom tells us you lost your job, so why are you still there?" Caleb says.

The machine's not the only force wanting to divide me from my children.

"Hey, Kiddo, you know how hard it is to pass through the partition walls. They're monsters and totally blocked off."

"Okay, bye. I love you," Caleb whispers.

Carrie comes back on the line. "Are you done?"

"Yeah, hey, you may hear about me in the near future. Stay tuned."

Silence of death. End of cat-scratching.

The sad emptiness of the call weighs down on me. But it also is an added stimulus for me to engage fully in my planned trip. To make something of myself. I would give my life if Caleb and Ellie could experience what I saw in that blissful third space. That liminal place of freedom.

CHAPTER 47

I guess it used to be a bowling alley. The sign outside hanging by a thread had line drawings of a ball with thumb holes and a martini class. Now the place is a cavernous, bombed- out shell. The group of six sits restlessly on the remnants of the lanes where denizens used to enjoy nights of fun and drinking. Back when there was fun.

I'm nervous. This is my first chance to share my experience of the third space. The only person I know here is Allacia. It's good to see her rotund figure and playful demeanor. The others are also organics, except for one paragon who proudly identifies as such. The paragon has creepy, half-closed eyes, which make me uncomfortable. Since he's here, I guess I need to trust him.

I stand in front of the group and start right off. Time is limited. Introduction would be unimportant. "I've been to a place in the machine that is not war-mongering. It's a place of peace and where you can think on your own. The path toward this place is accessible. At the moment right before you are taken over by algorithms, if you react not out of reflex and fear and look widely, you can find this space. It's within the algorithmic machine, but free of its malicious storylines."

I'm saying something of great drama, yet I see blank stares and even yawns as I continue.

"I never knew such a place could ever exist. It's even better than thinking outside the machine. There's a transcendent quality to it. This place doesn't have the random noise of our normal thinking. I was in the bliss of a natural meadow, the enjoyment of conversation, and I experienced an enchanted neighborhood. It felt like hours went by.

"This changes everything. It can be the savior for our country."

The audience remains quiet. Then I see reactions to this good news that I didn't expect. I see furrowed eyebrows, squinting, and sideways glances. Did they not understand what I just said?

"Who are you to tell us such a thing?" says a plaid-shirted middle-aged man. "Your background doesn't build trust. You've been with the killers. You suffer from split-brain seizures. You haven't fully trusted organic thinking in the past.

"Now you come to us with a farfetched story about a magical place that somehow exists within the hate-spewing machine. I have got to question your motivation."

"But wait," Allacia chimes in quickly as if she were expecting this man's reaction. "He has been with our activist network enough to know. He has experienced every aspect of *interconnect*. He was put through a horrendous withdrawal program few of you folks would put up with. That proves to me his integrity."

Gruff sounds of disagreement meet Allacia's proclamation.

A bearded, rough-looking older man speaks: "You got to understand, this is pretty hard to believe. Peace within the machine goes against everything we've seen for all these years. Tell us more about this space."

"It's a source of light," I reply. "Not outside the machine, but not part of its hate storylines. A third space. It's a place of individual freedom, of fulfillment. I could have stayed there forever. I was fully conscious, not in some fabrication, I'm sure of it."

I feel inadequate in describing it, and I think I'm losing my audience. I've got to find a better way to describe it in future meetings.

"I met two organics there who, physically, are incarcerated. Elijah and Anya. They knew all about this space and how to get to it."

I'm pretty sure I shouldn't have mentioned that. It sounds wacko to me too, but I know it's real.

The plaid-shirted guy throws up his hands, sporting a smirk of *Can you believe this!* His look is met by others in agreement.

A middle-aged woman wearing dangling leather earrings yells out, "You've been reading too much 20C science fiction crap. Two places at the same time. Ooh, wow!"

Laughter.

The paragon stands and apparently has something to say. He seems more engaged with what I'm expressing than most of the others. "When you were in this third space, was *interconnect* aware of it?"

This guy seems like he knows what I'm talking about.

"When I first entered this space of peace, the blackness was lurking and, after a while, I could feel its anger directed at me. So, it must have been aware. When I later got into other parts of the third space, though, I didn't feel it was there. That was a big part of the joy. It's absence."

The paragon responds, "You talk about a feeling of freedom in third space. Since you were chipped-in, though, don't you think the machine may have been involved in producing this space?"

The paragon is specific with his queries. It's clear he is

after something. It feels good to have someone interested in engaging with me further.

"If it's involved, it's a whole different stream of influence than what we so far have experienced," I say.

"When I'm chipped-in, I normally have this vibration that penetrates my head, like part of my mind is attached to some lever and is being pushed forward. In this space I'm describing, I didn't feel any of that. It was like thinking organically, but even better. Enhanced and clarified in some way. Gosh, it's hard to describe."

A large woman has been having some internalized conversation during our discussion. I tried not to stare at her at first, but she's an eyeful to behold. Sun-baked face, lime green bandanna wrapped around snow white hair, wearing some type of jumpsuit. Eccentric at best, mental case at worst. "Why do we persist?" she barks.

"Why do we play around with false hope? We, as organics, have always had this belief we could save the country from hell. Look around, my mates. Our ranks are plummeting. We're nearing extinction.

"Yet, here we are with the latest installment of hope. Our cause is over. We've been decimated by the devil Prince and his puppets. Fuck, Prince himself is the ultimate puppet, licking the machine's ass to stay in power.

"The only way we can survive as individuals at this point is to become a hermit or recluse, live in the mountains, and hang out with coy-wolves, hard copy books, and hot tea. If we're lucky enough to have a partner, fuck when we want, enjoy life as it comes.

"This is all we have left."

Our time allotment is near the end. Like all organics' meetings, they end abruptly with no time for synthesis, fuller discussion, or goodbyes.

I expected celebratory fireworks with my sharing of the good news.

I got doubt and suspicion from the organics.

As I scatter to the wind and fight off disappointment, I develop a mental checklist. Forester knows about third space. I've got to find him. Elijah and Anya know about the space, but no way I can find them outside *interconnect*. Besides Allacia, that paragon (damn, didn't get his name) seemed at least open to my message.

I go into hyperdrive. This first setback will not slow my evangelism. My energy for this cause will outlast any disappointment.

However, that first meeting turns out to be a prelude to a series of discouraging encounters with resisters. My proselytizing is met with disbelief, mistrust, and indictment.

At a wasted old circus site: "Our narrowing because of fear cuts out what we need most. There is a path to a place of free human thinking within *interconnect*. This liminal space occupies a position on both sides of the boundary between human and machine. It is the 'in-between' space."

In a crypt shot to hell: "In the machine is a freedom even greater than what exists out here. We think we are free out here, but we are determined by external forces. In the machine, in this third space, exists genuine freedom."

In a darkened, rat-filled, long-abandoned transport tube: "When the mind is occupied by fear and threat, there is no space. We're in the privacy of our own blindness. The occupied mind is disordered and not free. When the mind has space, it is aligned with a larger, peaceful flow. Such a mind provides the opportunity for evolution in human thinking."

At a chemsynth distribution den.

At a coy-wolf fight cockpit.

At a ghostly college cafeteria.

Many of my organic listeners had closed ears to anything that was associated with the machine. I can understand their resistance, but they are missing out on something big. Others get angry at my lecture tour, feeling that my activism is adding to the group's susceptibility to regime surveillance. They feel that I am producing a target more easily identified.

The Prince Proclamation of 4th quarter/81d 2045 is also obstructing my message. I get many questions about whether my third space is one of Prince's new 'learning modules.' These modules have been met mostly with condemnation by organics. They view it as one further disguise by *interconnect*, creating the illusion of free-thinking within the manipulative superstructure.

Again and again, I reply that it isn't that. It felt too unhooked from machine supervision. But the more questions I get, the more I start to wonder too whether I'm falling prey to the machine again.

It is simply too disheartening for me to even consider that this third space is another algorithmic trick. I've got to believe it was real. My mental state depends on it.

Only the few paragons in attendance respond in constructive ways to what I'm preaching. The fact of free-thinking within the machine does not seem too farfetched to them. Their questions are more probing and detailed than the organics' skeptical declarations.

Chapter 48

I suffer an emotional hangover after my excitement over the third space lecture tour crashes and burns at the feet of the resisters. My enthusiasm about spreading the good news about the third space has been met by hesitance and skepticism by the organics. Even those few organics that believed in my message deemed it as too risky a proposition for collective action.

The fog and ashes of war match my mood. An intensified surge of fighting in the Jeim region reinforces my sense of detachment from life. My feeling that I would finally bring meaning to my life has dissolved. I'm also embarrassed about my grand "save the country" rhetoric. I cringe at the thought that Caleb and Ellie heard such pompousness.

Without organics' commitment, I don't see any way that I can advance us toward a new form of free human thinking. The wars will surely continue with *interconnect* fully in control. We, as humans, appear to be cooked.

I walk the mean streets of Jeim. The masochistic part of me

wants to be eliminated or captured. I'm on dangerous streets I wouldn't have been previously. Enough of this life and its constant suffering. Life teases me using a devious device—hold out hope, then dash it.

I'm drifting, mentally and physically.

I have thirsted for some meaning in my life, and it has always eluded me.

My despondency is consuming me.

Exploding fin bombs, clouds of smoke, and the clipped sounds of gun battles encase the dying city. A stalemate in who exactly is winning this war adds stimuli to both sides—Pirner and Mage—to increase their attacks and counterattacks. The entire southern periphery of the city, formerly home to working-class denizens, has been razed to the ground and now resembles the lunar service.

Rumor on the street is that organics are nearing extinction. No wonder my audiences were so resistant to hope. They felt impending defeat. The always evolving, massively funded, and expanding surveillance tools of the regime are apparently succeeding. Incarceration facilities are filling with those denizens who believe that humans should be able to think on their own. New torture techniques by the regime are better able to extract from captives the whereabouts of those deemed "terrorists" by the regime.

Despite my constant efforts, I get no alt-x replies from Forester, Seyh, Nicolai, Jai, or Remy. I did get a response from Allacia, but it was a brief warning message not to contact her again electronically.

Meanwhile, new types of killing machines are constantly being purchased from foreign countries that are interested in nothing but profits. AGM-114 missiles and Lucifer drone warplanes are flooding into our country. Militia fighters have enhanced their wardrobes. Many combatants are now exoskeleton-equipped and carry machine guns formerly found only on vehicles. Tanks are now armed with M777 and ERCA canons. Sarin bio-attacks have become normalized warfare, although their targeting ability remains inexact.

There is a growing sense that our country may disappear entirely from the face of the earth. The protection domes over the regions are wearing out, fueling speculation that our intra-regional wars will morph into a country-wide apocalypse. Other countries are becoming bolder in sending invading forces into our country, typically to claim rights to our precious natural resources.

The Prince regime appears either incompetent or unwilling to prevent our country's dismemberment. I guess *interconnect* somehow feels that this amputation is consistent with its goals. Building community, my ass!

I feel the chaotic anxiety of war as I walk down Wythe Avenue. This intensifies my internal desolation. I walk past the few remaining intact buildings on the street. Militia fighters guard them with rifles poised and ready. There are numerous fins nearby in slow-moving traffic. There arises in me a sudden but passing panic that there might be a fin bomb about to detonate. The scene seems set. I start to feel nauseous being in this ripe environmental setting. My pace quickens. The feeling passes almost as quickly as it came. Part of me is disappointed that no bomb ripped me apart.

I've seen and felt too much of the sad architecture of urban warfare through the years. Militia fighters, sandbag barricades, barbed wire, and tanks have become like furniture in a house that I take for granted. It's as if they are required constituent parts of a city. Coverage on eVision of the conflict tinderbox is like a daily soundtrack that is always playing.

Yet, I'm also perversely drawn to this shitshow. It may be to prove to myself that life is not worth living. It has been one struggle after another for me since '32, and I don't see to what end. My mind's sanity level fluctuates. I can't detect truth from fabrication, nor do I necessarily want to anymore.

My trip into third space exposed that a better life is possible, yet it highlighted how far we are from that today. We spend all our time in this country unraveling.

The sole consolation I have is that I have a surprisingly less destructive co-existence with the machine these days. Ever since my experience with the third space, my chip-in experiences have been more manageable.

I effectively regulate my chip-in durations and responsibly chip out when the alarm sounds. A few times I successfully find the blessed space of free-thinking, but there now seems to be something missing. There is no longer the excitement of discovery, but rather a certain unhappiness that I can't bring this space to our citizenry. I've become less dedicated to finding the pathway of light. And this passivity seems to enable the blackness to terminate my searches more readily.

When I find myself in the blackness, the experience is not a ball of fiery hatred. Rather, the storyline is more of loneliness than hostility. I'm an observer rather than a participant. Long, depressing walks through war-destroyed terrain. Bloated dead bodies lying on streets and at building entrances. Torn apart children's toys submerged in cesspools of excrement. Used chemsynth canisters everywhere. Spent fragments of GBU-14 bombs at the rims of street craters.

The machine visions these days, far from pumping me with the adrenaline of battle-ready self-righteousness, now create a dull, numbed neutrality in me, a deliberation on the absurdity of this life. Although certainly not pleasant, these algorithmic entanglements are less difficult to emerge from and give me the sense that my *interconnect* use is now manageable.

I wonder what game *interconnect* may be playing with me now. Is it reducing stimuli strength to increase my craving for a more intense experience? Does it no longer need this floundering, depleted man to engage in its war?

Whatever the reason behind it, this new relationship with the machine seems like a shallow, even irrelevant, accomplishment. At this point, both realities have become watered-down and boring. When non-machine reality is so demeaning and ugly, and the machine's negative storylines have become pro forma experiences, I wonder if it matters whether I'm organic or chipped-in.

I flinch at the loud beginning of a nearby gun battle at the nearby Whyte/Ironwood intersection. I head back in the direction I came. I stand on a street corner amidst random bullets flying by. I bend down, hold my knees, and hate myself. I feel aimless, my big plans gone to dust. That familiar feeling of failure and emptiness pervades my mind. My organic thoughts have dimmed.

I want out of these cycles of worthlessness and self-criticism. All my grandiosity about saving the country now seems like self-delusion.

Who was I fooling that I could achieve something meaningful in this life? I'm a selfish skunk, a self-serving fake.

I need a darker blackness so I can feel again. It promises to fill the void. A deeper step into *interconnect* will provide me the energy so lacking in my life these days. These reassuring voices of justification come ever so gently to the front of the stage. I know once they are front and center, I'll be done for. I've already decided where I'm going.

Once home, smelling of war and looking like shit, I take my self-condemnation out on Raven. I project my internal turmoil onto her, the action of a coward. A minor disagreement about where to put our dwindling food supply ends up with me shouting out a full array of hurtful things to her. I feel out of control and regret immediately the nasty comments I'm making. But I cannot stop. She runs to the bedroom and locks the door. Her sobbing is non-stop.

My head is on fire and I have no idea how to extinguish the searing flames on my own.

This reality is too much for my mind to handle.

I need a different one.

Chapter 49

Thanks to my hostile outbreak, Raven has left home for once. Now I have an opportunity.

I am weak.

I am vulnerable.

I am being pulled toward a destination that will make me feel better and more alive.

I remember when I was trying to stop during my drinking days that an inner voice in my mind would convince me to take that first drink well before I actually reached for the bottle.

That inner voice still has persuasive power.

I crave the depths.

I chip-in and want to fully embrace the blackness.

I seek its intensity, its clarity, its authority.

It is waiting and reaches out to me.

It is comforting.

I see the light on the side but no longer want it. It leads to hope that cannot be fulfilled.

My need for the powerful surge of self-righteousness is greater than my desire for individual freedom.

Free thinking is pleasant, but adrenaline is more addictive.

The impulsive energy of righteousness and hatred fixes me quicker.

Power is more compelling, more seductive, and more addictive than freedom of thought.

Ego has greater magnetism than humility.

I fall further into the black darkness. An intense screaming vibration immediately annexes my brainstem. This violence is of much greater intensity than earlier chip-ins. I'm fully conscious of the pain and agony. A tsunami, volcanic eruption, an avalanche.

Power flows into my veins.

All feelings of self-doubt, inadequacy, fallibility, and fakeness fall away.

My blood gets enriched by cortisol and adrenaline.

My feelings of being less-than dissolve.

I open the utility storage closet and grab my militia supplies, equipment, and weapons.

I am out in the city, feeling like a hungry predator on the prowl for prey.

I know where to go. I know where there will be action.

Blurry images, charcoal-like in texture, come into my helmet viewscreen. I'm moving with military exactitude through an urban warfare zone. My ShadowTrax8 weapon is on ready-mode and my Armatix grenade launchers are an arms-length away. I'm locked and loaded.

I shoot at anything that moves. I don't care about the victim's cairn lineage. Pirner, Fronter, and Mage. It's killing that matters. Only it supplies the power I need. I continually squeeze the trigger. Thunderous blasts. I spray the general area where I saw most of the movement. Reload. Multiple rounds in seconds. All sorts of movement and yelling now.

I feel untouchable.

Super-human.

I have an identity.

Meaning saturates my being.

I have a reason for living.

I'm hiding behind a battered block of concrete as return fire comes at me in splatter droves.

Live or die, it doesn't matter to me anymore. Suicide by fabrication sounds cool.

This feels great, like a hundred simultaneous orgasms. I was made for this, not the wishy-washy uncertainty of regular life. That is all slurry, slimy stuff. This is concrete and real.

As I'm about to rise out of my hiding, I see images of light, of third space, of color emerge in my viewscreen. I then get alternating blasts of color followed by black images. Then, my sight is split between color on the left and blackness on the right. This whirling disorients me and I stumble, trying to get up. Knockout dizziness then puts me flat on the ground.

The pain increasing in my brain stabs at its core, like a metal rod being drilled into my very being. I try again to get up but I full-body collapse. I shake involuntarily on the ground, my body stiffens, my arms and legs jerk wildly. A large bowel movement explodes out of me and soils my fighting clothes. I smell burning flesh.

I lie flat on the ground, embarrassed by my condition.

I feel the presence of fighters coming up to me. When they see me, they laugh at the jerking menace on the ground. One lizard-looking guy kneels down and spits on me. A bunch of Dragunov sniper rifles are pointed right at me.

"Leave him, he's done for," says an authority voice. "Living life in this condition is a far greater penalty than death."

As they move along looking for targets, they sing some Pirner patriotic jingle that I partially recognize.

I exist unconsciously, a voice inside me says.

Chapter 50

Life is good. When Raven opens the shades each morning, the new day looks inviting. She reminds me that I need to stay in bed most of the day. We have a ritual where she brings me steel-cut oatmeal each day in bed, and we curl up and cuddle after my breakfast for the remainder of the morning.

In the early afternoon, she escorts me outside for a short walk. I notice pretty flowers starting to grow in between the concrete blocks. Sometimes we see a wild coy-dog, and I enjoy watching his alert face as he moves about. On our return to our apartment complex gate, we play a game each day where I try to guess the number of steps up to our floor. I get it right about half the time. When I do, we celebrate.

She counts the days. The note attached to the icebox says today is 94. When I ask what she is counting, she quietly says, "Since you came back."

My mind doesn't stay on one thing for very long. Then it's off to something else new. I don't know whether this is normal. Raven seems to be able to stay focused for longer periods than me.

I ask Raven when Caleb and Ellie are coming to visit. She is quiet and hugs me.

Raven regulates the amount of eVision we watch and she is always beside me when we do. It's all flashy stuff. Little of it I understand. There are times when she quickly turns off the images. I don't know why and I feel I shouldn't ask.

It seems preposterous that there is war outside. It all looks so beautiful when I pay attention to details—flowers, coys, children, stooped elders intermingling, Raven's smile and the warmth of her hands, the joy of being able to walk.

We enjoy our life together, although there are times when I see Raven crying in private. She doesn't know I see her, but I do. I wonder what she is sad about. She never says anything to me that would be worth crying about. She seems to be holding sadness within. I look at photos of us from years ago and she looks so much younger than now.

I find it boring when I'm connected to the machine. It's also too fast, I can't keep up. The black-and-white images are far less interesting than when I'm not connected to the machine. I really don't know what the purpose of the machine is. People talk about it a lot like it's a big deal. I don't see why. Raven calls it evil.

I sleep well most of the time. When I have dreams, they make me sweat, but I have no idea what they're about.

Life is good.

Day 98

I got the number of steps correct today. It is beautiful outside. Even the smoke has an attractive, wispy, painted quality to it.

That afternoon, a man visits us. We don't get many visitors.

"Jared, so good to see you," he says.

He reaches out to hug me. I turn it into a handshake. I'm a bit lost.

Raven says to the man, "Go ahead, I'm curious how he might respond. Just go a tad slower, okay?"

"Jared, my name is Forester. We met in the past and talked about a project we were both working on. It was to help our country."

"We were part of the Prince team," I say, totally guessing.

"No, just the opposite. We were against Prince and the machine."

"I can't stand the machine. Tedious stuff. I ignore it. It gets in the way of the good stuff in life."

I see the man look at Raven in wonder. Raven gently smiles back. I see her eyes. They are wet.

"I wanted to tell you something. That's why I'm here. We now have a group of people who we plan to send into the machine and find the nice part of it. A better part than the stuff you see now. You met a woman once, her name is Allacia. She will be part of the group.

"We call this nice part of the machine 'third space.' You helped our group locate where it is and how to enjoy being in it."

"I was part of a group? Did we go on field trips?" I say.

The man stops and turns away from me. "I can't do this, Raven."

"Go on, Forester."

"You found a special place, and now others are finding it too."

"When did we meet?" I ask. I need to say something to keep my focus on track. I was drifting off while this man was speaking.

"It was about a quarter and one-half ago. In the old days, we were both teachers."

"I loved teaching young people about cities. I remember my favorite book was by Jane Jacobs," I say. "I was teacher and students learned new things. I did so much enjoy that life. I wonder what became of it."

I look at the man and I introduce myself. I think he wants to say something but seems to hesitate. His head is down and his right hand is massaging his forehead.

Raven says to me, "Honey, do you mind going into the bedroom and relax for a while? Your doctor says that rest is the most important thing you can do, remember."

"Will do, sweetie. You are the best."

I walk past the man and lie on our soft bed. I always enjoy that feeling. There are no soft beds when I connect to the machine.

I am drifting off to sleep. But I hear the man and Raven talking in the next room. I'm interested in what they're saying.

Raven's voice. "I've seen him in bad shape before this, like when he came back before the withdrawal program. But never like this. His body was even more beaten up than that time. Last time, he was somewhat aware, although really messed up mentally. This time, his mind was gone. He didn't know who he was, and he barely knew me."

Man's voice: "I don't think he understood anything I was saying."

Raven's voice: "I don't think so. Forester, in many ways he's like a boy now, an unstained man. He relishes simple pleasures in life. And his memories are mainly of the good things in life. You saw he was positive about his teaching days. And when he remembers his children, he smiles.

"Can I tell you something?"

"Sure, Raven, anything."

"I feel a bit guilty, but I enjoy him like this. He has been through so much shit in his life. I've seen him tortured inside so many times. Now he smiles and seems to be free of all the trauma.

"Is it bad that I enjoy him like this? I mean, I wouldn't want him this way if I had the choice. But given that he is like this, I see in many ways he is happier."

"Raven, you both deserve to be happy."

Silence.

Man's voice: "What did the doctor say about his condition?"

Raven's voice: "He has brain damage, a lesion caused by a split-brain seizure when he was on *interconnect*. It makes it difficult for him to focus. It's hard for him to process thoughts.

"His understanding weakens when he's presented with different topics. It's like he's still processing one topic—stuck on it—while the conversation has moved on to another topic. He's also unable to connect two different thoughts into a higher level. Doctor calls it 'integration.' He can't do it."

There's a long pause. I enjoy the softness of the blanket that is atop me. I drift closer to sleep. I don't understand the words.

Raven's voice: "He was so energized and hopeful when he shared his discovery with members of your group. He was happy."

Man's voice: "Yeah, I think we let him down in how we received his news. That hurt him. I think it sent him into a spiral of despair. With Jared in that state of despondency, the machine may have been able to lure him into its depths.

"I'm sorry to tell you this, Raven. But I also think he may have opened himself up to the machine in an intentionally hurtful way. It seemed like he wanted to punish himself."

Raven's voice: "That's the man I know. His ability to go into dark places has always been his burden."

Man's voice: "Some in our group feel that *interconnect* sensed Jared was a threat when he was galivanting all over the region talking about his discovery of third space. That the machine intensified its input into Jared so much that it created his incapacitation.

"The machine is diabolical.

"Jared may have known too much. He had to be disabled."

Raven's voice: "I don't know for sure, but I don't think he remembers any of what happened before, you know, with the machine and all."

Silence.

Tick-tock of the clock for several minutes.

The door creaks open.

Man's voice: "You know, it is astounding that he made it back to you. His wandering in the dark spaces of the machine ironically did him one benefit. His Mage crux—look at it as a kind of war shield—protected him when he collapsed. Apparently, it was a Mage unit member who brought him back to you."

Silence.

Door closes.

Chapter 51

4th quarter, 7d, 2046

I like to call this place a hospital, although the 24/7 armed guards outside my room belie my label. I've been told I've been here coming up on one quarter-year. The nurses are a nice group, wiping my ass and dealing with morose bedsores with a smile. They come and go but I've gotten to know several of them. They break rules for me often, bringing me ice cream and other treats. They even let Raven in during some nights so we can cause havoc under the sheets.

I was apparently a sorry sot when I came here. I'm pretty sure it was not voluntary. I don't remember anyone asking my permission. I recall looking up at the bright ceiling lights and feeling empty. The intake counselor, Owen Pollard, asked me what I was in here for, and I had nary a clue. I felt scraped of most of my memories. When asked about my past, my recollection was scarce. I felt some meaning in my life had been voided. I didn't really know who I was all about. This lack of meaning echoed within me like this was a feeling I knew well.

The doctor, a wiry guy with a weasel look to him, calls it a split-brain or duality seizure. Apparently, my mind has split into two perceptual fields at war with each other. Because I am at an advanced stage of this cognitive split, I need constant surveillance. My next brain eruption may be my last, I'm told. This would explain my circumstance. In a semi-drugged consciousness only a few feet from medical help.

The armed guards undoubtedly tell a different part of this story. You'll have to ask them.

All in all, my rehabilitation over the past quarter has been cloudy and banal, yet I am showing progress in regaining some semblance of mental stability. I'm loaded on brain medicine, the pills of which are too difficult to remember their names.

I have daily walks in the garden to regain some physical tone. I put up with all sorts of mental and psychological tests by meddlesome technicians. I'm given constant assignments to do, such tasks as crossword and jigsaw puzzles. Each Friday night, I get to play the old 20C game, *Stratego*, with a nurse and practice my flirting ability, which seems to be quite developed.

My memories consist of shadowed images and are fragmented into multiple segments that don't readily align. I have become re-acquainted with the machine and its strong influence on our denizens. Black, noir-like images come to me as well as colored visions. I don't know which ones come from within the machine and which ones are outside the algorithms.

The nightmarish memories have a potency stronger than the benign ones, but I'm usually unsure which recollections are real and which are fabricated. In other words, I'm a mess concerning my past. Part of me is grateful for this unknowingness.

"We want information about all the resister friends you have, Mr. Rohde. Alt-x codes, safe houses, terrorist affiliates, and future plans," comes an abrupt voice, waking me from a restful nap.

A man in full regime uniform stares down at me. He's got an apex predator look to him. He's frightful in his perfectly pressed black outfit and shiny helmet. He has a polished SigXMacro weapon (it's weird that I recognize it).

Only his slightly protruding nose hairs tarnish the look of tight-ass precision. I wonder about this guy. Whether he sleeps wearing immaculately folded pajamas and penetrates his spouse with military precision. Something about this guy repulses me.

"We have given you enough time to heal your damage. We have helped get you back on your feet. Enough is enough! It is now time for you to serve the regime. To repay us for what we have provided you."

He holds out a piece of paper and forces it into my hand. I groggily look at it.

Seyh Maki
Nicolai Lovaas
Pavo Molimo
Allacia Talae
Remy Rajohnson
Jai Dos Santos
Jason Forester
Lydia Mahina

"As you can see, we are well aware of your little network of terrorists. I've got to say, they are experts in eluding us. Most terrorists do stupid things that give themselves away. Not your little tribe."

There is a troubled urgency to this regime bully's demand that counters his outer polish. His furrowed brow betrays his know-it-all demeanor. I'm loving this because right off I hated this guy. All spit and polish.

Even more enjoyable is the fact that I have an opportunity to fuck with this tight-ass. Time for fun. This is better than crossword puzzles.

I scratch my head and use my best stupid look at the paper. The scowl on the predator bully's face makes me happy. "Let me see, I think I remember one name."

"Which one!"

"Mai."

"Mai? You dim wit, you mean Jai?"

"No... um... I don't know a Jai. That's a funny name. It starts with J."

"Look again, you fuckhead."

I methodically say aloud each of the names, pronouncing a good number of the family names like a mental basket case. The bully's face is getting red at this point.

"I don't know. I notice they're not in alphabetical order. Do you want me to say them in order? I like games."

At this, the thug calls in the doctor and rips him a good one. "I thought you said by now he would remember. He's been treated like a fucking hotel guest, and all we get is some guy acting like a retard!"

The doctor, cowering, replies, "Sergeant, Sir, Mr. Rohde's condition is very extreme. I said it would take a while for the brain to heal. He still has scars deep in his hippocampus. These still need time to heal."

"We have intelligence about an imminent terrorist action," predator shouts. "We can't wait around forever. We'll give this terrorist two weeks to function. If nothing at that point, we eliminate him."

The bully slams the door so hard on the way out that its glass panel cracks. The doctor looks at me like a beaten-down puppy and leaves with his tail between his legs. In the hallway, I hear him say to a nurse, "Increase memantine dose 3x."

*

I slowly rise, stretch my legs, sit in a nearby seat, and request a cup of espresso from a passing nurse.I deserve an award for my acting role with the regime jarhead. When I looked at that list, there was a clicking into place in my mind.

I know those names, surely yes.

The espresso comes steaming hot. I kiss the nurse on the side of her cheek as she reaches down with the cup.

"What's that for, Mr. Rohde?" she says softly.

"Celebration, my dear."

Now the hard work of remembering the details linked to each name.

I have all night. I even cancel a Raven tête-à-tête. This is something important.

The memories come. Some quickly, others slowly. I recall my first acquaintance in a weirdly formal meeting with Seyh and Nicolai (and two others whose names escape me). They were organics, resisting the machine for some reason. I remember further meetings with the two of them and others in strange places, more hurried and we were facing threat.

I met Allacia, Remy, and Jai to plan something. I recall Lydia as a frothy prostitute who helped me escape. Jason was a close friend, I think, and he told me a secret. At first, I recall Pavo as a spy for the other side but on further thought, I think he was with us.

A second cup of espresso is beside me now. These nurses are the best. I relish having memories. I relish these specific memories. A recollection of a sense of purpose in my life warms my heart. I was part of a group trying to do good for our country, I am now sure. Exactly what, I am less sure.

Along with these positive memories come dark thoughts. I feel remorse as a turncoat to the cause. I think I have killed people. I don't know why. These memories have a heaviness the other ones don't possess.

The positive memories have a natural, flowing quality to them. The darker ones have a hard-edged, spikey texture to them. The positive ones invite me in. The dark ones frighten me.

316

Chapter 52

4th quarter, 19d, 2046

It's a late, hazy afternoon, the kind of day when one's mind wanders. My ability to solve crossword puzzles is unsurpassed. My walks are longer, and my physical stamina is increasing. I feel fuller as the finer details of my involvement with the organics emerge.

I'm sleeping better but I'm drinking way too much coffee along with nicotine supplements. I think an addictive personality has been part of how I lived life.

The dark memories are associated with the machine, which I now know to detest. It had power over me that reduced me to animal behavior. Flashes of hatred and righteousness flood in with those memory bits.

I try not to focus on the dark too much. I don't want to get stuck there. When I chip-in per regime-required durations, I'm involved in mundane activities of no interest. The machine seems to not want to remind me of my past derelictions.

I do remember that in the darkness there was also the presence of light. I get the sense the machine does not want me to revisit that place.

Then one day, it comes back into full focus. I'm busy putting on presentable clothing (I call it my gentleman outfit) getting ready to roam the hospital hallways for exercise and to tease the nurses. My favorite nurse, sleek and radiant Kima, comes in. She discreetly slides a small piece of paper on my lap as she noisily busies herself with medical details in my room.

"This came through alt-x, pretty sure you don't want anybody else with eyes on it."

I squint through my visual aura, a feature that the doctor says may be permanent.

Sender: Seyh

Thanks to you, good man, we have cracked interconnect. Team of five went in together. Found third space and created dedicated pathway for others to follow. It is a place of learning and cognitive development. This is a huge victory for organic movement and possible development of independent thinking in our country. Without your heroic efforts, we never could have succeeded. Forester sends congrats and best wishes for full recovery. Kima will assist. We will need you soon.

Chapter 53

Given the presence of armed thugs outside my room, the escape from my incarcerated hospital stay was surprisingly easy.

Kima had tantalized not only me but also the guards, who, by this time of my uneventful stay, were a sleepy, bored bunch. They had become experts in securing doughnuts from the facility's cafeteria and regularly left their positions.

Kima, a provocative sight in her tight-fitting nurse outfit, had the guards at her beck and call. She had them going to all parts of the facility to bring back needed medical supplies. They would readily agree, anything to fight the boredom of sitting in a sterile, brightly lit hallway.

The guards had seen enough of my behavior to believe I was docile and slightly demented, surely someone not in need of close monitoring. In the days before the escape, I reinforced this impression by acting particularly weird in front of them.

I mumbled to them about my love of flowers and children's smiles and of watching sunrises through my window. With my best half-crazed look, I told them I had never been so happy in all my life. One day I even reached out and tried to kiss one of them.

Thus preoccupied and bothered, the guards had no interest in monitoring my afternoon walk in the garden. Kima even wore a canvas bag type outfit so the guards' eyes wouldn't follow her as she joined me amid the dogwoods and junipers.

"We're going to move fast when we get near that gate," Kima says, eyes directing me to a medium-security apparatus just past a row of prickly pear cacti.

"I want to thank you for your care, Kima. All this time, I had a sense that you were special. You looked after me more than the others."

"We organics sure had to wait for you, dear man. You took quite a while getting back some of your brainpower.

"I enjoyed you, though, even when you were a basket case. You were one gentle soul back then, you treasured the smallest things in life. Geez, if your Raven wasn't around, I might have jumped on top of you those days. Add to your enjoyment, you know."

We bide our time, slowly meandering toward the prickly pears. The slower the better. Any random eyes on us would soon lose interest.

My pulse races as we get closer to the gate. The thought of freedom from this facility energizes and scares me. I know I won't be going back to the old apartment. The regime would easily find me there. Raven said to me two visits ago that she found another place far from our old place and she has moved most of our meager personal effects there already.

Emotions flood in as I take one last look at the 20C brick façade of the facility. I rose from the ashes here and feel an odd attachment to the hulky building. Kima moves so quickly that I hardly notice when she taps open the security gate. She pushes me outside. I'm immediately pulled into a van-fin with Renfro Medical Supplies written on its side. The driver pushes the accelerator switch, and we explode down the gravelly dirt road.

I look out the back window as we shoot over rocky patches. Kima has already turned away and is walking back toward the facility. In my turbulent life, it seems that saviors consistently emerge who rescue and assist me.

If I didn't know better, I would think that some higher spirit is shepherding me toward greater things. I laugh at the thought.

PART IX

A PATHWAY TO LIGHT

2049 and 2051

CHAPTER 54

3rd quarter, 66d, 2049

To excavate a reliable path within *interconnect* that evades its intelligent darkness has seemed, at times, a near-impossible task. One step forward, then one step back as the machine learns our techniques and adapts accordingly. Its constantly-learning algorithmic network sends us increasingly sophisticated and disguised stimuli that trick us into the black and discourage us. A light space appears but is actually an appendage to a greater blackness. Blackness disguised as light. Darkness inserted into third space. Fabricating the sense of being lost while on the pathway to light.

We counter in response. Ever so incrementally through the past three years, we have chiseled out a resistant and dependable route. We have created mental signposts that others can follow.

We have suffered heavy personnel losses. The slaughterbot attack on an organics meeting last year killed beautiful

Seyh, Nicolai, and Allacia. We think Jai and Remy are now captives. The regime's years-long obsession to eliminate organics finally paid off. Other cells of our network have been decimated. Prince went on eVision and disgustedly boasted about his latest anti-terrorism victories.

Nonetheless, I feel good about what we have done. I was a part, although an erratic one, of this endeavor to sustain human thinking in this algorithmically determined country.

The fact that the paragons are the ones moving forward now makes me sad, but also proud that we were the pioneers who initiated the openings. Unlike organics and our dedication to non-machine free-thinking, paragons advocate for a computer-human symbiosis in which the machine would support human thinking, not manipulate it. They now seem to have the momentum of activism, not us. I wish them well, although their goal still seems strange.

Quarters after their deaths, I remain deeply sorrowful over the loss of the freedom fighters whom I consider friends. They believed wholeheartedly in our cause and gave their lives in pursuit of it. At this time, our best estimate is that about five percent of our original group size is still free. A good number of them have likely retreated to the mountains out of fear. I have not heard of Forester's status and this gives me some hope amid the otherwise despairing situation.

I had the joy of being together with Seyh in third space. It felt like a culmination and celebration. We did our necessary work on our mission—to add data to the "light protocol" that would help others avoid the darkness. But, we also rested and took in the beauty and calm of this special place. We were embedded in a living and breathing natural ecosystem. We witnessed huge forests growing before our eyes in a time-lapse fashion, the creation and erosion of great mountain ranges, the meandering and changing of waterways, and the intricate behavioral routes of beasts, large and small.

We looked at this all in silent wonder, gently holding hands in reverence.

I also joined Allacia and Nicolai on two other expeditions, working on the protocol. The joyful laughter by Allacia in third space was something to behold. And, I never saw Nicolai show such emotion as when he wept in the face of the light's grandeur. All told our work on creating a pathway to the light that others can follow has proceeded well.

We have created the "light protocol" as a user manual for accessing third space. We have outlined the steps to follow and the mental traps to avoid.

The machine's darkness manipulates us into thinking that each of us is a big person in a small, competitive world.

The under-explored chamber of light in the machine lets us know that each of us is a small person in a big, wonderful world. Connected to each other in a truly human community that spans across the algorithmically created false divides.

The darkness feeds ego and conflict. This third place illuminates humility and awe.

What makes the death of my compatriots, and many others in the organics' cause, so untimely is that, as we have made inroads into the machine, there are fewer willing travelers. It's not really unwillingness. Most denizens no longer exist high enough on the cognitive ladder to even exert will. Most denizens have become fully incapable of comprehending anything not produced by the darkness in *interconnect*.

This is understandable. Denizens are not to be blamed. Nearing two decades of addictive dependency on machine storylines to define their reality, there is a strong likelihood of severe erosion in most denizens' prefrontal cortexes. An old

20C saying was, "Use it or lose it." Well, our denizens have not been using their prefrontal area for independent processing for years now. It's even worse than that. With such a passage of time, we now face the possibility of an inter-generational transmission of decayed prefrontal cortexes.

Our population has been indoctrinated into a life determined by emotional reflex rather than deliberative, higher-level thinking. Their lives are more and more confined to the "fight or flight" stress response elicited by *interconnect*'s dark stimuli. They're unable to gain deeper insights produced by higher reasoning. They're living inside their brain's limbic system.

We organics have worked tirelessly to create a widening and more accessible pathway to the light within *interconnect*. Sadly, it may become a little-traveled route trekked by only a few enlightened hikers still able to think on their own. Hopefully, the paragon group can effectively use our light protocol.

Despite my gloom about our numbed-out population, I do recognize that there are new shoots of promise. The paragons are a younger, feistier group than we were. They believe in more ballsy efforts at disrupting our catatonic country. They have engaged in the first-ever public protests against the regime and machine. They are expertly managed and scattered throughout the country in a well-integrated super-cell. They also actively engage in public criticism of the regime, painting them in posters and clandestine one-second eVision inserts as being appointed puppets unrepresentative of the country's denizens.

I should not get so pessimistic that I don't see that there are small changes afoot. There are smatterings of hope.

I still turn on eVision, but I feel like a masochist doing so. Raven may be smarter. She goes into another room when I turn it on. The last three years have been wither and waste in our country. Dragging along in its 17th year, our conflicts seem to be horribly self-perpetuating. A conflict without end.

The original fabricated causes of the wars have transformed into a complex and incomprehensible set of rationales, justifications, and equivocations. Simple-minded slogans are bandied about by militia leaders. These mantras have no logical meaning but contain emotional triggers that keep their followers' amygdalas inflamed.

There exists a whole stratum of conflict-breeders who profit from prolonging the wars. Conflict has become a source of their wealth and identity. Any efforts at communication between the warring sides would threaten their ability to maintain these advantages. Sustaining conflict becomes their strongest weapon in preserving their privileged status.

Each conflict has its own specificities, but they share the common sorrow of mass killing and catastrophic disruption of normal life. War has a deadly logic that continues to tear at the heart and soul of our society. I wonder if, and how, we can ever rebuild a country after nearly two decades of hostilities.

In Heartland, Centrals clearly dominate the Zonal population. It's an obscenely unequal region with a massive separation barrier between the advantaged Centrals and the marginalized Zonals. The whole region continues to be unilaterally controlled by a murky coalition of Central militia leaders and entrepreneurs. In such a setting of deeply embedded inequality, I wonder how we would ever create a more just and fairer region.

In Birthplace, Turmoil violence between Eastern and Western militias has produced a jigsaw pattern of partition walls that have unsuccessfully stemmed ongoing violence. In any effort to build peace there, I wonder when these walls of division and hatred would come down.

In Sesperia, violence is less an everyday occurrence, yet breaks out in deadly episodes between the two groups seeking greater autonomy and the centralist group fighting to maintain its political control over all of the region. How, I think, will we ever be able to reconcile these intractable desires for separation and unification?

And in the Northwoods region, my home for way too long, unending Pirner attacks on Jeim and counterattacks by Mage and Fronters have produced nothing other than substantial loss of life and withering destruction of urban assets. I saw an image the other day of Elderwater—where I was a visiting professor years ago—and it was shocking. Almost all of the city has been reduced to rubble. The site of my former host university is unrecognizable, characterized by hundreds of acres of jagged concrete slabs. In this most devastated region, I ponder how we will interrupt the transmission of war memories and trauma to future generations.

Despite the depressing state of affairs, I maintain some hope. It may be only a survival technique on my part. I cannot allow myself to be influenced by the darkness. I've learned that I must keep myself above the mire to maintain my sanity and preserve some normalcy in my life with Raven.

My hope finds justification in certain gradual changes that I perceive.

I have to trust that I am seeing a reality that is truly there.

CHAPTER 55

The day begins like any other. Itching and scratching. Touching Raven's warm body in bed. The daily soundtrack of bombing percussions in the distance. Coffee and nicotine gum to wake me up.

A knock on our door. I look through the viewscreen with trepidation. We don't get many visitors.

I see a smiling, excited man, something unusual these days. I cannot believe it. His face has lost some of its sharp, chiseled features, but those dreamy blue eyes are a giveaway. I open the door quickly.

"Forester!" I shout.

"Indeed, you didn't think we were done with, did you? Damn, it's good to see you, you old dog."

We hug each other and I protectively close the door.

"Old academics never die, we just become irrelevant," I joke.

"Ain't that right?"

We share egg breakfasts ala Raven style and settle into the warmth of friendship.

"Jared, not to rush things because this meal is great, but I'm here also to show you something."

"Oh, yeah. What might that be? I can't imagine what you have up your sleeve now, you scoundrel."

"It has to do with *interconnect*. I have seen something different during my recent excursions into third space. At first, I didn't want to admit it because it might raise false hope. But I am convinced it's there."

Ten minutes later, we chip-in simultaneously to ensure concurrent experiences. Not with complete confidence, but with secure footing on a path I have visited several times now, I venture forth with Forester.

We make sure to adhere to proven methods.

A meditative relaxation upon entering to avoid an immediate reflex-based reaction that would attach us to the blackness. A gaze not directed at the dominant blackness but to the side. Then walk slowly to the light and enter it calmly. Don't look back at the blackness or anywhere except at the threshold to the illuminated corridor.

A cool breeze brushes by us as if it is a messenger. "Let's wander a bit and see what happens," Forester whispers.

We are in a shopping area of some type. The trees nearby are deep green and blow in the wind.

We watch an older man push his full shopping cart out toward his auto-fin in the parking lot. He is bent over, of craggy physique, and moves extremely slowly across the lot. His face is hardened by a life dominated by machine-driven conflict. His whole appearance suggests that he lives a lonely life. Yet, his eyes have a curious luminosity to them, as if he is seeing beyond life's heaviness into a source of light. Several fins wait patiently for his gradual path to be complete. Two fin drivers wave at him. We come up beside his fin, where he is painstakingly lifting his bags into the back compartment.

Forester asks, "Sir, may I help you with your bags?"

From his bent-over posture, we see the smile of a young man break through. "No thank you, you are a good man, Forester," he says with a flicker of a smile that suggests that the offer of assistance is prize enough. The joy of human connection is sufficient and fills the air.

We walk down a bustling city street. I feel part of a living tapestry.

Young people escorting the elderly across crosswalks.

A freshly painted 20C phone booth relic packed with books free for anyone to borrow.

Denizens bending down to talk to unsheltered street residents.

Colorful stalls and food carts lining the sidewalk, each filling the air with enticing aromas.

An impromptu street dance in rhythm to the sounds emanating from a parked auto-fin.

People in finely-tailored wardrobes having lunch in streetside cafes seated next to denizens in soiled, tattered clothing.

An enchanting puppeteer woman dressed in rainbow colors holding the rapt attention of about 20 children with a story apparently about humans with wings.

This is not a place of individual atoms in collision and competition, but a place of mutually interacting parts. We're witness to communitarianism and collaboration.

Later in our pleasant wandering, a middle-aged woman wearing athletic workout clothing is observing us from a sidewalk bench. We are intrigued and come up beside the woman.

"Excuse me, good woman, are you watching us from this spot," I say bravely, possibly too brashly.

"Oh, indeed I am. Now that you are closer and I see your eyes more clearly, I know that I am right."

"What are you correct about, friend?" I ask.

"I see myself in your eyes," she says to me. "I remember you. I know you. You have overcome several challenges in your life but now have some hope, even some sprinkling of joy."

It is as if she can read my mind.

"I too have dealt with several hardships," she says. "Divorce, domestic abuse, a dead child. But, these have led me to discover the light, the joy, in life. Without the darkness, I would not have opened to the light. The simple ability to persevere is proof of light and love. I saw this same life story in you when I saw your eyes. Not the specifics you know, but the general trajectory of life."

Our walk continues into a natural area with running water cascading down a waterway. Families are enjoying picnics on the grass and on tables. Coy-dogs are having great fun running excitedly after each other.

We sit on a bench, in wonder.

Forester softly enters the quietude, "In my first few excursions into third space, I was awed by the calmness, the beauty, of this place. I was obsessed with observing everything I could and was blown away by what I was witnessing. But, I stayed a distant observer of this miracle.

"Then, in later expeditions, I explored beneath the surface, and what I found was even more magnificent.

"What did you notice about the denizens we interacted with?" he asks.

I think of the old bright-eyed man and the observant workout woman.

"There was human connection."

"Go deeper, Jared. Human connection can be of any quality. Someone yelling profanities at you is a type of human connection."

"What I saw on the man's face was an opening," I say, "a response to a simple act of compassion. What I felt with the woman was a deep identification. Acknowledging each other and our common humanness—warts and all. A knowingness of each other. An understanding of the human condition."

"Good," responds Forester as he smiles at a toddler tumbling down a play sandhill. "I don't want to put words in your mouth, dear friend, but may I suggest that what you saw were compassion and empathy."

My eyes moisten upon hearing those words. Forester is right. Those qualities of life had been so long closed off by the dark machine that I had difficulty recognizing them as human traits when I experienced them. Far from foreign, these traits are authentically human ones.

"This third space allows for compassion and empathy!" I declare. A teenager passing by smiles at my pronouncement.

"Jared, third space is not only a joyful place of peaceful co-existence. It's different not only in terms of denizens' behaviors. There's something deeper going on here. Beneath the surface. It may be a place where consciousness itself is advancing.

"It's important to remember that we are within the machine. This shows that it is capable of enabling a different reality, one that supports the good qualities of humankind. A humane reality. One that may be even better than organic reality.

"An evolved consciousness!"

We look at an intricate layering of clouds that refracts the sky's golden light and creates a beautiful painterly image. We sit in quiet awe. I think about the implications of what Forester just said. This could be a game-changer.

"You know, it's sad to think how many of our group are no longer with us," Forester says. "But what we started, I think, may have set things in motion. It's not a lost cause.

"These paragons out there are growing and in some ways are picking up where we left off. They're a different breed, for sure. Not so much the 'old arts' focus, they're more technically savvy and don't see *interconnect* as the devil.

"They think that the machine is capable of change and that they can somehow force it to adapt into a human-compatible apparatus.

"Finding this third space, this humane reality within the machine, makes me think they may be on to something."

"I hope you're right, Forester. I'm excited about what we found, too.

"But let me tell you. Years ago I had hope that I could save this damn country. I was intoxicated with hope. But experiences since then, including a total breakdown, have made me hesitant to fully grab onto hope. I have been fooled so many times. I feel wiser now, possibly more realistic.

"Call me skeptical, but I don't entirely trust anything connected to algorithms. The machine is expert in manipulation and fabrication. What exactly is it up to in allowing this humane reality to exist within it?"

While we've been talking, I've noticed that a small group of men and women have arrived and are now seated in a circle on the grass near us. We can't help but listen in on their engaged conversation.

"We are similar in our differences, aren't we? Or is it that we are different in our similarities?" a trim, sandy-haired woman proclaims, followed by friendly laughter from the others.

"I just kept coming back and found freedom from my old self. I have the strength of acceptance now, not the old strength of self-will which put me in bad situations. You guys have been a lifesaver." A wave of emotion seems to come over the speaker—a middle-aged man with long, pony-tailed hair.

"When we learn to smile and relate to the other, we will have mastered our problem," says a white-robed older man.

I've been in such groups in the past, so I know what this is – a support group of some kind.

There is companionship and community right before our eyes. Not the fucked-up community fabricated by the machine through hatred of others, but community that connects, not separates.

We're both smiling at the joy of humanness these denizens are sharing.

"I understand your doubt, Jared. Maybe this will change your view. Something else I've detected recently inside the machine. Did you notice something about the blackness when we first entered? I know we are not to look at it, but I have and I noticed something different."

"I'm not brave enough yet to look at the blackness," I reply.

"It seems to be a lesser darkness. It's not solid black. I see waves or, I don't know, striations in the blackness. It looks like there is light shining through the blackness."

"Are you suggesting that the blackness is cracking open?" I ask.

"Geez, wouldn't that be something! I don't know. Let's hope so.

"Best case, I guess, *interconnect* may be loosening its grip, maybe our trips into third space are changing it. That it may be opening to the possibility of fundamental change."

"Are you suggesting that humans are capable of changing the machine?" I say with a skeptical tone.

"I'm no expert, Jared, I'm just throwing out stuff here. But couldn't it be possible that we are disrupting the algorithms in some way through our intentions? Maybe our actions are leading the machine to explore human free will. Maybe it's experimenting."

The thought of the machine allowing human independence is a bit much for me. But I stifle my default skepticism and listen with interest.

Forester continues, "Anyhow, the reality on the ground would support my interpretation that there is a fundamental change in how *interconnect* is operating. I saw an eVision report the other day that stated that fatalities this quarter are at their lowest level since Turmoil began.

"When I walk around Jeim, sure there is still routine, pro forma raids and killing. But, the militias are acting like they are past their prime. A lot of them are staying in place and biding their time. They're acting like they're already part of yesterday."

"I get what you're saying, Forester, but that's pretty hopeful. To imagine that the machine may be in the process of restructuring itself. But, and this is a big 'but,' we have no idea about the goals of its re-tooling.

"I just don't trust such an intelligent machine. It may have motivations to protect itself that we know nothing about. What you see as positive change may be a temporary phase during which it is developing a new manipulative scheme. How can we predict what it might do in the future?"

I look out at the beautiful serenity of our surroundings. I feel the warm embrace of optimism, yet nagging doubt interferes with my acceptance of such hope.

"Forester, if *interconnect* transforms into something different tomorrow, what would it all mean?

"That we've started momentum toward a more human-compatible machine or that it's off on its own, devising something that meets its own needs, not ours, and that we'll not be able to understand?

"How will we know *interconnect*'s motivation?

"Based on the machine's actions in the past, can we really hope?

"I guess I just can't yet fully trust."

CHAPTER 56

Two years later.

*** 2nd quarter, 81d, 2051. *Interconnect Transmission.* 07:00

Interconnect sends message to all denizens that it will deliver in the future a new algorithmic modeling package, to be called ReStart, that will help denizens in re-gaining independent human thinking abilities.

Machine-based re-cognition training will be delivered from basic through advanced levels. Levels I and II will be fundamental indoctrination training on how to think independently and will be provided to all denizens. Level III will train denizens in applying cognition to different scenarios.

Level IV will emphasize training the mind to form integrating thoughts that organize separate thought patterns into a higher frame of understanding. This training will educate denizens on how to link separate thoughts into a larger whole in order to achieve a higher level of conceptualization and abstraction. Levels V and VI will focus on analytical thinking and decision-making ability and will be delivered to those denizens showing the most potential for leadership in our society.

*** *2nd quarter, 82d, 2051. Interconnect Transmission. 09:30* **President Prince announcement.**

Dear fellow denizens,

It is with a heavy heart that I report an important development to you at this time. At 7:00 this morning, I received a Level 1 message from our master machine that I am to resign my position as your President effective at 24:00 tonight.

Pause.

Interconnect e-delivered to me 23,000 words detailing several practices of the regime, initiated by me personally, that are contrary to the machine's goal of building community.

The machine requires me to publicly state that if I was not to resign, then it would transmit these indictments to all denizens.

Pause.

Garbled sound.

I am disappointed with the machine's conclusions. Yet, I know that interconnect is perfect.

Pause.

I will thus accept the machine's verdict and resign as set forth.

Pause.

Upon my resignation, the colossal machine will appoint a caretaker government to lead us in the days ahead. I will work to achieve a smooth transition.

Long pause.

It has been my high honor to serve you these past 10 years as your guardian and leader. We have done great things together as we move into our bright tomorrow of community with separation. I bid you good morning.

Garbled sound.

May your stories be fulfilling.

*** 2nd quarter, 83d, 2051 at 03:20

Interconnect shuts off completely.

To be continued in
ReStart: Stories of the Cairn Age (2021)

About Atmosphere Press

Founded in 2015, Atmosphere Press was built on the principles of Honesty, Transparency, Professionalism, Kindness, and Making Your Book Awesome. As an ethical and author-friendly hybrid press, we stay true to that founding mission today.

If you're a reader, enter our giveaway for a free book here:

SCAN TO ENTER
BOOK GIVEAWAY

If you're a writer, submit your manuscript for consideration here:

SCAN TO SUBMIT
MANUSCRIPT

And always feel free to visit Atmosphere Press and our authors online at atmospherepress.com. See you there soon!

About the Author

Scott Bollens is Professor of Urban Planning and Public Policy and Warmington Endowed Chair of Peace and International Cooperation, University of California, Irvine. For 25 years, he has studied urbanism and political conflict in contested cities throughout the world. His most recent scholarly book is *Bordered Cities and Divided Societies*. *Precipice* is his third novel. It is inspired by today's troubling and unquestioned insertion of artificial intelligence into everyday life. It is the prequel to *ReStart: Stories of the Cairn Age* (2021) and *ReForm: Combating the Algorithmic Mutation* (2023).